A THEATRE FOR ALL SEASONS

NOTTINGHAM PLAYHOUSE
THE FIRST THIRTY YEARS
1948–1978

A THEATRE FOR ALL SEASONS

NOTTINGHAM PLAYHOUSE
THE FIRST THIRTY YEARS
1948–1978

JOHN BAILEY

Foreword by Dame Judi Dench

ALAN SUTTON PUBLISHING LIMITED

NOTTINGHAM PLAYHOUSE

First published in the United Kingdom in 1994 by
Alan Sutton Publishing Ltd · Phoenix Mill · Far Thrupp
Stroud · Gloucestershire
In Association with Nottingham Playhouse

First published in the United States of America in 1994 by
Alan Sutton Publishing Inc. · 83 Washington Street · Dover · NH 03820

British Library Cataloguing in Publication Data
A catalogue record for this book is available from the British Library

ISBN 0–7509–0636–7

Library of Congress Cataloging in Publication Data applied for

Typeset in 10/14pt Sabon.
Typesetting and origination by
Alan Sutton Publishing Limited.
Printed in Great Britain by
Redwood Books, Trowbridge, Wiltshire

CONTENTS

FOREWORD
by Dame Judi Dench

Something like 29 years ago, I went up to Nottingham. It was so exciting to be working in a new theatre with a really great and enthusiastic group of actors. I never remember empty seats in the theatre at all – I am sure this isn't an exaggeration – and the foyer always seemed full from early morning to late in the evening with people meeting for coffee and drinks, seeing an exhibition, just coming in for a chat.

It was a wonderful experience and something I look back on with great affection. It was what I have always believed a theatre should be.

This book is a record of an enormously exciting and innovative period, and I am sure that everyone who ever worked or visited the Playhouse will be proud of its place in the history of theatre in Britain.

ACKNOWLEDGEMENTS

My first thanks are to my wife Barbara, for her patience and understanding, not only during the work on this book, but throughout many years of close involvement in the affairs of Nottingham Playhouse. I thank also the rest of my family for their interest and encouragement.

I am grateful to Dame Judi Dench and Richard Eyre for their delightful contributions, written amidst their very busy lives. And my thanks to the following for their help and co-operation: Ella Hugman, for meticulous preparation of the script, and her general support; Ruth Mackenzie, Stuart Rogers, and staff at Nottingham Playhouse; John Plumb, of Nottinghamshire County Council; Dorothy Ritchie, and staff at Nottinghamshire Central Library; Emrys Bryson; Alan Guest; George Hagan; John Harrison.

JOHN BAILEY

INTRODUCTION

This book is about the founding of a theatre and its growth to become one of Britain's leading regional playhouses. In chronicling those experiences which, as a member of the Founder Board, I have been fortunate to share from the beginning some forty-five years ago, I suppose care is needed about what E.M. Forster called 'the personal memory-sogged past' for which he thought there was neither time nor room. Perhaps such indulgence could be avoided by concentrating only on cold, historical fact, but a theatre's life-story cannot by its nature be confined to that.

It is true that the first phase of a theatre is inanimate enough, starting with buildings and the hard cash to achieve and continue them. Even in that sphere Nottingham had incident sufficient to fuel several dramas, complete with dialogues of success and disappointment; good luck and bad; the flood and ebb of inspiration. Those elements have their place in the objective record, but the story of Nottingham Playhouse is dominated for me, as I imagine it is for all contemporaries involved, by the people on, behind and in front of our stage, a host of theatricals tumbling through the years, bringing the venture to life, giving miraculous effort and wondrous delight.

That enthusiasm, still sustained, has influenced my approach to this account of the Playhouse. I have, of course, included the historical background, the developments and main events, but I have not provided solely a strict chronological recital of data and dates. I have imagined a query: 'What was so special about your theatre? What for instance in the earliest years would my 2s. 7d. Stall ticket admit me to?' I wish this could be shown by a Priestley time-experience, taking us to far-away productions, but sadly J.B.P. is no longer with us to conjure the trick. I have to answer by attempting to convey the atmosphere. A theatrical creation is a compound of several arts, which is its distinction and fascination, and first homage is to the writer, with whom it all starts; the begetter. So sometimes in these pages I stay with our enquiring patron to discuss playwrights and their work, and how it was done here. To that extent the book is occasionally as much a companion to Playhouse theatre-going as it is a history.

During the fifteen years in its first building, Nottingham Playhouse presented 320 productions and, to take a mark, some 300 in the next twenty years at the new theatre (where conditions gave a welcome emancipation to longer runs) from Shakespeare to *Charley's Aunt*, Ibsen to pantomime. Most of the standard and modern classics have been done, very many new works and a huge general roll of plays of the time. All these are listed in the Appendix, and through the text a few are recalled in detail. Those examples of range and style illustrate the environment during the founding of the Playhouse. There was input of many kinds, but the prestige came above all from the principle of 'the play's the thing'. The faith of our initial theatre directors and their guidance in programme building was our theatre's immeasurable good fortune.

In retracing early years one hopes to have evaded the negative nostalgia which Mr Forster probably had in mind, but memory can be fickle at such a long distance and, to strengthen it, extracts from production reviews by independent critics have been quoted. I have taken the risk of giving an impression of Playhouse self-acclamation. I make no apology for being a devotee of the artists who built our reputation. I witnessed intimately the selfless dedication which went into their achievements. I have sympathy with the feelings of a certain flamboyant trade union leader when I heard him accused of being an uncompromising partisan where his members were concerned, and he replied, 'I should bloody well think so.'

However, I trust the general secretary fell short of claiming infallibility for his union. There were bound to be mistakes and unevenness among so many Playhouse productions, especially during the fortnightly-run days. Audiences were tolerant of occasional lapses among so much high-standard work. Many enjoyed the convention of having a settled company for a season or two, watching its members mature in a medley of parts. The situation has changed because actors are less willing to commit themselves to a long-term arrangement, which indeed might be difficult for them financially and for their careers.

These are different times from the forties and fifties, when Nottingham Playhouse was being established. The television and film industries have a strong influence, and the British theatre itself is more complex, with a proliferation of regional theatres some of which have policies very different from the old repertory concept. Such a fluctuating structure dilutes the tradition that, after drama school, the best training and luck for a young student was to be admitted to a reputable repertory company under an experienced director and, after learning via stage chores how a production works, and being given modest opportunities on stage, progress from an attendant lord or lady to playing Benedick or Beatrice. Certainly that pattern has been seen often at Nottingham, and people still watch with interest and pride the advancement of stars who learnt some of their trade here. Sadly, there is space to feature only a few of the legion of players and staff who have worked in our two theatres, and to whom we owe so much. To the very many whose names cannot be listed we should express sincere collective recognition of their unforgettable contribution, given for little material reward.

Similarly it is impossible to detail the service which has been donated to the administration of the Playhouse since 1948, especially in negotiations for the two theatres. From time to time there erupts controversy on the role of theatre boards. They exist for constitutional reasons and I relate in the first section how Nottingham Theatre Trust Ltd came into being. Using it as an example, it is first the mechanism for receiving and being accountable for public money, i.e. grant aid from the Arts Council of Great Britain and local authorities, and for sponsorship. It appoints its professional staff which manages the theatre with an agreed policy and budget. They control running expenditure and the board has financial responsibility at balance sheet times, and indeed for all transactions in its name, exactly as with the board of a commercial undertaking. Board members adjust to working in a unique field with an end product far removed from a manufactured article in a store. It is an activity in a highly sensitive unpredictable arts world, with its own creations and creeds requiring freedom in their unfolding. So the answer is not too complicated; one devises a partnership in which each recognizes and respects the other's areas and duties.

Boards vary in size and composition according to particular policies. Nottingham Theatre Trust has had representatives from the local authorities, national and local arts associations, supporter associations and independent members from occupations such as business, education, law, accountancy and academia. Sitting with the board are the theatre director and administrator, the secretary, a representative of (and elected by) the main house company, the director of the Theatre-in-Education company, assessors sent by the Arts Council – London and Regional, and advisers on special matters when required. Normally there is a monthly meeting of the full board and a smaller number elected from it would meet when necessary. This means that some board members are required to give a considerable amount of time to the work which is, of course, entirely voluntary.

Nottingham Theatre Trust has been fortunate in its chairmen. The first, John E. Mitchell, was Lord Mayor of Nottingham at the time. He did much to give confidence and standing to the new venture. In the 'make or break' early days important doors were opened with his influence. He was followed by the then Vice-Chancellor of Nottingham University, B.L. Hallward, for fifteen years. That long period covered all the remaining time in the old theatre, and the opening of the new building. Mr Hallward was generous in the enthusiasm and commitment he gave to the Playhouse. It required all his remarkable energy at a time when he also had responsibility for the university's development. Mr Hallward was succeeded by C.T. Forsyth, who joined the board in 1964, and this again was a lengthy chairmanship, lasting thirteen years. Cyril Forsyth was one of the best-known personalities in the business and political life of Nottingham. He brought to the Playhouse great attachment to the theatre, a quick grasp of its economics, and a sagacity which facilitated the handling of some testing situations. He retired in 1977, and the chairmen following in recent years have been David Corder, David Edmond and John Taylor. Thus over forty-five years Nottingham Playhouse has had the stability and continuity of only six chairmen.

The position of Theatre Director has been held by André Van Gyseghem (1948–51); John Harrison (1951–7); Val May (1957–61); Frank Dunlop (1961–64); John Neville (1963–8); Stuart Burge (1968–73); Richard Eyre (1973–78); Geoffrey Reeves (1977–80); Richard Digby Day (1980–3); Kenneth Alan Taylor (1983–90); Pip Broughton (1990–). (Peter Ustinov was a joint Theatre Director in 1963–4).

These tenures range from three to seven years and average about four years. Occasionally we heard the somewhat insensitive theory that after such a period it was time for a theatre director to move on, but that criterion was not imposed at Nottingham Playhouse. Circumstances of change were varied, and they developed in a natural way. In our Theatre's first years, when finances were low and staffs small, the work required in maintaining the system of fortnightly runs to a high standard was formidable. Also the factors of a very meagre stage space and minimal technical resources led to frustration over limited staging possibilities and a personal feeling of the need for new challenges elsewhere. Just as a departed director refreshed another theatre with the experience he had gained at Nottingham, it was in turn interesting for us to welcome new personalities, styles and different policy on play choices. From those areas come the all-important product which arrives on the stage and the theatre director, having responsibility for that, is able to make an obvious mark on the theatre's development more spectacularly than those in the other key position of administrator or business manager. This is a background activity but equally vital for a theatre's success, and increasingly so as the financial structures and controls become more complicated. Over the years the post of business manager has had different titles but the following have served the Trust: Ronald Masters, John Snaith, Robert Sayer, Edward Holton, Gordon Stratford, Peter Stevens, George Rowbottom, Peter Bentley-Stephens, Ian Simpson, Jean Sands, Stuart Rogers, culminating in the appointment of Ruth Mackenzie as Executive Director of the Playhouse.

Finally, why thirty years? This period provided a balance of fifteen formative years in each of the Playhouse theatres. These were its 'golden decades', a time when the Playhouse saw the most exciting theatre in the country, and comprised a substantial example of post-war changes in the structure of British theatre. During these years, the Playhouse was host to some of the best directors, writers and actors then working, and the book was able to take the story to the end of Richard Eyre's acclaimed directorship.

CHAPTER ONE
THEATRE LIFE OF NOTTINGHAM

About one hundred years ago a theatre, known as the Grand Theatre, opened in Hyson Green, Nottingham, in an unlikely position well away from the city centre. In its early years it presented a wide range of work with visits from the D'Oyly Carte and Carl Rosa Companies, variety performers including the great Marie Lloyd; many stock repertory companies the best known being the Ben Greet which brought to the Grand H.B. Irving, son of Henry Irving, and other names which to older theatre enthusiasts still have a ring – Lillah McCarthy, Granville Barker and Sam Livesey. For years much of the fare was a succession of melodramas, their titles and players long-forgotten. There was a period when the building functioned as a cinema.

The theatre finished as the Grand in 1920 and was re-opened in that year, renamed The Nottingham Repertory Theatre, by a well-known theatrical family, then performing as the Compton Comedy Company founded by Edward Compton and his wife Virginia Bateman. In Nottingham Mrs Compton headed the organization, with two daughters Viola and Ellen, whose husbands were also leading members of the company. (There was a third daughter, Fay, the most famous member of the family who by then was playing leads in London at the beginning of what was a very distinguished career in the English theatre, ranging from pantomime principal boy to playing Ophelia to the Hamlets of John Barrymore and John Gielgud.)

The Comptons reconditioned the Grand Theatre in courageous style: redecorating internally and externally; refurnishing with every seat tip-up; putting down new carpets; providing a new green drop-curtain with an emblem of three Cs for their name; placing oil paintings, antique clock and furniture in the foyer. The stage set for the first production, *The School for Scandal*, had furniture of the period; silver candelabra and tea-service were used.

The occasion must have glittered. Dignitaries and notables of the town were present, many in evening dress. The performance went well, with Ellen Compton as Lady Teazle and Viola as Lady Sneerwell. 'At the end,' said a contemporary account, 'Mrs Compton went on stage and made a graceful little speech, referring touchingly to her husband. She kissed both her daughters, all being in tears.'

The same writer described the Comptons' start as excellent. But he was 'doubtful if the audience will be as good as the plays'. He thought the venture would have a 'sporting chance' in the town, but felt people would want a strong inducement to journey regularly to this location.

Alas, he was quickly proved correct. Only one week later, for a production of *The Rivals*, the balcony was well attended but the rest of the house half-full. However, audiences were improved in the following week for a piece entitled *Columbine* when the theatre was as full as on the opening night with 'evening dress and taxis atmosphere'. Again there were excellent stage furnishings, and a grand piano. Compton Mackenzie was visiting his family and was persuaded to speak at the end.

But an uneven pattern continued for three years, in both audience support and strength of production. Mrs Compton had made too lavish a beginning and after six months changed her manager and ran the theatre on cheaper lines. She struggled on, providing a splendid training for the younger members of the company, especially in frequent Shakespearian productions and good plays of the time such as *Hobson's Choice*, *What Every Woman Knows* and *Trelawny of the Wells*. Still insufficient Nottingham people attended habitually and in an endeavour to improve the situation the Comptons, like many theatrical managements since, and no doubt against their inclination, put on plays deemed to be more 'popular'. Gradually they lost touch with the public and in spite of appeals for funds found themselves in a financial plight. The last season, their fifth, had opened in September 1922 with audiences in good numbers but the old lack of loyalty reappeared in the following year, and finally the Comptons closed their Nottingham Repertory Theatre in May 1923 leaving for many years a gap in Nottingham theatre-going opportunities.

With all its faults it had been an oasis in a fairly drab desert. No longer would one alight from the trolley cars which thundered down the dull road, walk over a black pavement, enter the theatre and cross Mrs Compton's foyer carpet through to her magic carpet which could transport her audience to Illyria and Duke Orsino bidding his musicians. For some there was left a void which would not be filled for many years. This is the link between the old Grand and the Nottingham Playhouse and why the former has its place in an account of the latter.

The achievement of the Comptons was a foundation of significant repertory theatre-going in Nottingham. Perhaps young people of the time could not realize how fortunate they were to be audience-apprenticed to them, but in a short time they had put down distinct roots. Apart from development of personal attachment to drama there was an influence on the amateur acting companies. These became strong and were stimulated to produce good work. Members of these groups retained relationships long after the Grand had disappeared and the site become shops. They shared an ideal that another repertory of that excellence would one day be possible in Nottingham. Many years later some of the same people were still unified in a Civic Theatre Movement which had no official status but kept the concept alive. Indeed, a committee formed a practical plan to adapt an existing hall and its report was put before the city council, but it found no interest. One supposes it was rejected as merely the dream of a few enthusiasts.

This was discouraging at the time and there had to be a few more years of quiet probing. In fact the realization was nearer, in relative terms, than could have been hoped, though sadly since it was due to the outbreak of the Second World War and the accelerated circumstances arising from it.

The first months of the war in 1939/40 were uncertain and drastic for places of entertainment. Theatres were closed and it was some time before authority recognized that provision of music, drama, etc., was an important constituent of morale. The nation was hungry for diversion. To its lasting credit the government took important and imaginative steps which founded the state financing and involvement in the arts now taken for granted. This was done first through the Ministry of Education and later by the Treasury direct. The Council for the Encouragement of Music and the Arts was launched early in 1940 and CEMA was reorganized in 1946 as the Arts Council of Great Britain.

It would be difficult to overstate the impact of that body on the theatre of this country, especially in the regions. It is the subject for a book in itself, but at least it can be said here that Nottingham was an example of how vital the Arts Council became. Close connection with the establishing and maturing of the Playhouse during its years of association with the Arts Council has proved this. The alliance was an example of the council's achievement in the arts. Nor were the benefits confined to financial support. The experience and friendship of the council's officers were of great value over a long period. In our early days the council maintained regional offices one of which most fortunately was in Nottingham and run by Frederic Lloyd and N.V. Linklater.

However, before all that could take place the Playhouse had to be in existence, first and foremost as 'bricks and mortar' without which everything would continue to be dreams. I have mentioned the dismissive response of the city council to the efforts of the local Civic Theatre Movement. In spite of the new atmosphere and post-war opportunities for regional theatre there were no signs whatever in Nottingham of change of heart or interest in providing a theatre, and it would be many years yet before such an item appeared on a council meeting agenda. In the meantime Nottingham did not have the good fortune of Manchester and Birmingham whose repertory theatres came from the dedication and financial resources of, respectively, Miss Annie Horniman and Sir Barry Jackson. But if a single such benefactor did not exist the solution still had to be reached by a private route, and this became most fortuitously possible. A brief account of how this happened is justified because otherwise the prospects were bleak, probably for another generation.

One of Nottingham's first cinema buildings, in Goldsmith Street, had a small stage of sorts and underneath it a warren of compartments adaptable as dressing rooms, again of sorts. It is not indelicate, but a striking example of the conditions, to mention that the lavatory was at stage level and its use disconcerting during performances!

During the Second World War it was known as the Little Theatre in which a weekly repertory company played, run by the cinema proprietor. There was nothing here of the past delights of the Comptons' theatre. The shortcomings of the fare were matched by those of the building which, apart from stage problems, had no foyer facilities and no bar. It was, however, situated in the city centre, had quite good seating with Stalls and Circle for about 460 and, above all, the auditorium had astonishingly a true theatre atmosphere. So an affection for the place grew in the city and there was much regret when the management encountered postwar difficulties and announced imminent closure and reversion to cinema.

A small group led by Mr Fred Leatherland who was well known in local theatre, felt deeply that it should be saved as a theatre and was prepared to provide finance. A limited company was formed with Fred as chairman and subscriber of a major part of the capital. My wife and I were among the other shareholders. I recall the interview when Fred and I, representing the group, conducted the negotiations. The owner of the theatre had a long, silent think about the proposition, the clock ticked in the tiny office, and here in the balance was a decision which, though we could not know it, founded the pattern of theatre in Nottingham up to the present day. Our offer for the lease of the theatre was accepted and the little consortium set out, in retrospect fairly bravely, on the hazardous road of theatre management.

The first requirement was to get the box office selling as quickly as possible, so arrangements were made with a repertory organization which came in for a season immediately after some preparatory refurbishing had been done. Later there were negotiations with an enthusiastic group of ex-Service professionals who had set up a company called Re-Union Players, led by Campbell Singer, and including several members who became well known. The standard was good and there were satisfying highlights. One remembers a Christmas with the young Vivien Merchant as a charming Cinderella.

There was much fun and excitement from it all but also we had hard lessons, in both company management and theatre finance. Moreover, competition became stronger with increasing activity when the commercial theatre was re-forming after the war, for example the large theatre in the city again received its star-cast 'No. 1 tours'. Another major problem was the crippling burden of Entertainment Tax. These factors, together with the handicap of limited working capital, meant that eventually the venture had to be closed.

But something very important had been achieved. The building was still there and had been preserved as a theatre, not a warehouse as it is today. And, most significantly, it was there at the right time, ready to start the next and final phase of its theatre life as the Nottingham Playhouse.

Although the management could not continue, still it was determined that their much-loved Little Theatre should not disappear for ever. There were vague ideas of patrons being brought into closer relationship with the running of the theatre and perhaps having a financial involvement.

Public meetings were held at the theatre, addressed by stage personalities including the actress Freda Jackson, an old friend wanting to see repertory preserved in her home town and knowing from her own experience at Northampton how valued it was. An important ally was found in Councillor John E. Mitchell, the then Lord Mayor of Nottingham, who took the chair at one of these meetings. His support was valuable in publicizing the crusade in which more and more influential people became interested.

The management of the Little Theatre indicated that it was prepared to negotiate a tenancy of the building to a new organization able to continue its use as a theatre. An interim committee was elected from the meetings to work on the task of constructing a new administration, and in due course it became the first Board of Directors of Nottingham Theatre Trust Ltd.

We heard of a formula known to have been successful elsewhere which required the setting up of a non-profit-distributing limited company under the Companies Act 1948. Constituted in that way, not established or conducted for private gain, it was possible for the board to apply to HM Customs and Excise for exemption from Entertainment Tax. Also, and most importantly, such a company was eligible to seek association with the Arts Council of Great Britain.

Guidance was obtained from an organization called the Conference of Repertory Theatres (CORT) which federated the welfare of such theatres. Much help was given by its Director, Patrick Henderson, who had become an expert on the subject. He supplied a model Memorandum and Articles of Association and with this aid Nottingham Theatre Trust Ltd was formed.

Interviews took place with Customs and Excise and the Arts Council. It was a smooth passage, the first giving the tax dispensation, and the second agreeing to formal association, subject to the Arts Council's approval of the board's choice for the post of artistic director. This will be explained later.

Nottingham Theatre Trust had a nominal capital of only £100 and the first problem was the financial requirement to take over the theatre lease and create the Nottingham Playhouse, as the new venture was to be named. It was necessary to have improvements to the stage and dressing rooms; redecoration of the auditorium; new stage lighting installation, etc. A public appeal was sponsored by the Lord Mayor, Councillor Mitchell, who had accepted chairmanship of the Theatre Trust board. The target was £4,000 and the Arts Council, with the first of its benefactions, offered £1,000 if the appeal could raise the balance. This was achieved and the building work accomplished.

These facts give a very bare outline indeed of the immense amount of work done in a very short time to convert the vision into reality. It was all severely practical without any degree of theatrical glamour. The building work costs had absolute priority on the appeal proceeds and there was nothing available for preliminary administration which for weeks was done voluntarily in the small office containing a card table, chair, a few filing boxes, portable typewriter (all borrowed), and a telephone as the only expense necessarily but grudgingly incurred.

The initial meeting of the Theatre Trust board took place on 18 August 1948 and the opening night, with Shaw's *Man and Superman*, was on 8 November 1948. On that occasion my programme note had this paragraph:

> *It has been a long and sometimes difficult road to the point when the reader of these pages may put down his programme and look around the freshly-decorated auditorium of the Theatre in which he sits, The Nottingham Playhouse. As we wait for the commencement of the opening performance some of us will lean back, close our eyes and wonder whether it is a reality.*

In four months a theatre had been acquired and restored; an artistic director appointed and company formed together with design and stage staff;

wardrobe; front-of-house. Behind the scenes an efficient start had been made by the first board of directors of the Trust. These were:

Councillor John E. Mitchell, Chairman
W.A. Anderson
J.J. Bailey
W.J. Bennion
Sir Jack Drummond
Councillor M. Glen Bott
J.E. Mason
M. Pilkington
V. de S. Pinto
Councillor W.A. Rook
Alderman R. Shaw
A.J. Statham
F. Stephenson
R.J Willatt
J.J. Bailey, Hon. Secretary

Here was a representation from the professions, business, academic life and local government (e.g. the directors of education for the city and county). All these functioned in a private capacity, but their vocational experience and influence in the community were always available and of great value. They and their successors over the years have given an enormous amount of service to the Playhouse. Perhaps this is the place to say that the board saw its task as primarily to control the business side and have minimal input on artistic matters (not excluding expressing personal opinions), but to appoint the professional, provide a budget, agree a general policy, and leave him to carry it out. In any case, only in this way would the position interest a person of distinction.

This, then, was the background and the foundation. Ahead lay fifteen years of incredibly hard work in that first Playhouse building, in conditions having all the physical and financial constraints imaginable. But everyone, those responsible for the theatre and audiences alike, was constantly sustained by the marvellous first companies whose names read now like a theatrical *Who's Who* in themselves. Every few weeks they produced new miracles of beauty and quality on that tiny stage and acquired a national, indeed international, reputation. By 1963 their efforts had gained from the people of Nottingham sufficient regard and respect with which to persuade the City Council to provide a new theatre.

CHAPTER TWO

ANDRÉ VAN GYSEGHEM, 1948–51

I have referred to the Arts Council's wish to be involved in the appointment of the artistic director, or producer, as then called. The successful launching and future hopes for the Playhouse depended on making the correct choice for this vital position, and the Theatre Trust, only recently formed and with limited experience, welcomed having access to the Arts Council's advice. The board had interviewed two applicants each with long and distinguished previous connections in repertory theatre, but both were at an age when they might have found it difficult to generate the energy to meet the demands which undoubtedly lay ahead.

The name which the Arts Council then put forward may well have occurred to the board as ideal, but unlikely to be within its reach. This was André Van Gyseghem, eminent in the British theatre as producer, actor, writer, and established as a busy freelance director of plays. The Arts Council, in its first and arguably most significant service to the Playhouse, had with great foresight sensed the possibilities at Nottingham and persuaded Van Gyseghem to consider taking a new course in his career.

Now was a favourable time to be part of the new movement, eventually almost an explosion, in regional theatre. Also this opportunity to direct a theatre, to shape its growth and style, to control the plays and players, was unique since the actor-manager era, and the few special instances of drama-inspired individuals whose private sponsoring resources (or dynamic drive like Lilian Baylis) synchronized with their aesthetic taste. The proposition must have had its attractions for Van Gyseghem, and above all it was shored by the association with the Arts Council. He came to Nottingham for talks and viewing of the theatre, to listen to the board's ideas for it, and so accepted the challenge.

In a history of Nottingham Playhouse it is impossible to exaggerate the contribution of André Van Gyseghem to the founding of the Playhouse and the rapid achievement of its reputation. Any renown we acquired over the years, and may still have to this day, has its source in the work of Van and his company from 1948 to 1951.

André van Gyseghem

He left his assured place in the profession and came to blaze a new trail. He created fame from nothing and, every two weeks, himself directed a new production and occasionally played leading parts. He was indeed the Playhouse's inspiring leader and artistic mentor. He wrote at the time:

> *In gathering the company together at the opening of this, our first*
> *season, I had three main objects in view. Firstly to create a group of*
> *artists who would work together with the good of the Theatre as*
> *their main objective, putting their own personal advancement*
> *second; secondly to surround myself with actors who were*
> *interested in the quality of the play they performed rather than*
> *seeking 'good' parts in poor plays; and thirdly, in achieving a*
> *balance between actors of experience and young, little known*
> *people whose talent needed a vigorous theatre on which to sharpen*
> *itself. Some of the artists had worked for me before – George Hagan*
> *and Rosalind Boxall were in my productions in the Birmingham*
> *Parks the year before. Michael Aldridge I had seen give admirable*
> *performances with the Arts Council Midland Company, and I*
> *counted on these three, together with Maxine Audley whom I saw*

only once some years ago, but whom I had never forgotten, to
provide the hard core of my company, sharing the big parts equally.
If we have achieved anything during these few months it is first and
foremost a team of actors who are devoted to their work, whose
loyalty and support have overcome the difficulties of pioneering in a
Theatre where the conditions backstage make every production a
major undertaking. Finally I would like to acknowledge the work of
my designer Mr Anthony Waller, whose imaginative settings have
contributed so much distinction to our productions.

On another occasion in 1948 he had summed up his basic approach:

One of the most far-reaching effects of the War on our English
theatre has been to de-centralize it; to remove the centre of interest
from London, and spread it out over the country as a whole. Before
the War the provincial repertory theatres which were doing work of
a really high standard, could be counted on the fingers of one hand;
now this number has more than doubled itself.

It is now generally recognized that there is a big provincial public
for plays with an international reputation, for world classics, and at
the same time managements and producers have realized that these
plays cannot be prepared and rehearsed within the limits of weekly
repertory. More time is required for careful, concentrated and
detailed study of the plays, if the actors are to present them
truthfully. So now we see a growing number of repertory theatres
rehearsing for two and three weeks; changing over alternate weeks
with neighbouring companies, or using one town as a centre and
visiting surrounding towns; and we see their repertoire of plays no
longer slavishly copying the successful West End play but widening
to include the great dramas of the world.

A theatre which provides the chance for citizens to see and enjoy
the finest plays of all countries, old and new, played by a group of
professional actors who take their work as artists seriously is what I
hope will be achieved. Such a theatre can be an important, creative
and inspirational force in community life.

Nottingham Playhouse was indeed fortunate in having found a theatre director
committed to such a foundation testament and with the ability to put it into
effect.

Van Gyseghem's reference above to the importance of purposeful play study should have emphasis. On the occasions when he put forward his thoughts for another season it was stimulating to experience his learning and expertise. I suppose those first months of working with him amounted to a course in drama theory and practice, the former round the table and the latter by blazing fulfilment on our stage. Perhaps the habit of play research in early days explains why some productions specially considered in these pages include discussion of the play's content and background.

Van Gyseghem undertook the post of artistic director on 16 July 1948. At the time he was casting and rehearsing a new play by Bridget Boland entitled *Cockpit*, presented by the Arts Council and the Western Theatre Company for production in Manchester and a tour in Wales and the North-East.

A journey to Manchester for discussion with Van was combined with a visit to the play and I found it satisfying to feel that the person shortly to take charge of the Playhouse was responsible for such an exciting production. The play's circumstances required difficult integration of stage with auditorium. The *Manchester Evening News* said:

> There are limitations to the removal of the barrier between actor
> and audience. Here the method is a triumphant success. Why?
> Because this is not so much a play as an experience. . . . Cockpit *has
> been beautifully produced by André Van Gyseghem. . . . Bridget
> Boland's play draws half its strength from its dispassionate
> marshalling of facts. It leaves comment to the audience. And it
> demands that the audience give as well as take. The result is an
> evening as exciting as it is thoughtful.*

Later Van Gyseghem contemplated making *Cockpit* the opening production at Nottingham Playhouse, saying in a letter: 'I think its shock tactics would liven everyone up and attract a lot of attention to the Theatre.' But there were several changes of mind ahead before the final decision was made.

Before Van came to Nottingham in late September 1948 he was busy at auditions in London forming the company. He received over one hundred applications for the places remaining after the four or five key people he had already engaged. During negotiations with the latter he sent several to Nottingham to look at the theatre, which was still in the hands of contractors with the stage area looking like a building site. But apparently none of this deterred the visiting actors who stood reflecting on it all and said to me: 'Fine, I'll come.' George Hagan, who became a leading member of the first company, says:

Auditorium – old theatre

*I liked the little theatre the moment I saw it. I liked its warmth, its
intimacy and its shape. It was a real theatre despite its size, and was
easy and rewarding to speak in. Of course, things back stage left
much to be desired but in retrospect, who cares? The dressing rooms
were microscopic and quite airless and were situated immediately
under the stage, so that every cough or comment, seeping upwards
like the murmurings of so many Hamlet ghosts, could be clearly
heard by the frantic actors above!*

The stage alterations led to an awkward situation which nearly caused the
loss of Van Gyseghem and therefore very different fortunes for the Playhouse.
When Van first saw the stage he was understandably anxious about the
extremely limited space, but was comforted somewhat by a plan to which he
gave great importance, that is the construction of an apron stage. However,
there was a calamitous later discovery that the Circle sight lines made the
scheme impracticable. His letter replying to this news told its own story:

I am more depressed than I can say about the stage. I feel that I have fooled myself by not testing the sight lines myself when I was there. Now I am left with the original dimensions, and I feel like throwing the whole thing up. I would but for the fact that it is my own fault, and because we have gone so far. The Arts Council have been so decent about it, and so many people seem to be looking forward to the work I am supposed to do there.

However, this storm was weathered. Van's confidence was revived by the fact that his designer, Anthony Waller, was not daunted by the obstacle. And so the busy weeks went by to the point when Van and his staff arrived to live and start their adventure in Nottingham.

When Van Gyseghem came to Nottingham he was a very erect forty-two, at the peak of energy and purpose. His manner could be rather peremptory and he had limited patience with administrative hindrances. I had first met him eleven years earlier at a theatre summer school in Suffolk where he was teaching and lecturing on, among other things, the Russian theatre, on which he was an expert. To mark the beginning of his stay in Nottingham he sent a copy of his book *Theatre in Soviet Russia*, inscribed 'From Moscow to Nottingham via Leiston!' He was a fluent speaker, commanding in manner, and conveyed the same authority which, together with his distinguished position in the theatre, enabled him to attract the superb team he referred to above: young and mature actors, designer, technical staff, all eager to put themselves in his hands at this new enterprise. George Hagan:

We were very lucky in having André Van Gyseghem as Director. He had just the right qualities for the job. A fine dramatic flair, long experience in the theatre, boundless enthusiasm and an excellent visual sense. He had too that indefinable and most valuable quality of good theatrical taste.

The crusading excitement may have sustained them during the first months but eventually only dedicated professionalism maintained that standard. Van Gyseghem had made his own condition of appointment; namely, that productions must run for two weeks, but though this seemed a deliverance from the inhuman grind of weekly repertory, the high quality he set in all departments required even more constant effort.

Certainly there was little motive in the pay, which was very moderate indeed. A request from the stage manager, and another from a member of the

Exterior – old theatre

company, for an increase of £1 weekly were considered at board level and rather gravely at that, but one is glad to say both were granted! Similar authority was required for the purchase of a second-hand sewing machine and vacuum cleaner. On another occasion Van Gyseghem telephoned to say: 'For *The Apple Cart* Tony [Waller] can hire a set of Regency chairs which would make all the difference in the Cabinet scene. The cost will be £12 for the fortnight and we must know now. What about it?' Immediate backing was given and blessing contrived at the next board meeting. All this of course was not a question of meanness but plain necessity in administering small resources.

These very limited funds, providing production budgets fortnightly, were viable only with co-operation from company and staff. Solving the problems demanded all reserves of ingenuity. A major example was design and staging, in which Anthony Waller was outstanding. In a very interesting note he said,

> *The stage designer today is a specialist. He is no longer simply a pictorial artist who paints elaborate backgrounds for the actors; he must be well versed in all the mechanics and technicalities of the modern stage. A stage setting should not only be an interesting picture framed by the proscenium opening, but a three dimensional thing in which the actors can move and have their being. The designer has first to convey the mood and atmosphere of the play, so that when the curtain rises the audience is immediately transported into the world the dramatist has peopled with his characters. But that is only the beginning of his job; he must also provide a set which gives the producer full scope for grouping his actors, arranging effective entrances, and any other stage 'picture' that is necessary. If the play is one requiring changes of scene, the designer must contrive a workable method of doing it within the limitations of his theatre. Frequently he will have to make a virtue of necessity, so that a simplicity enforced by lack of space and stage machinery may produce a more effective and truly theatrical decor than a far more elaborate method would have done. Since the cinema has it all its own way with naturalism, the stage designer has come to rely more and more on his imagination and ingenuity rather than the cumbersome realism of forty years ago. And in so doing he allows the audience to use their imagination too, which, as I have discovered while working at the Playhouse, they are perfectly prepared to do!*

This theory was impeccable for the Playhouse's situation. Tony Waller had to engage his imaginative gifts with the practicalities of a stage with a depth of 12 feet from the setting-line; a wing space of 4 feet on the O.P. side; minimum stage equipment and lighting; and makeshift workshops sited inconveniently away from the theatre. The results were always admirable, as illustrations show, and on many occasions quite wonderful.

The first words spoken on the stage of Nottingham Playhouse were the commonplace 'Show him in'. It was a fancy in one's mind, while waiting the few moments for his appearance, that dear Octavius Robinson might be a symbol of our new theatre which, like him, would enter shyly but with sincerity.

The atmosphere on that first night of Shaw's *Man and Superman*, on 8 November 1948, was very tense. My programme note said:

> *It is no longer a question of people reading or hearing of preliminary plans for the Playhouse, and expressing this vague doubt or that tentative approval. Our doors are now open and our wares are displayed.*

But the audience's reception was enthusiastic. The next day a critic wrote, 'From the moment that the curtain rose . . . Nottingham realized that here was something new and exciting.'

Maxine Audley as Ann Whitfield and Michael Sherwell as Octavius Robinson in *Man and Superman* (Shaw)

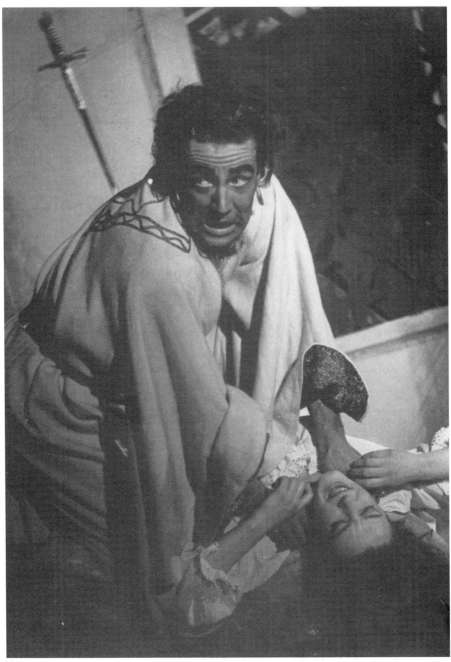

Michael Aldridge (Othello) and Rosalind Boxall (Desdemona) in *Othello* (Shakespeare)

The second play was *Othello* and these first two productions were seen as being together the opening 'display of our wares'. There was no doubt about the good impression they made on first audiences. Van Gyseghem had chosen his company well, with built-in leading casting geared perfectly to the style and pace required. George Hagan and Maxine Audley were a joy as Tanner and Ann; Michael Aldridge's Othello was superb. Van's productions were always tasteful, but he was not afraid to include touches of deliberate theatricality. Tanner, pressed by Ann into the service of holding a skein of bright red wool for her to wind, provided business simulating the playing of a hooked fish which gave the audience much amusement. A small red spot mounted at the proscenium base caught Iago's bearded and hate-contorted face, perhaps not very subtly equating him with the devil but supplementing the passionate lines. (Maybe Van recalled from his Russian theatre studies Stanislavsky's comment that Iago is 'possessed by satanic energy'.) Occasional indulgences of this kind could be afforded because the basic acting strength was dominant.

There were three other highlights in the opening season. The first came from the Playhouse's good fortune in having Van Gyseghem, when he presented his wife, Jean Forbes-Robertson, in *Twelfth Night* and Priestley's *The Long Mirror*. We were able to witness why she had been called the most enchanting

Jean Forbes-Robertson (Viola) and Maxine Audley (Olivia) in *Twelfth Night* (Shakespeare)

Viola of our time. She had a mysterious quality in both plays, but during *Twelfth Night* there were moments in her performance when the simple little playhouse was transformed into an ethereal, timeless place. Does this seem like an exaggeration? Here is James Agate, the best-known drama critic of his day, reviewing *Twelfth Night* at the New Theatre, London, in 1932:

> *The point about Miss Forbes-Robertson's performance . . . is that its sum is absolute and flawless perfection however attained. One spectator, who has seen this performance three times, is always at Viola's first entry brought to the verge of tears, with the rest a mere blur. What other tribute could Viola have? I can only salute and call attention to a perfect and perhaps unintentional thing.*

Van Gyseghem himself played Malvolio and Michael Aldridge, Aguecheek. We felt it an honour to have staged such a wonderful production. Also, it was one of the happy (but too rare) occasions when artistic perfection was matched by virtually maximum audience response. The house was completely full for ten of the twelve public performances, with an attendance result of 94 per cent. The six additional school matinées gave a total of eighteen performances in the fortnight. Simultaneously, of course, rehearsals were happening and sets being built for *The Long Mirror*.

The second outstanding feature of the season was a production of *The Apple Cart* with Van playing King Magnus. He enjoyed this enormously, yet it was difficult to comprehend how he could do the directing and also play such a heavy part. The king has one of Shaw's longest speeches and Van joked at the time that he had spent every night of the prior two weeks learning it with a wet towel round his head. The cast was very strong, including Maxine Audley as Orinthia; Leo McKern as Boanerges; George Hagan as Proteus; Elizabeth McKeowen and Rosalind Boxall as the Post/Power Mistresses. The play's staging, with the scene changes in our small space, engaged Anthony Waller in one of his hardest challenges at Nottingham Playhouse and he met it with his usual skill. Perhaps the set of chairs did help after all.

The third major production was a colourful account of *The Merchant of Venice* presented and costumed in such a way that the board of directors could hardly believe its eyes, though accustomed by now to budgetary marvels. Maxine Audley's Portia was perhaps her happiest part during her time at the Playhouse and, like Aldridge's *Othello*, does not fade in the memory.

Towards the end of the first season came an accolade, as surprising as it was encouraging. This was an invitation from the Arts Council to be one of the

André Van Gyseghem (King Magnus) and Maxine Audley (Orinthia) in *The Apple Cart* (Shaw)

four companies chosen to perform in a Repertory Theatre Festival at the Embassy Theatre, London, the others being Manchester, Glasgow and Bristol. For Nottingham, only a few months old, to be given a place beside those established theatres to represent the country's repertory was by any standards a considerable achievement. The decision to take *Othello* was made possible by Sir Barry Jackson's temporary release of Michael Aldridge who had by then joined the Birmingham Repertory Theatre. The other principal parts were played by Maxine Audley, Rosalind Boxall, George Hagan, Elizabeth McKeowen and Peter Wyngarde. We were told the production had been a strong feature of the festival. Here is George Hagan's recollection of the occasion:

> *Van liked clear and well pointed speech. When we went up to Swiss Cottage with* Othello *Stephen Williams wrote of us – 'These players are Shakespearian actors in the true sense of the term. They do not "throw away", or gabble, or chop up the verse into prose as though they were ashamed of it. They hurl it at us with the full power of their lungs and glory in its opulence.'*

The visit to the Embassy must have been particularly pleasant and evocative for Van Gyseghem who was a member of the repertory company there for four years in the thirties.

In its early months the Playhouse had been consolidated in the community by another development which, in some ways, was the most satisfying feature of all. This was the foundation of what has been claimed to be the first professional theatre performing regularly for children as part of their school life. The Directors of Education for the city and county, F. Stephenson and J. Edward Mason, were from the beginning enthusiastic supporters of the Playhouse and served on the board. They had persuaded their committees to each subscribe £500 towards the appeal fund. This was generous in itself, but co-operation continued and in January 1949, within two months of opening, an arrangement was made with the two education authorities for each of them to take, for secondary schoolchildren, three matinées of productions selected (with their agreement) from the normal repertoire, at a cost of £60 per performance. In July 1950 Mr Mason wrote:

> *So far there have been some 26,000 attendances to see* Twelfth Night, Tobias and the Angel, The Merchant of Venice, Pygmalion, The Guinea Pig, The Taming of the Shrew, The Rivals, A Hundred

Years Old, and Doctor's Joy. *Reports received from the teachers to date are most encouraging. The children have been critical but appreciative. Already a new zest has been given to literacy and dramatic studies in the schools, and there is real evidence of a newly awakened appreciation of the art of drama. Furthermore, a small itinerant company will take selected plays to audiences of rural children outside the City boundary. In addition both City and County Education Committees have sponsored visits to the performances at the Playhouse, by members of their respective Youth Groups. Already other Education Authorities are showing a developing interest in these schemes. All this means not only a more informed and more practical aspect to educational study, but the gradual building up of a mature and educated adult audience. The school children and the young people of the City and County are not only supporting the Playhouse, they will eventually help raise and carry its standards even higher.*

The county Education Director was correct. There was nothing more rewarding, or refreshing to the spirit, especially when circumstances were worrying, than calling at the Playhouse in an evening and seeing young people newly left school paying their own money to continue their theatre-going, initiated by school visits. This was obviously the basis for the Playhouse's reputation of having for years the youngest theatre audience in the country.

During the discussions with Van Gyseghem on choice of plays for schools work there was a passing reference in a letter to a concept which, to the Playhouse's lasting misfortune, never materialized. He said: 'I suppose the first play for children might be *A Midsummer Night's Dream.* Jean [Forbes-Robertson] says she will come and play Puck if she is free. Incidentally, she is trying her hand at a dramatisation of *King Solomon's Mines* which might be fun if she can do it.' Although neither of these projects was achieved Jean did visit the Playhouse once more. George Hagan salutes her memory: 'We were lucky too in having three visits from that lovely actress Jean Forbes-Robertson. It was a wonderful experience for an actor to play opposite her and to hear Viola's marvellous lines spoken as one had never heard them before, or to witness the icy intensity and cruel wit of her Hedda Gabler.'

The first season came to a close having forged a beginning for Nottingham Playhouse which was certainly successful artistically. 'But,' said Van Gyseghem, 'it was uphill work for all of us. Nottingham was no quicker than other cities to respond to its new Theatre. Audiences were thin and variable, expenses were high and at the end of the season we were in a serious financial position. It called for great courage, faith and vision for the Board of Directors to offer a second season.'

There were two simple and familiar reasons for the board's dilemma; inadequate working capital and, as Van said, an insufficient level of hard-core audience. The uncertainty about this is shown in the attendance percentages for the first six productions:

	%
Man and Superman	63
Othello	42
You Can't Take It With You	50
Arabian Nights (Christmas)	66
The Torchbearers	53
Guilty	47

Variable audience response depending on a play's appeal is, of course, a fact of life which will always be with us, and annual budgets must be compiled accordingly. To cope as the year progresses with fluctuations of between 10 and 15 per cent needs resources which the Playhouse required more time to build. But the board, on a wing and a prayer, sanctioned plans for a second season.

When it came in September 1949 there was a reversal of box office fortune which left everyone delightedly amazed. Here was an example of theatre at its most capricious. There had been a revision of seat prices, to provide better opportunity for school-leaver and student playgoers, but this was hardly sufficient explanation for the surge in attendances during the early part of the season. There was even a thought that being closed for six weeks in the summer had made the heart grow fonder and led people to realize what they were missing. No doubt the reasons were much in Van Gyseghem's mind while he was away in South Africa during the break. He had been given leave enabling him to accept an invitation to produce in Johannesburg where he had previously directed a pageant.

The second season programme was well chosen, but the first six plays did include a consecutive three from Shaw. The first two, *Pygmalion* and *Arms and the Man*, were directed by Robert Quentin during the absence of Van Gyseghem who on his return did the third, *Mrs Warren's Profession*. These three followed by *Present Laughter* (in which Van played Essendine) were the plays mainly attracting the excellent business and as a group resulted in a

The Glass Menagerie (Williams), with Jane Holland (Laura) and William Patrick (The Gentleman Caller)

surplus of £600 which, in 1950, was a very acceptable sum indeed. One dared to wonder whether the city had now become aware of its repertory theatre.

After a Christmas *Treasure Island* and then *The Taming of the Shrew* there was a welcome development which at last made Van Gyseghem's working circumstances more humane. This was the arrival in the company of Leon Gluckman, an actor whose great additional value was his ability to direct, and he was appointed Associate Producer.

Apart from the three productions by Robert Quentin and two by Douglas Seale, Van Gyseghem had up to that point directed all the remaining twenty-four. He continued to do much the major portion of that work, but it was a relief for him to have an assistant director on the staff. During his year's stay Gluckman directed on eleven occasions including a fine *The Glass Menagerie* with Barbara Everest and Jane Holland which was performed when a production of *The Rivals* (with Van as Faulkland) had been honoured by an invitation from the Dutch equivalent of the Arts Council to tour in Holland for two weeks, preceded by the Birmingham Repertory Theatre and followed by an Old Vic company. This was another indication that the Playhouse's reputation was widening, this time internationally.

During that season business had another stimulus when David Tomlinson, at the time a very popular film star, expressed a wish to join the company for

Design for Living (Coward), with
David Tomlinson

two plays, most generously waiving payment. Van Gyseghem acted with him
in *Design for Living*; the second play, less well attended, was *The Petrified
Forest*.

Another guest star occasion was the production of *Hedda Gabler*, but the
return of Jean Forbes-Robertson, magnificent as she was in the part, did not
repeat the splendid audience response of her first visit. In fact, in spite of
continued acclaim for the quality of the work, attendances had again become
erratic, and in some end-of-season comments Van Gyseghem discussed the
subject. He questioned his audience, and reaffirmed his ideals for the
Playhouse:

> *Would it seem to indicate that you come, not out of love for the
> theatre and the artist's exhibition of his craft, but out of curiosity,
> and once that is satisfied the interest fades – or is it again the choice
> of play? You see how frequently the phrase 'choice of play' crops
> up? Yet I believe that if we take the Box Office receipts as our sole
> guide to this important question we should not be sailing a true
> course. We should be forsaking an ideal for immediate gain –
> hugging the coast instead of venturing out across the ocean, braving
> unknown dangers in a voyage of discovery. For that is what every*

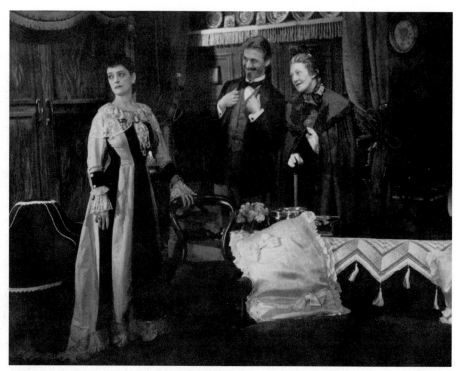

Jean Forbes-Robertson as Hedda Gabler (Ibsen)

visit to the theatre should be – a voyage of discovery and revelation.
No we are not nearly there yet. There is so much more to be done.
We must discover new playwrights, attempt new methods of
production and design, we must feel free to experiment if need be.
We must take the long view in building-up theatre lovers of the next
generation, and get our plays seen by more and more young people
and school children.

Here was the Van Gyseghem the Playhouse had always known, still
enthusiastic and eager to continue towards his heart's desire, after two years
toil and some disappointment.

Almost symbolically the third season opened in cheerful fashion with *The
Happiest Days of Your Life*, with Van directing and playing.

In what was to be his final period at Nottingham Playhouse he applied all
his experience in assembling a balanced programme. There was some
compromise with the inclusion of several 'popular' plays, but they were the
best of their genre and always done with full care and sincerity. They were

The Lady's Not For Burning (Fry), with George Hagan (left) and Ursula O'Leary (centre)

alongside two Shakespeares (including *Hamlet*), two Shaws, Barrie, Wilde, Bax, Miller (*Death of a Salesman*) and the premiere of one new play, *Here Choose I* by Yvonne Mitchell. From September 1950 to July 1951 there were twenty-two productions. Van Gyseghem had by then begun to feel the strain of overwork and finally, temporarily exhausted by it all, he announced that he must leave the Playhouse at the end of the season.

His last production was Coward's *Private Lives* and the forty-eighth he had directed himself out of a total of sixty-four in two and a half years. The personal achievement was inseparable from that of his stage designer, Anthony Waller, who did every production but one! All this work must rank among the best examples of concentrated theatrical effort made for an ideal; for the benefit of a community.

It was good to know that this achievement was recognized away from the Playhouse. Greetings came on the theatre's second birthday from John Moody, then Drama Director, Arts Council of Great Britain: 'The Arts Council offer the Nottingham Repertory Company their warmest congratulations on the work of their first two years. From an uphill start they have made remarkably rapid progress and are now regarded by the Council as a model repertory theatre.'

When he left Nottingham, in July 1951, Van Gyseghem knew that he and his company had accomplished the objective of establishing the Playhouse among the country's leading regional theatres, and they were aware also that they left with the admiration and profound gratitude of their audience.

In fact it was not a last farewell. Van Gyseghem returned as a guest director on several occasions, and for a special period in 1963. But now the board had the responsibility of finding a successor as able and unsparing of himself, company and staff.

CHAPTER THREE
JOHN HARRISON, 1951–57

There was no relaxation for the board during the Playhouse summer recess in 1951. Finding the replacement for Van Gyseghem was a difficult matter within the short period up to the start of the new season in September, and to give more time for a permanent new appointment the board made temporary arrangements to the end of the year.

Guy Verney, with Pembroke Duttson as designer, staged a group of five productions: *The School for Scandal, Captain Carvallo, A Midsummer Night's Dream, Dear Brutus* and *Venus Observed*. Following these Joan Swinstead directed two plays, *The Barretts of Wimpole Street* and *The Holly and the Ivy*, leading neatly to a lively Christmas season of *Aladdin* and *Charley's Aunt* done by Leslie French.

Thus four months were gained and during that time a new Director of Productions, John Harrison, was appointed in December 1951. He stayed in

John Harrison

Nottingham for five and a half years and it can be stated unequivocally that the Playhouse was as fortunate in its second director as it had been in its first, and for twice the length of time.

John Harrison started his theatrical life at Birmingham, first as a member of the Repertory Theatre School and soon as a regular acting member of the company. In 1946 Sir Barry Jackson became Director of the Shakespeare Memorial Theatre at Stratford-upon-Avon and took with him from Birmingham three members of his company. They were Paul Scofield, Peter Brook and John Harrison. It was while playing in Peter Brook's production of *Romeo and Juliet* that John met his first wife Daphne Slater, who was the youngest Juliet ever at Stratford. He played Ferdinand to her Miranda in the Stratford *Tempest* of 1948. In 1948–9 he made a tour of Australia with Anew McMaster's Shakespeare Company, playing a large number of parts and was associate producer. On return, and having decided that production was to be his aim, in 1949 John Harrison succeeded Kenneth Tynan as Director of Productions at the David Garrick Theatre, Lichfield. Later he produced at Guildford and Leatherhead, and had a particular success in 1950 at the Rudolf Steiner Hall in London with a production of Shakespeare's *Pericles*. Paul Scofield played Pericles and in the cast were Beatrix Lehmann, Mary Morris, Donald Sinden, Daphne Slater and Peter Bull. A second Shakespeare production in London was *Hamlet* at the New Bolton's Theatre with David Markham, Rosalinde Fuller and Andrew Cruickshank.

John Harrison brought to Nottingham Playhouse the stimulating impact of a different style in production, play choice and personnel. It was, perhaps naturally, as the new director's age was twenty-seven, a noticeably younger approach, which had also a certain poetic quality. (But in addition the leadership was technically hard and demanding. John describes himself as being in those days a 'considerable termagant'.) The play lists, while continuing with standard classics, began to include the names of Anouilh, Eliot, Bernard, Whiting, Morgan, Greene, Lorca, Betti, Fry and Ustinov. But the likes of Rattigan, Agatha Christie, Ben Travers and Coward had their place also. A group of six consecutive plays taken from the middle of the first season was *Murder in the Cathedral*, *Ring Round the Moon*, *The Seagull*, *The Cocktail Party*, *She Stoops to Conquer* and *Six Characters in Search of an Author*. This weight of work, undertaken in three months, would not be contemplated today, and it is unlikely that there would be sufficient volume of audience support for it. Theatre everywhere now has to face the new ingredients in our rapidly changing life and times; the range of entertainments and diversions available in the growing array of contemporary venues and in the home. When asked about the old fortnightly achievements John Harrison said it was possible because

> *We were all young, serious-minded (a few larks apart) and*
> *ambitious. . . . We lived and breathed nothing but theatre. We had*
> *our heads down. Also, of course, actors did a considerable amount*
> *of work for themselves and on their own. A director concerned*
> *himself with the broad sweep rather than the detail. We were all*
> *jolly glad to be doing something we wanted to do and were so*
> *totally escapist that it is shocking to contemplate. Immoral and*
> *wonderful.*

Concerning problems with present-day counter-attractions, one keeps faith in the power of an audience's unique involvement during live theatre. No other experience has such warmth and heart or that alchemy which can occur between players and audience.

However, there was sorcery of a different and unwelcome kind hovering over John Harrison's first production at the Playhouse in January 1952. There is a theatrical superstition about the staging of *Macbeth* and ill-luck duly arrived at dress rehearsal when the leading actor, John Lindsay, fell from a rostrum and broke an ankle. Bernard Kay, cast as Banquo, heroically studied Macbeth's lines through day and night, and the substitute for Banquo conned that part on a train bringing him from London. As often happens in such adversity the first performance was stirring and received enthusiastically. John Lindsay, with plastered leg encased in velvet and black-robed for further concealment, quickly returned. Perhaps this actor could be forgiven for recognizing the supposed shadow round Macbeth, for which he had been cast at Oldham four years earlier. On that occasion he had to drop out and the actor who replaced him died later from blood poisoning after a sword thrust in the duel with Macduff. The Playhouse setting, by Henry Graveney, was open and plain, making an effective background for the lovely Jacobean costumes obtained from the Stratford Memorial Theatre, and it allowed the action to be flowing and continuous. One critic thought the audience had been given some idea of how the play looked when it was originally presented in 1610 and said, 'It will be a change, at least, from the Gothic gloom which so often obscures, in the swirling mists of the blasted heath, the essential tragedy of the conscience-tormented opportunist, Macbeth.' The mishap to Lindsay was the only cloud over a powerful production which launched John Harrison's long regime at the Playhouse.

Denis Quilley and Daphne Slater in
Colombe (Anouilh)

Other new names in the company were Basil Hoskins, Patricia Kneale, Hazel Hughes, Richard Gale, Lee Fox, Colin Graham, Ewen Solon. At the end of the season they were joined by Daphne Slater who in many memorable parts became for several years the essence of the Playhouse style, and there is lasting affection for her. One of those occasions was the first provincial production of Anouilh's *Colombe* about which the *Manchester Guardian* said:

> It will be remembered for Daphne Slater's playing of the flower girl
> who marries the penniless musician, falls into the claws of his
> ranting actress-mother and trips with such devastating innocence to
> the bad. Here is a performance that not merely charms, but
> convinces you that it is right. Miss Slater puts on corruption as if it
> were a new hat, or the last unsold bunch of her own flowers. It is
> like an awakening: Blake's dreadful light is breaking upon her, and
> she basks in it like a child at the sea.

Two more 'natural' parts for Daphne had been the leads in Ibsen's *A Doll's House* and the play which Barrie wrote for Elisabeth Bergner, *The Boy David*. The latter performance was quite special and inspired the critic J.C. Trewin to include it in his 'most valuable experiences in thirty-three years of steady playgoing. . . . Daphne Slater as David and John Harrison as producer showed how the play could rise from the text.' Also, the critic from *John O'London's Weekly* recalled the anti-climax of the first production of the play at His Majesty's Theatre in 1937 after 'woes of every kind' in the planning, and its withdrawal after a dull run of only six weeks, not to be performed again for many years. The review of the Playhouse production continued:

> *spoken by young players in the city where Barrie was a journalist so long ago . . . the dialogue came through with singular freshness. . . . I left the Theatre feeling that if it had been suitably presented in London, without premature fanfares, and with a David of Daphne Slater's radiant simplicity, Barrie's last work might not have been so sadly and unkindly shelved. . . . It can wheedle without being sentimental, it is a clear, delicate story-telling, a sketch in pastel. No need to blame Barrie for having failed to reproduce the bold colours of the Bible; he did not try to do this. Here I want only to note how Daphne Slater acted David with an unstrained faith in the part, a natural appreciation, a quick boyish fervour that never approached archness. She is one of the young actresses to whom we look for the future.*

Looking back at the end of his time at Nottingham Playhouse John Harrison said: 'I know we should like you to remember us for *The Boy David*, and for Betti's *Summertime*.'

During the second season John had directed a production of *The Tempest* using Loudon Sainthill's costumes from Stratford-upon-Avon and with Robert Eddison as Prospero. There had been a further influx of players into the company and in the cast were Denis Quilley, Graham Crowden, Dennis Woodford, Judith Stott, Jeremy Burnham, Julian Somers and these became the core in many plays. Reviewing *The Tempest*, the *Manchester Guardian* (NMR) was again well pleased with

> *a distinguished production. . . . Mr. Harrison, abjuring tricks, has striven first for the clear and vital speaking of the play. The result, as the phrases are knit up tautly, is a mounting excitement. . . . Few of the Company which serves his intentions so faithfully have been imported for the occasion. One of the exceptions is Robert Eddison's majestic Prospero, whose gravely cadenced voice makes memorable his flattest tracts of verse as his presence ennobles every*

Daphne Slater as David in *The Boy David* (Barrie)

scene in which he appears. But Judith Stott, whose Miranda seemed
not to have trod the earth until the curtain went up, was playing
Cinderella in last week's pantomime. This is an exquisite
performance. To hear Miranda's 'What is't? a spirit?' is to watch a
flower opening, infinitely fragile yet perfectly Trusting that the day
will bring only sun and beneficient dews, which are provided by the
wondering tenderness of Jeremy Burnham's Ferdinand.

Henry Graveney's decor had 'a deep-sea shimmer'.

It is more satisfactory to quote these accounts, particularly as they have
such critical skill, than using, after so many years the conjured memory of one
closely associated with those days. Enchantment there certainly was, but the
view is at a long distance and there might be exaggeration. So it is good to find
favourable confirmation of the work's quality to complement the quantity
already described.

Robert Eddison as Prospero, Judith
Stott as Miranda and Patricia Kneale
as Ariel in *The Tempest* (Shakespeare)

John Harrison opened his third season with *As You Like It*, for a run of
three weeks which at that time was fairly bold. Maybe a line in the first scene
of this play set the mood: 'Fleet the time carelessly, as they did in the golden
world,' or perhaps it was a feeling for the freedom of Arden, but John called
his production 'A Musical Comedy of the First Elizabethan Age'. It had
costumes of the Charles I period: knee-breeches, high boots, cloaks, plumes,
and it was all very gay and gallant. Daphne Slater was Rosalind and Jeremy
Burnham Orlando and among the new names were Michael Barrington and
Margaret Wolfit. Diccon Shaw wrote new settings for the lyrics sung by
Norman Platt, the Sadlers Wells baritone, as Amiel. Bernard Shaw said of
Touchstone: 'Who would endure such humour from anyone but Shakespeare?
– an Eskimo would demand his money back if a modern author offered him
such fare.' On this occasion Graham Crowden gave an unusually urbane
interpretation of him whom John Harrison saw as 'a gentlemanly fool, as well-
bred and intelligent as any of his companions but forced to turn an honest
penny by jesting. . . . I have tried to get an intellectual quality to his wit.'

   This was a happy start to the season which went on to include Sheridan's
The Critic ('Now then for my magnificence!' exclaims Mr Puff at the rehearsal
of his play, 'my battle! my noise! and my procession! – You are all ready?').

Derek Godfrey as Gaveston and
Robert Eddison as the king in *Carnival
King* (Treece)

There was a British public premiere of the play by Alfred Adam, *Sylvie and
the Ghost*, in a new translation by John Harrison; another premiere
Carnival King by Henry Treece, a poet who chose prose to tell the tragic
story of Edward II. This was a significant occasion and the play must have
recognition here. There was a certain aptness in Treece's piece being
launched in the city, although he does not make the point that Nottingham
Castle was the place where retribution finally caught up with Roger
Mortimer, the disaffected noble who was involved in Edward's murder. He
was also the seducer of the king's wife Isabella, who was goaded to
submission by Edward's rejection of her and her hatred of his favourites.
The most colourful of these was Piers de Gaveston whose relationship with
the king is taken to have been homosexual. There was an artistic
temperament in Edward II, as in his great-grandson Richard II. Intrigues,
banishments, treachery and the failings of unfitted occupants in a kingly
office thrust upon them by the accident of birth; with such dramatic
materials it is surprising that Edward II has apparently been neglected by
playwrights since Marlowe. Henry Treece's writing was a mixture of
poetical prose with anachronistic inclusions reminiscent of Christopher Fry.
Here is Gaveston with the king:

GAVESTON

> *There are some men who chop down trees, or chop off heads, or read the stars, who come at the end of the day to some warm blankets, where they rest their limbs, or assuage their curiosity in sleep. They live to seventy and gradually become less able than they were. . . . And when at last we hear that they've gone, we say, 'well fancy that! Old Jenkins down the street passed on last night. Cerebral thrombosis, so they say. He hadn't looked himself this month or more. He had a stroke, you know, when the last war broke out!' Yes that's Jenkins, and Jones, and Johnson! Their fingers are thick and they like cabbage. They pay their taxes regularly and never read a book that isn't about animals or the way men die! But what of the others Ned? what of the boys who sniff at mignonette?*

EDWARD

> *I love 'em all Peter! Those who love musk or medlars; and those who dream of flags or shepherd's pie!*

Earlier in the same scene the poet in Treece rises:

EDWARD

> *Oh Piers, Piers! Peter, Peter! You stand at the gates of Heaven and let me in! Peter, you have fished for my soul and caught it in the net of your eyes! Yes, Peter, the rock I'm founded on, my rock of lapis lazuli, of agate, or of diamond – how could my heart beat on if you were gone?*

With such a husband Queen Isabella had her problems and some felt that she was a more interesting character in Treece's play than in Marlowe's. She was played movingly by Daphne Slater, and Robert Eddison returned to play Edward with his customary graceful authority and beauty of voice. One remembers a superb Gaveston from Derek Godfrey, and these three were at the heart of strong casting in a production which attracted the national critics who generally praised it, though there was some doubt about the epilogue, and feeling in other respects also that the play required 'revision and clarification'. But it is good that this script was brought to life at the Nottingham Playhouse.

The play following *Carnival King* was the first professional performance in England of Anouilh's *Waltz of the Toreadors*; then *Julius Caesar* sandwiched between *Rookery Nook* and *Dandy Dick*. It may have been that the

Shakespeare felt uncomfortable between these bedfellows, but putting it into Elizabethan costume and convention was not well received and one critic thought that for Julius Caesar 'there is, after all, something about a toga which is fine, fine, fine'.

The French writer Baudelaire has a purple paragraph:

> *Julius Caesar! What a sunset splendour this name sheds upon the imagination! If ever a man on earth seemed like a God, it was Caesar. Powerful and charming, courageous, learned and generous, he had every power, every glory and every elegance! He whose greatness always went beyond victory, and who grew in stature even in death! He whose breast, transfixed by the blade, could find utterance only for a cry of a father's love! He to whom the dagger seemed less cruel than the wound of ingratitude!*

Perhaps experiment in non-classical treatment is difficult in such a context. Years later the Playhouse tried a production in modern dress. With what does one relate frock coat, striped trousers and spats? The Cabinet Room? The board room? The Stock Exchange? Certainly, there would seem to be something incompatible in Mark Antony saying to Caesar's dead body clad in formal morning dress: 'Thou art the ruins of the noblest man / That ever lived in the tide of times.'

The next season was another plum pudding of choices and no compromise with anxious theories about audiences being unsettled by mixed extremes. *See How They Run* stood between *Marching Song* and *Romeo and Juliet*; *The Cherry Orchard* next to *The Cat and the Canary*; *The Burning Glass* between *Toad of Toad Hall* and *Nightmare Abbey*. On the latter play the *Manchester Guardian* said: 'The brightest jewel of this production was Derek Godfrey's Scythrop Glowry. Mr Godfrey is a master of the curling lip, the flared nostril, the swivelling eye-ball, and his performance an enchanting essay in the precious ridiculous.' Those of us who knew this distinguished actor and dear colleague will recognize how exactly those words caught Derek Godfrey's touch in so many parts during the fifteen months of his unforgettable contribution to Nottingham Playhouse. Other names in the company at that time were David Aylmer, Diana Fairfax, Jane Wenham, Kendrick Owen, Jill Showell, Barbara New, John Nettleton, Dierdre Doone and, in Ustinov's *No Sign of the Dove*, Joan Plowright made her first appearance at Nottingham.

Also there had been two important staff changes in the appointment of Kay

Gardner as Associate Producer and the designer Voytek to replace Henry Graveney. Voytek stayed for over three years and was one of the Playhouse's most resourceful designers. Born in Warsaw in 1925 and living there until 1943, he was active in the Polish Underground Movement and was captured by the Germans but later fought with the British Eighth Army in Italy. After the war he came to England and studied at the Old Vic Theatre School. He had first met John Harrison for the production of *Pericles* and before Nottingham had worked with the West of England Theatre Company and at York. Kay Gardner was an experienced producer who had been at Guildford, Dundee, Salisbury and Carlisle. In the previous season John Frankau, the Stage Director, had taken an occasional production, but Miss Gardner's arrival gave John Harrison additional relief.

The new season had started very light-heartedly with Anouilh's *Thieves Carnival*, ideal, as one critic said, for 'anyone feeling frivolous, or down in the dumps and wanting to feel frivolous'. Among the several Anouilh productions of those days this was perhaps the most completely uninhibited, free for example of the dark elements in *Waltz of the Toreadors*.

John Harrison described *Romeo and Juliet* as a 'dramatic poem of classical simplicity which must be left to speak for itself' on which he based a straightforward production. In this he was near to William Hazlitt's placing of the play as being 'The only tragedy which Shakespeare has written entirely on a love story. . . . There is the buoyant spirit of youth in every line, in the rapturous intoxication of hope, and in the bitterness of despair.' Hazlitt quotes another critic: 'Whatever is most intoxicating in the odour of the southern spring, languishing in the song of the nightingale, or voluptuous in the first opening of the rose, is to be found in this poem.' Romeo and Juliet are in love but they are not love-sick, so Derek Godfrey and Diana Fairfax played with fine control, without sentimentality. The production contained some remarkable staging – fourteen people grouped naturally in the tiny space, still leaving room for the duellists.

The Christmas play, anticipating the future with a run of five weeks, was *Toad of Toad Hall*, the adaptation by A.A. Milne. Derek Godfrey was a joyous Toad (the versatility of repertory – after Romeo!) with David Carr, David Aylmer and Michael Barrington as the other famous animals. Box office business was prodigious, so an all-round happy Christmas.

In the early part of 1955 came a particular example of John Harrison's adventurous play-choosing, with the rarely performed Jacobean tragedy *'Tis Pity She's a Whore*, of which its author John Ford said 'the gravity of the subject may easily excuse the lightness of the title'. That subject, as the

Left to right: Badger (Michael Barrington), Toad (Derek Godfrey), Mole (David Carr) in *Toad of Toad Hall* (Milne)

producer said, expounded with frankness and sympathy by the most fearless of the followers in Shakespeare's tradition, is the incestuous love of a brother and a sister. The play was printed in 1633, and, after a few contemporary productions, had stayed unperformed until Donald Wolfit's revival at Cambridge in 1940. In a letter to the press Gareth Lloyd-Evans, then on the staff at Nottingham University, said:

> *I beg space to thank the Nottingham Playhouse Company and its*
> *producer John Harrison, for the performance of John Ford's 'Tis Pity*
> *She's a Whore. As well as overcoming such technical difficulties as a*
> *small stage, the company succeeded to a large extent in dealing a*
> *hammer-blow to a tradition of criticism which has sought to judge this*
> *play (among others) as virtually unpresentable to present-day audiences.*

The *Manchester Guardian* (NS) in another of its urbane notices said 'the grasp of this production is firm. Derek Godfrey and Diana Fairfax are a

Derek Godfrey as Giovanni and Diana Fairfax as Annabella in *'Tis Pity She's a Whore* (Ford)

shining, haunted pair who succeed in the testing task of conveying a passion at once bright and damned. Elizabethan gilded youth has grown old; what we have here is Romeo and Juliet gone bad, a golden apple rotting at the core.'

Two months later we staged the premiere of a play commissioned for the Playhouse by the Arts Council from Henry Treece, *Footsteps in the Sea*. This was about the Viking invaders of England in the ninth century, a much less immediately dramatic situation than in *Carnival King*, Treece's previous play on Edward II and his court, compared with which the Vikings and the Saxons were, in one critic's words, 'a rather plodding earthbound lot'. Another recalled Chesterton's comment on 'those great, beautiful, half-witted men from the sunrise and the sea'. Perhaps the choice of subject should not be attributed to Henry Treece. It was reported that he had wanted to write a play about the Wars of the Roses but John Harrison had seen a children's book by Treece called *Vikings' Dawn* and asked for the new play to be about those people. The first draft was judged by author and producer to be unsuitable and several revisions were written before the final script. It seemed that uncertainties appeared also over the design. Voytek said that one of his difficulties had been to prevent himself making the Viking invaders look too much like characters from *Prince Igor*. In his settings he made an effective use of fisherman's net. After the impressive impact of *Carnival King* the national critics were in full attendance and, although their reactions this time were generally less eager, there was recognition of the quality of Treece's work. *The Times* referred to 'an opening act in which great surges of speech in verse and rhythmic prose burst in words like the smarting spray of the North Sea. . . . In performance the play splits into brief squalls of violent action and long spells of speech-making. Some of these passages, such as the girl's glimpse of England at Easter, sing in the ear.' But in spite of the lustrous verse and imagery it was felt that there were weaknesses in dramatic construction; in longship terms an occasional loss of rudder. One remembers strong and sincere acting from Dierdre Doone and John Turner. The success of *Carnival King* may not have been repeated, but the Playhouse was glad to have given another opportunity to this playwright. In all producing theatres the encouragement of new work should be a principle, materializing as often as deserving scripts and funds allow.

New members of the company for the season opening in September 1955 were Bernard Horsfall, Roger Gage, Freda Gaye, Mavis Edwards and Frederick Bartman. Joan Plowright returned after playing in the Orson Welles production of *Moby Dick* at the St James Theatre, London.

At this time it was Nottingham's turn to host the Conference of Repertory Theatres, and to mark the occasion permission was obtained from Jean Anouilh to present the English premiere of his play, *The Ermine*. It cannot have been a light-hearted night out for the delegates but as theatre specialists they probably found interest in what a critic described as 'a morbid yet dramatically exciting exercise in psychology with love and murder as its fulcrum', which towards the end became starkly melodramatic. But it was also summarized as 'a night of theatrical fire and a credit to Nottingham'. The audience level of 66 per cent for this production is interesting. Because of it being a premiere occasion there had been more publicity than usual and there were national reviews, but it was fairly testing dramatic material and the very reasonable attendance figure indicated that an enlightened and loyal audience had emerged.

After a charming Goldini *Mirandolina*, in which Joan Plowright was a vivacious mistress of the inn, came an important production of *The Winter's Tale*. The style of this was signified in a programme note by John Harrison describing the play as 'fairy-tale, simple, mellow as old wine, ripe as a

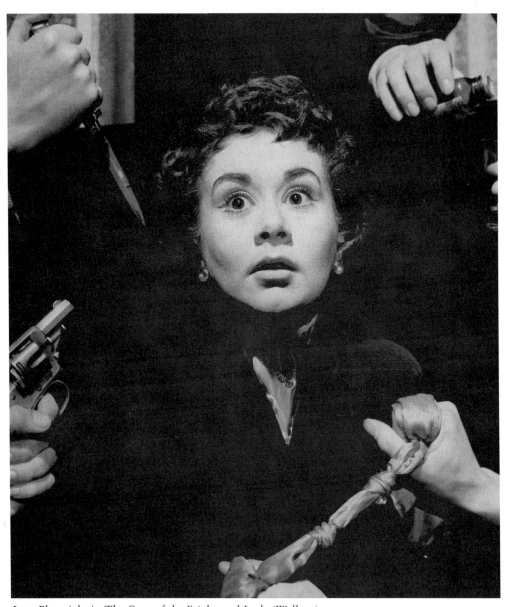

Joan Plowright in *The Case of the Frightened Lady* (Wallace)

Daphne Slater as Hermione in *The Winter's Tale* (Shakespeare)

peach . . . the rich autumnal Shakespearian medley of court tragedy, low comedy, pastoral song and young love, with the pervading message of forgiveness and the righting of wrongs'. It is also, as someone has said, 'saturated in the English countryside', inspiring some of Shakespeare's most enchanting lyrics. Daphne Slater (who about this time was said by Kenneth Tynan in the *Observer* to be 'the best ingenue in the country') played the wronged queen as 'the embodiment of all that is sweet and stately in womanhood', and in one critic's view was 'the best Hermione in [his] recollection'. Joan Plowright was a gentle and gravely moving Perdita, and also arranged the dance. Diccon Shaw again composed the music for a Playhouse Shakespeare. Voytek's costumes were particularly effective; Hermione in 'the white and silver of a snow queen'.

In April 1956 this production was taken to the Zagreb Dramatic Theatre, Yugoslavia, as part of an exchange (the first of its kind between the two countries) arranged by the British Centre of the International Theatre Institute. To Nottingham came two plays, Lorca's *Blood Wedding* and *Blizzard* by Pero Budak, acted by Playhouse companies and produced by Kosta Spaic, a director at the National Theatre of Zagreb. The designs for settings and costumes were Yugoslavian. No English version of *Blizzard* was available, so a special translation was made by Professor V. de S. Pinto and a colleague at Nottingham University. This reciprocal theatrical event was no doubt a contribution to international understanding and had some cultural value, but its economics were somewhat disastrous for the Playhouse which by reduced box office levels, and other costs, incurred a loss of £1,400.

John Harrison had been away to direct Ben Jonson's *Volpone* at the Bristol Old Vic, working again with Derek Godfrey as Voltore. Eric Porter was Volpone, Peter O'Toole Corvino, and Alan Dobie Mosca. The invitation to direct this major production was a recognition of John Harrison's standing and confirmed a London critic's description of him as 'one of the best young directors in England'.

At Christmas 1955 Nottingham had the benefit of Harrison's writing talents in his dramatization of *Alice in Wonderland and Through the Looking Glass*. The local press referred affectionately to 'Daphne in Wonderland' and Miss Slater was indeed a truly Tenniel Alice in her pink and blue dress and white apron. To see her was 'to slip decades off one's life and imagine oneself back on that hearthrug with the book opened for the first time'. This production was an example of repertory team-work. Several members of the company played two or three parts, for example Kendrick Owen took the March Hare, Tweedledum and Haigha; Graham Crowden played the Mad Hatter and Hatta; Joan Plowright was the Mouse, the Cheshire Cat and the Red Queen. Jill Showell played three parts while rehearsing a major prize in the career of any actress – the title role in Shaw's *St Joan*. *Alice* played to 80 per cent audiences over the five-week run and made a profit of £700, a vital result in a season which fluctuated considerably financially. Paradoxically, the company's success and reputation, which encouraged boldness in play choice, heightened the problems. The 'House Full' occasions of a heavy production could not, in the small capacity auditorium, recoup the shortfall on less popular nights of the week. So *St Joan* played to 80 per cent capacity but lost £131. The production, in February 1956, was the first Shaw play since May 1952, and the last of four during John Harrison's five and a half years at the Playhouse. It was the only performance of Shaw's masterpiece during fifteen years in the old Goldsmith Street theatre, and appropriately marked the centenary of his birth. Its staging problems in the cramped conditions ranked with those encountered for the Shakespeares, and the designer's ingenuity was crucial. Voytek deployed all his experience in castle, cathedral and courtroom. Jill Showell's Joan was stronger on the earthy, soldierly side than the spiritual. One remembers fine speaking from the men; David Aylmer's Inquisitor, Frederick Bartman's Cauchon. There was a spirited and convincing Dunois from Roger

Gage. It is satisfying to recall also that *St Joan* was a Children's Theatre production giving a rare opportunity for young playgoers to see one of the great plays of our time.

The schools matinées were still proceeding, in spite of an occasional difficulty in agreeing the plays with the education authority. The work was supplemented by an annual county tour to schools in Mansfield, Retford and Newark. The productions taken over six years were:

1952   *Twelfth Night* (directed by Val May who later became Producer at the Playhouse)

1953   *Noah Gives Thanks* by Eric Crozier

1954   Scenes from *A Midsummer Night's Dream*

1955   *Lady Precious Stream* by S.I. Hsuing (a full-scale company prior to Playhouse production)

1956   *As You Like It* (another full production after an Arts Council tour of theatre-less towns in north-east England)

1957   *Noah* by André Obey

In mid-1956 a well-contrasted exchange was arranged with the Sheffield Playhouse company who brought their production of *Misalliance* directed by Geoffrey Ost while Nottingham took Ugo Betti's *Summertime*. John Harrison had an affection for this charming Italian comedy about young love; the sensitive, ingenuous girl next door helping the wayward boy playmate out of his scrapes, and when he talks of leaving home for the big city realizing her love and the need to steer him towards their happy ending. Dirk Bogarde and Geraldine McEwan acted these parts in London. At the Playhouse Alberto and Francesca were Frederick Bartman and Daphne Slater who 'imparted a witty maturity'. It was all enchanting, sweetly nostalgic and played under a blue Italian sky within Voytek's set featuring wicker frames and recalling Chianti bottles.

The season ended with a popular comedy of the time, André Roussin's *The Little Hut*, directed by David Buxton thus enabling John Harrison to leave for a much-needed holiday. Five years' heavy work and responsibility had left him tired, drained and, as he said in a letter, 'at the stage when I would consider paying someone to give me a break'. He hoped that 'having lain fallow for a bit I shall be ready to grow some new ideas'.

The past year had certainly been arduous. It had included two premieres, four classics, two Shaws including the *St Joan*, and six other plays of significance in a total of twenty-three productions, which had meant great

Daphne Slater as Francesca and
Frederick Bartman as Alberto in
Summertime (Betti)

pressure on every department of the theatre. This had been the situation over
the eight years since the Playhouse opened, and of course in one hundred and
fifty productions there had been times when the overwork showed. All the zeal
of Van Gyseghem and Harrison and their teams could not avoid some
unevenness, but no relaxation was implied on these occasions. They had
required the usual amount of planning, rehearsal time, line study, design and
provision of set and dress.

The average attendance of 69 per cent for 1955/6 was good, but rising costs
and loss on the Yugoslav episode badly affected the year's financial result.
Concern about that influenced the next year's choice of programme which
appeared to be rather less adventurous, though it hardly deserved an Arts
Council stricture that they 'felt some misgivings and it was not nearly so
exciting compared with the previous year'. However, it included what became
fine productions of Shaw's *Caesar and Cleopatra*; *Twelfth Night*; *The Servant
of Two Masters*; *The Country Wife*; *Miss Julie*; Betti's *The Queen and the
Rebels*; *The Matchmaker*. The drama critic Eric Keown, writing at the time
about the Playhouse, said:

> *Experienced repertory managers do not underrate their audiences.*
> *Naturally they know that an unalloyed diet of Brecht, Beckett and*

Ionescu will produce indigestion in the most enlightened customer
as quickly as an unbroken run of lobster thermidor and creamed
duck, and so they sandwich the menu judiciously with lighter fare;
but they also see to it that they give their fortunate audiences a
selection which in quality and interest should be more than a match
for the ogres on the other side, television and the cinema.

Mr Keown ended his piece by referring to his faith in 'the imagination and thoroughness of John Harrison's methods. His company works as a team, and a winning team; and when one considers the desperate rush of repertory life, even on a fortnightly basis, the results seem to me both baffling and wonderful.'

The new season commenced in September 1956 with Molière's *School for Wives* in the version by Miles Malleson. The part of Georgette was acted by a newcomer to the company, Pat Heywood, who had played it also at the first performance of Malleson's adaptation when he himself acted the aged husband, Arnolphe. At the Playhouse the anguished old man was Peter Duguid, sparring with Ruth Meyers as his tantalizing young wife, Agnes. Duguid had joined the company as actor and Assistant Producer. He was a very able aide and during the year directed eight plays including the second of the season, *I Am a Camera*, John Van Druten's adaptation of Christopher Isherwood's novels on his adventures in the Berlin of the early thirties.

Thus, after the pressures of setting up the new season and directing the Molière, John Harrison was given more time to prepare the next production, Shaw's *Caesar and Cleopatra*. His comment on this play was an example of his lively approach:

Egypt under the Roman occupation – that has almost a headline
ring about it! But this witty oriental extravaganza about the ageing,
balding Caesar and the Egyptian child-queen is more like an
Edwardian Scherezade – a Shavian Night's Adventure. Shaw's
humorous, original Caesar lacks nothing in greatness, but it is the
greatness of a godlike liberality. And his kittenish Cleopatra is
spitfire, rather than the serpent of Old Nile. It is an eventful,
colourful play with much more action than we expect from Shaw. It
is indeed a marriage of the Edwardian Theatre of Spectacle with the
budding Theatre of Ideas, and as such unique.

How difficult it must have been at times to sustain enthusiasm and originality of thought! The labour of building that same production involved the stage staff and technicians working non-stop from the time of striking the old set on Saturday evening until a first dress rehearsal on Sunday evening; then a second on Monday and first performance at 7.30 p.m. The difficulty of maintaining standards in such circumstances was put to the board and arrangements made that when a production ran for three weeks its opening should be deferred until the first Tuesday, but an extra matinée played in the second week. It had taken eight years to arrive at that concession, if such it was.

However, about this time morale had been lifted by important developments which had followed the growing confidence flowing from the successful first years. The Playhouse's secure place in the life of the city, and its national reputation, justified a decision to achieve drastic rehousing. A by-product of the groundwork accomplished by Van Gyseghem and Harrison was an increasing awareness of the theatre's physical limitations, and frustration from feeling that all possible variations of staging and design had long been exhausted. Successful solving of the problems could not continue indefinitely.

The subject first appeared regularly at board meetings in late 1955 and early 1956 with discussion on, firstly, obtaining the freehold of the existing lease and, secondly, acquiring adjoining property. These were ambitious projects for an organization struggling constantly even to balance its day-to-day finances. But negotiations for the freehold interest succeeded in October 1956 and, in January 1958, came the adjacent premises. This was good progress, though both transactions required, of course, loan arrangements. In the case of the adjoining property the owner, Nottingham Co-operative Society, agreed a very reasonable purchase price and simultaneously granted a mortgage on remarkably indulgent terms. The Society had also been by far the largest single contributor to the 1948 appeal for foundation capital. (There was more collaboration in 1963 in connection with the new theatre and generally it seemed that the Society was the very good friend always quietly ready to help.) It should also be recorded that the financial transactions were assisted enormously by a most substantial legacy to the Playhouse in the will of Mrs F.M. Taylor of West Bridgford, Nottingham.

The first reviews of better accommodation were linked to the strategy of acquisitions with which to base a reconstruction on the existing site, and as early as December 1955 it was agreed that a preliminary survey of that possibility should be made by Mr Peter Moro. But only five months later preliminary talks were being held with city officials regarding the prospect of another site being available to the Theatre Trust within three years, and thenceforward the emphasis was on an entirely new theatre.

But in the meantime there remained further years in the old building. This was too heavy a proposition for someone who had already experienced the wear and tear of six years, and John Harrison announced his resignation in January 1957. He said: 'I am my own sternest critic and I know that I have achieved the most it is given me to achieve under the conditions of work and time obtaining here, and that the most I could hope to do under these continuing conditions would be a repetition. The new building is perhaps only a few years away, but, much as I should give to be its heir, I cannot – in honesty – believe that my work and health could do anything but deteriorate in the intervening years.' The board had no alternative but to accept the situation, with great regret, and said that the period of John's directorship had been an exceptionally happy one for the board, whose difficulties had been faced and solved with his co-operation, and tribute was paid to the atmosphere he had maintained in the company and the high standard of professional work which he had required and obtained.

So, after closing 1956 with a rousing four-week Christmas season of J.B. Fagan's adaptation of *Treasure Island* (resulting happily with a profit of nearly £400 worth of doubloons!), John Harrison opened what was to be his last season with, appropriately enough, Daphne Slater's return to play Viola in *Twelfth Night*, a part and a play crying out to be a swan song for this particular player and producer. In a valedictory note later John said: 'I have always enjoyed the Shakespeares and none has come closer to my intentions than the most recent, *Twelfth Night*.' Indeed, there were so many touches of inventiveness it was like seeing the play for the first time, though not all ideas worked for everyone. For instance, 'She pined in thought' was sung by Viola to a setting by Haydn, and this caused doubt among critics, including J.C. Trewin, though he did say 'a director must be allowed a foible – Mr. Harrison has uncommonly few – and, in any event, we know that Viola can sing. Does she not say so on the Illyrian shore?' On Daphne Slater he said: 'She has become one of the best young actresses of her day. Nottingham, I hope, was grateful for her performance, so warmly in love, so gentle and so true.' I am quite sure Mr Trewin's hopes were met. Daphne had been away from the company for eight months, playing leads in television including *Jane Eyre* in a BBC serialization. The added fame, and the recollections of her many fine performances at the Playhouse, made her reappearance an exciting occasion in Nottingham. Following *Twelfth Night* she played Strindberg's *Miss Julie*, the tortured aristocrat driven by irresistible sexual impulse to a betrayal of the fundamental values of her class. Audiences, which showed some embarrassment, fell to 58 per cent for *Miss Julie*, paired in a double bill with another unusual piece, Ionesco's *The Bald Prima Donna*. We had seen an impressive example of a fine actress's wide range of portrayal, but probably there was a general feeling that Viola would have been preferred as Daphne Slater's final performance to leave in Nottingham's memory.

Goldini's *The Servant of Two Masters* was produced by Peter Duguid with much gusto, led by a romping Truffoldino from Bernard Kay who, after setting a Playhouse record of appearing in thirty-eight productions (thirty-two of them consecutive) left to join the Stratford-upon-Avon company's continental tour of *Titus Andronicus* led by Laurence Olivier.

John Harrison returned from producing Shaw's *Pygmalion* at the Bristol Old Vic to direct Sheila Burrell in Ugo Betti's *The Queen and the Rebels*. In Wycherley's *The Country Wife*, surprisingly the Playhouse's first Restoration comedy, Horner was played by Emrys James who previously had done Claudio in *Measure for Measure* at Stratford-upon-Avon where he returned later to become a leading actor at the Shakespeare Memorial Theatre.

Another old Playhouse favourite, Kendrick Owen, returned as Sakini in John Patrick's enchanting *Teahouse of the August Moon*, one of the most heart-warming comedies of modern times. Kendrick stayed to play in Samuel Beckett's *Waiting for Godot*, John Harrison's last production at Nottingham Playhouse. On this milestone occasion the cast was: Estragon, Kendrick Owen; Vladimir, John Southworth; Pozzo, David Phethean; Lucky, Emrys James; The Boy, Raymond Lee.

At the time, July 1957, *Waiting for Godot* was a theatrical talking point concerning whether this was the clever work of a dramatic virtuoso, or confused gibberish masquerading as a play. Audience reactions were (and probably still are) as extreme as that, and as the debate was in its first flood, the play having had its London production only two years earlier, John Harrison may have felt that he would light a beacon; an adventurous torch for the future, though he would be as aware as anyone else that for some the illumination might be very dim indeed. In the latter group was the drama critic, the late Ivor Brown; in his notice of the London production he wrote:

> *On the stage were a couple of tramps resting amid the detritus of a dirt-track with a background supposed to be sky, and looking like Lincrusta. There was a withered tree which was discussed as a possible gallows for suicidal uses, but was never, alas, so employed. The two 'bums', Estragon and Vladimir, in the intervals of discussing body odour and sore feet and slouching off to relieve themselves, remarked with devastating iteration that they were 'Waiting for Godot'. Godot. Godot. Godot. He never came and nothing happened. Patience was never more in demand.*

But Kenneth Tynan's review included this about the play:

> *I care little for its enormous success in Europe over the past three years, but much for the way in which it pricked and stimulated my own nervous system. It summoned the music-hall and the parable to present a view of life which banished the sentimentality of the music-hall and the parable's fulsome uplift. It forced me to re-examine the rules which have hitherto governed the drama; and, having done so, I declare myself, as the Spanish would say, godotista.*

A personal reaction is somewhere in the middle of these. At the Criterion Theatre I had no wish to follow the considerable number who left after Act I. I recall the pathos of Hugh Burden and Peter Woodthorpe as the tramps. Drifting between hopelessness and hope, and the yearning for a sign, are universal predicaments. Among these tensions comic relief is not unwelcome. Perhaps *Waiting for Godot* in the theatre touches the unconscious too deeply.

So John Harrison's final production prodded his audiences into discussion and controversy, and no doubt it pleased him to leave on such a note. Before his departure there were occasions to celebrate his achievements.

John Harrison's farewell message included: 'It is difficult to build atmosphere, and I hope that when you go to the new Theatre something of the Goldsmith Street atmosphere will be put into a package and taken into the new building.' And we still value highly his statement: 'These have been for me happy and fruitful years, and I greatly prize the faith in me, and co-operation with me, that this Board of Directors has shown.'

CHAPTER FOUR

VAL MAY, 1957–61

The successor to John Harrison was Val May who was offered the post on 5 March 1957 and commenced in September 1957. He trained at the Old Vic Theatre School before working at Dundee and Salisbury and becoming Director of the Ipswich Repertory Theatre in 1953.

The project of a new building for the Playhouse had been started prior to Val's arrival, as we have seen, and the continuing developments were a background to the whole of his Nottingham four years, the later of them being part of the transition to the new theatre. Thus, before discussing the work of Val and his successors during the remainder of the time in the old Playhouse building, this seems a suitable place to record the happenings which made up the background. One cannot attempt to cover the mass of detail which coursed through five years of striving for a new theatre, but a broad account may conjure the *mise en scène* against which those years were played out.

Val May

At the time of Val May's appointment negotiations had grown to the point where they were being conducted by a theatre sub-committee set up by the General Purposes Committee of the city council, and three alternative sites were under consideration. After a further six months a recommendation was made to the council on the site for a new theatre. In February 1958 a council meeting carried a proposal for a new Playhouse in East Circus Street/Wellington Circus and in June 1958 the council approved the choice of Mr Peter Moro as Architect. Mr Moro had made a special study of new theatre design in Europe and America.

To have reached this position in about two and a half years was very good progress by the council sub-committee led by Councillor C.A. Butler working closely with the Theatre Trust board whose Vice-Chairman, R.H. (later Sir Hugh) Willatt had been prominent in all the discussions, and was involved over a long period in the minutiae of negotiations. He later became Secretary-General of the Arts Council.

Normal progression was architect design, quantity surveyor costing and such matters as obtaining possession of existing properties on the site, but in fact the path was not smooth and ahead was a cloud which at times threatened the whole enterprise.

The building of a new theatre of the kind proposed was meeting great resistance from the Conservative group in the city council. There were debates revealing many doubts and disagreements with the decisions already made by the controlling Labour group, and references to 'a grandiose scheme likely to become a permanent and heavy burden on the ratepayers'. Opinion was influenced by political alignments, yet it is true that not all the objectors were without sympathy towards better accommodation for the Playhouse, but some thought the likely cost of this new building would be extravagant and made alternative rehousing suggestions of a modest kind. One of these referred to a somewhat curious letter he had received from a New Zealand correspondent who 'had made an intense study of civic and public theatres in various parts of the world and said that the scheme was too costly and a comfortable theatre could be built for about £50,000'.

In May 1960 municipal elections gave the Conservatives more seats on the council and they warned that if they gained control in the following year work on the new theatre would cease. The Labour group, while insisting that site preparation should proceed, conceded that there should be another full council debate before commencing building, though the contract was put out to tender in November 1960.

The resulting uncertainty aroused national and local concern. Petitions were organized; the press was inundated with statements and letters.

When Nottingham City Council accepted the policy of providing a new theatre the cost envisaged was up to £200,000. This money was to come from a city fund derived from the realization of the old Gas Undertaking and earmarked to be used on 'some special purpose for the benefit of the City'. The estimated cost had now risen over two years, and from a more comprehensive specification, and this escalation was ammunition for the guns firing against the scheme. In any case, the cost thinking of the Labour councillors themselves was limited to £300,000, and there was a major shock when the lowest building tender received, in January 1961, was £358,000. Newspaper headlines read 'Death Knell of Civic Theatre?'

Modifications to the design were sought immediately and two features removed were accommodation for actors' flats and an art gallery. After the revisions, and including the cost of fees and furnishings, there emerged a figure of £370,000, which was beyond council's bounds. Thus the whole venture was in jeopardy and at a meeting in February 1961 the Theatre Trust board decided to commit itself to raising £60,000 towards the cost. The Labour Group of the council accepted that this offer restored the feasibility of the project and resolved that the full council meeting on 6 February 1961 should make the final decision. This meeting was a legendary occasion in the city council's annals, becoming a full-scale political confrontation between two groups of nearly equal strength.

Regretfully the atmosphere had by then deteriorated and the general goodwill towards the principle of a better home for the Playhouse had become diluted amidst the political struggle. In the debate a Conservative maintained that it was not a matter of party propaganda but of economics, and confirmed that if his party obtained power in the coming elections they would stop the development and 'cut their losses to save the city an unwarranted and continuing burden'.

At least the essence of drama was preserved in the theatrical nature of events in the late afternoon of that day when the vote was taken and showed a tie of 33 to 33. From the chair the Lord Mayor, Alderman R. Green, finally gave his casting vote in favour of the motion to build a civic theatre. Objections and points of order sparked around the chamber, but the decision had been made and a contract for the construction was signed on 3 March 1961 with the Nottingham firm of Simms, Sons & Cooke Ltd. Perhaps Thornton Wilder's *The Skin of our Teeth* might at that time have sounded an appropriate title for the first production at the theatre-to-be.

This scenario continued when the Conservatives were duly elected to control of the City Council and, as expected, immediately dealt with the smouldering issue of the new theatre. By then much work had been done and was proceeding on excavation and foundation, but not yet to the point of building, which for the time being would not now commence.

New ingredients had entered the theatrical situation in Nottingham. The fate of the large 'No. 1' house, the Theatre Royal, was apparently also in the balance. The fine old theatre had become run down; back stage conditions were completely out-of-date, especially for the large-scale touring organizations some of which came eventually to the point of refusing to visit the venue until improvements were made. At the end of 1959 its owners, Moss Empires, having some time previously closed its adjoining variety house, The Empire, had sought planning permission to pull the Theatre Royal down for a development of shops and offices, with an intention to build a new theatre on another site. In January 1960 consent was given, but the owners decided that the Royal should stay another year and in 1961 extended the circumstances for a further year.

So the future of the Theatre Royal was still unknown when control of the City Council changed. The Conservatives saw a possibility of associating their resolve to scrap the Playhouse scheme with the new building requirements of Moss Empires, to whom the proposition was made that they take over the Circus Street site (still with foundations only) for their Theatre Royal rehousing, in exchange for accepting the contracts and obligations to which the corporation had been committed, on the assumption that these amounted to approximately the same as the estimated value of the site, about £75,000.

There followed six months of suspense during negotiations, and dismay that the new Playhouse was again caught in political turmoil. But of course the Conservative leadership was doing no more than it had warned, and the new circumstances of Moss Empires seeking a theatre site must have seemed like a lifeline, in a situation difficult for them financially as summarized by the Town Clerk, who was reported as saying that 'if the Conservatives carried out their threat to stop work on the Civic Theatre it would cost the city about £100,000 for fees, site clearance and compensation to contractors for loss of profit, etc.'

However, Moss Empires eventually withdrew from the exchanges, preferring to look at the possibility of rebuilding the Theatre Royal on its present site. This was not surprising because it had always been unlikely that a site planned to take a playhouse of under 800 capacity could accommodate a main touring house taking large-scale productions and seating about 1,800.

The loss of the Moss option left the Conservative group badly placed. It met the Theatre Trust board to propose another plan for the new Playhouse, limiting the corporation's liability to an interest-free loan of £100,000, plus paying fees of £35,000, leaving the Trust to find the balance of £235,000 to be raised, it was suggested, by the issue of debentures. The Trust would be entirely responsible for the running of the theatre, and pay a nominal rent of £100 per annum on a 99-year lease at the end of which the theatre and site would revert to the city. It was impossible for the Trust to contemplate these financial commitments, in particular securing such an amount by debentures, and the plan was quite impracticable. Matters drifted on until December 1961 when a discussion took place between the City Council and the Arts Council, that is, Lord Cottesloe and his drama director, J.L. Hodgkinson. It can be assumed that reassurance and confidence was imparted to Nottingham City Council as two days after the meeting it was announced that the theatre building would be completed.

However, when Val May became Artistic Director, this satisfactory conclusion was 130 productions away (ninety-two of them during his time), and altogether there lay ahead four more years of work in the old theatre. At about the half-way point Val wrote, in an article entitled 'Looking Forward', an interesting personal summary of the situation:

> In two years Nottingham is to have a new Theatre. It will be built
> by the City and run by the Board of the present Nottingham
> Playhouse, thus creating a unique partnership between the
> Corporation and a completely independent body with ten years'
> experience of running a Theatre behind it. It is significant that
> besides entrusting the future management of the new Theatre to the
> Playhouse, the City has sought its advice on planning from the
> inception of the scheme, and members of the Playhouse Board and
> staff have been working closely with the architect ever since,
> ensuring as far as possible that the building will exactly fit their
> needs. There are obviously great advantages in this. A team which is
> simultaneously facing the day-to-day problems of operating a going
> concern in bad conditions is in the best position to advise on the
> right solutions. It can not only foresee most of the snags, but also
> help to create an ideal machine for the expression of its artistic style
> in the future. This is what is happening now at Nottingham. What is
> the particular quality of the present Playhouse, what are its
> problems, and how will they be solved and its policy be developed in
> the new building? The Playhouse is now in its twelfth season of
> fortnightly repertory. It has built up a strong position for itself over
> the years by its adventurous choice of plays, its production methods,

*its link with the Education Authorities, and its policy of quality
before commercial expediency. The Playhouse production methods
are not unique, but over the years have developed some special
qualities of their own. The main aim has been to build up two
strongly interlocking teams; a group of actors who are kept together
for as long as possible so that a recognisable style may develop, and
a group of technicians who can use their materials creatively and in
close liaison with each other, so that every detail of the production
from a door knob to a sequence of* musique concrete *contributes
something positive and in the right way. There are great difficulties
on the technical side due to bad equipment, shortage of time, staff
and space. The stage of the present Playhouse is only 12 feet deep,
with 3 feet of wing space on one side, and no adequate flying
facilities, making it impossible to conceive any but the simplest box-
set plays naturalistically. This, in a way, is an advantage. It has
forced us to use our imagination and inventiveness to the utmost, to
experiment in all directions with stylised scenery and to develop the
lighting and sound far beyond their simple utility value. Out of this
has gradually emerged a style which is flexible, free and expressive
in what we hope is an exciting and truly theatrical way.*

Val went on to detail the existing production difficulties, and some of the
main features being built for the future ('The stage will be 50 feet deep, with
over 30 feet of wing space on one side!'). He concluded:

*In these ways it is hoped that the new building will carry on the
work of the old as a direct growth. But there will be one other
important development, in line with the new trend to make theatre
buildings not just places with seats and a stage, but centres for a rich
social experience quite different from that which can be had
anywhere else. A theatre is, after all, a place where human contact is
paramount – actors with audience and the members of the audience
with themselves. The theatre, also, is the one art which embraces all
the other arts. The new building will be a perfect setting for people
to meet and enjoy, not only the performance itself, but all the other
arts which contribute to it.*

During 1957–61 Val continued the general policy of his two predecessors
but again we had the stimulation of new characteristics in choice of plays and

Michael Malnick, Irene Hamilton and Brian Spink in *Our Town* (Wilder)

players. There were six Shakespeares, two Shaws, two Chekhovs, a memorable *Peer Gynt* and several other classics, and, significantly, eleven premieres, two of which transferred successfully to London. In addition to the new plays there were many instances of work by dramatists of the day – John Osborne, Robert Bolt, Willis Hall, and Playhouse audiences were well in touch with contemporary trends. Examples in Val May's first year were *Pygmalion* (the opening production), *Under Milk Wood*, *Look Back in Anger*, *Henry V*, *Three Sisters*, *She Stoops to Conquer*, *The Moon is Blue*, *Our Town*, *Summer and Smoke*, *The Banbury Nose*. This kind of repertoire offered many challenging parts which, added to the high reputation of the Playhouse and its Artistic Director, attracted some of the best young actors and actresses in the country. Among them were Peter Arne, Ann Bell, Brian Blessed, Peter Bowles, Donald Burton, Tony Church, James Cossins, Colin George, Bernard Kilby, Robert Lang, Rhoda Lewis, Gillian Martell, Julia McCarthy, Brian Murphy, Perlita Neilson, Siân Phillips, Bryan Pringle, Gillian Raine, Brian Spink, Clive Swift, Michael Williams and John Woodvine.

Voytek was succeeded as Designer by Mark King and Graham Barlow. The unsung stalwarts in the background continued to build sets, devise lighting

Michael Malnick, Brian Spink, Kendrick Owen in *Henry V* (Shakespeare)

and make costumes. Their work was part of a feature entitled 'How It's Done' in a Playhouse publication at the time.

Under 'Staging':

> *John Hilgers, Master Carpenter, worked practically alone in a cold, draughty garage, for more than three years, constructing all the scenery used by the Playhouse as well as many of the larger properties. The problems of scenery construction were intensified by the necessity of building each unit small enough to be moved from the garage into the Theatre. His workshop was so small that no regular piece of scenery could stand upright, while the whole of the stock of large staircases and rostra as well as the canvas-covered 'flats' were kept in the same place.*

Under 'Lighting and sound':

> *In a small windowless room, Tony Church (not the actor!), lighting and sound technician, recorded and edited the tapes which, more*

and more, are essential for the many types of sound effects used in modern production. When recordings of human voices were required this room served as a studio, but owing to the noise of street traffic, recording could take place only during the night. Tony Church operated the switch-board during performances and was responsible for all electrical work in the Theatre, especially the stage lighting equipment.

Under 'Wardrobe':

Audrey Price, wardrobe mistress, had two rooms one of which was almost entirely full of hats and boots. The other, holding the Playhouse stock of some 600 costumes of all periods, as well as sewing machines, tailors' dummies and Miss Price and her assistant, Anne Hobbs, was barely sufficient for a Company which presented mostly plays involving some sort of costume. Most repertory Companies and many commercial managements hire their costumes but the Playhouse found it more economical to make costumes and hold them in stock. This has the added advantage that unity of design can be maintained as well as guaranteeing fit. It has never yet been necessary to spend as much in making costumes as would have been spent on hiring for the same period.

It could have been added that the wardrobe mistress's contribution extended to providing her own sewing machine! Not until the board meeting of December 1959 was it agreed that a machine should be purchased and the private one renovated. In 1956 Audrey Price's costumes for a Nottingham University production so impressed John Harrison that he invited her to join the company as wardrobe mistress. (Later she became a designer and costumier at the Bristol Old Vic.) She was a distinguished member of the line of wardrobe leaders who have graced the Playhouse. The longest serving of them, Mrs Betty Dewick, came to us in 1971, and (in 1993) is still brilliantly in charge of one of the most efficient wardrobe departments in the country.

A production of importance in Val May's regime came in September 1958. During the summer the playwright Willis Hall (who at that time lived in the area) had regular contact with the Playhouse, to the point in June when the board had agreed to a proposal that he should be attached to the theatre as a resident playwright with access to rehearsals, for first-hand experience of theatrecraft. The Arts Council made a particular point of approving this arrangement.

Bryan Pringle, Brian Blessed, Bernard Kilby, James Cossins, Colin George, James Maxwell and Terry Scully in *Boys it's all Hell* (Hall), later known as *The Long and the Short and the Tall*

Willis Hall had completed a play, not yet finally titled (but first called *The Disciples of War*) which Val May thought would be ideal for opening the new season, and others who read the script concurred enthusiastically. The play concerned a group of soldiers in the Far East, and for its first professional production at the Playhouse it was called *Boys, It's All Hell!*, which was taken from an address to his troops by US General Sherman: 'Many a boy here today thinks that war is all glory but, boys, it's all Hell.'

Val put together a fine cast, worth recording. Corporal Johnstone – Colin George; Sgt Witham – James Cossins; Private Bamforth – Bernard Kilby; Private Smith – Bryan Pringle; L/Corporal Macleish – James Maxwell; Private Whitaker – Terry Scully; Private Evans – Robert Lang; the Prisoner – Brian Blessed.

When the title changed to *The Long and the Short and the Tall* the play became famous, opening successfully in London at the Royal Court Theatre in January 1959 and subsequently being performed all over the world, and filmed.

Bryan Pringle was the only member of the Playhouse cast in the Royal Court production where the company included Peter O'Toole and Robert Shaw.

Our premiere of the play had splendid reviews but did only 35 per cent business, which has remained an example of how unpredictable audiences can be. Perhaps it was an omen of the financial worries which beset the next few years, in fact generally for the remainder of the time in the old theatre. The Playhouse was well established; the plays could not have been more varied; there was no repertory company with better direction and acting quality, but often the situation was precarious and it was very limited comfort to be assured by the Arts Council assessors that most other theatres were affected similarly. Increasing costs were a large factor in the difficulty of maintaining standards in a small capacity house with modest seat prices, unable to redress sufficiently in the popular part of the week the shortfall at other performances. Had television already become a strong persuasion against leaving the home for a night's entertainment? In several of those years the television companies gave us generous donations but these were not seen as compensation for lost box office! A main purpose was to help sustain the repertory theatres in recognition of their essential part in the training of theatrical personnel, and in nurturing new playwriting. The money was timely and in turn the Playhouse could feel that it had generated an effective justification for it. This mutually valuable relationship had more possibilities and should have been developed. With adaptation to changed circumstances perhaps it is not too late.

For a three week Christmas season in 1958 an attempt was made to repeat the success of *Treasure Island* two years earlier with a version by John Blatchley and Willis Hall of R.L. Stevenson's *The Black Arrow*, but in spite of a lively production the less famous story was indifferently supported.

What was probably the first regional professional production of Ibsen's *Peer Gynt* was an outstanding occasion and indeed for this play a rare appearance of any kind. In 1896, when he was forty and writing weekly drama criticism, Bernard Shaw reviewed the French premiere of *Peer Gynt* and in his most mocking style said:

> *The humiliation of the English stage is now complete. Paris . . . has been beforehand with us in producing* Peer Gynt *. . . within five months of its revelation in France through translation. We have had the much more complete translation of William and Charles Archer in our hands for four years, and we may confidently expect the first performance in 1920 or thereabouts, with much trumpeting of the novelty of the piece and the daring of the manager.*

James Cossins and Julia McCarthy in *Peer Gynt* (Ibsen)

Shaw was made into a remarkable prophet, being exactly on target, by Robert Atkin's Old Vic production of 1922! The same theatre presented the play twice more, in 1935 (Henry Cass/William Devlin) and in 1944 directed by Tyrone Guthrie with Ralph Richardson's legendary Peer. So the Old Vic was something of a patron saint of this huge, sprawling dramatic poem. Val May's courage in contemplating the production on our tiny stage was almost audacious. He cut the length by about one-third but there were twelve scenes with thirty-six characters played, via hectic doubling, by sixteen actors. The production had several heroes, apart from Val. Mark King's setting was centred on a large wooden circle around which the play's progress was arranged, from representing a mill wheel to being a symbol of Peer's life cycle returning to its starting point. James Cossins led the company splendidly though the *Manchester Guardian* thought 'he was not quite fully in command of the middle-aged Peer (as perhaps Ibsen was not) but both the youth and the old man were beautifully done'. The scene with his dying mother Ase was very moving, by the bedside pretending to drive her in a silver-belled sleigh over the snows to 'a castle towering above us – now the journey will soon be over'. And after he has closed her eyes:

> Thank you for all that you gave me
> The beatings and the lullabies.

To portray Peer Gynt's strange adventures is demanding for any actor, and Richardson himself was felt by some critics not to have had the temperament to be effective in the fantasy world of the young Peer but was superb in old age. Our production also had a heroine, the ever-resourceful wardrobe mistress, Audrey Price, who created about forty costumes in a fortnight. With justification it was suggested that 1958 would be remembered as 'the year we did *Peer Gynt*'.

In the following March business was improved by a three-week production of *Hamlet*, confirming its reputation as one of the more profitable Shakespeares. Its setting in the early nineteenth century, with Empire costumes was very effective. The Hamlet, not particularly 'sicklied o'er', and looking romantically Byronic, was Colin George who became an important member of the company and had been appointed Associate Director, producing about twenty plays during the next three years. His first was N.F. Simpson's short comedy *A Resounding Tinkle* which was done in tandem with the British premiere of Arthur Miller's two-act *A Memory of Two Mondays*. This was a sombre piece which did not have the usual distinction of Miller's plays.

Another double bill contained a further premiere in Anouilh's *Cecile* or *The School for Fathers*, together with an instance again of Val May's courageous programming, Sophocles' *Oedipus Rex*. He made a prior announcement saying that 'he wished the public to know that Oedipus is one of the most horrific and sensational plays ever put on at the Playhouse, depicting murder, incest and suicide'. A review said: 'The Playhouse production pulls no punches, augmenting the oppressive, guilt-ridden atmosphere with such items as three gigantic figures of the gods, masked Furies in a blue light, and weird sounding recordings to convey doom, disease and the sort of crime that would make Agatha Christie recoil in terror!'

Perhaps these were shock tactics, but Playhouse audiences were not faced with long periods of heavy fare and during the three months following *Oedipus Rex* were entertained by *While the Sun Shines*, *Reluctant Heroes* and an American adaptation of *Mr Pickwick*. However, ten years' work had bred discerning playgoers and it did not ensue always that the lighter plays produced better box office results.

Between the *Hamlet* of 1959 and Val May's departure in July 1961 there were eight premieres, either world or British:

1 May 1959: *The Man with the Golden Arm*. Nelson Agren's novel dramatized by Jack Kirkland was a strong story set in the gambling and drug world of Chicago. As the card dealer Frankie Machine, Bernard Kilby's acting

was described as 'electric'. Here was a flamboyant character in seedy surroundings but the predicament was not trivial and Kilby gave a moving performance in the pathetic progress to inevitable disaster. After the Playhouse run the production went to Oxford Playhouse and earned much praise. (During the company's absence there was a joyous return of Derek Godfrey and Diana Fairfax in Jan de Hartog's *The Fourposter*.)

2 September 1959: *Take the Fool Away* by J.B. Priestley. It was an indication of the Playhouse's reputation for this British premiere to be agreed by the author. It is understood that the play was rewritten several times, and this, from a dramatist of such experience, might mean that the concept was difficult to express in the situation of a clown finding himself transported from Victorian London on the eve of the twentieth century to a (then) futuristic world of moon rockets and bombs, where he recognizes his Harlequinade companions in Orwellian circumstances stifling and debasing to the human spirit. The play was first performed in Vienna, then in several European cities and did not become one of Priestley's successes. The *Manchester Guardian* found it a 'curious and depressing experience'. Alan Dent in the *News Chronicle* said 'the rocket does not, so to speak, go into orbit'. In a supplement to a lecture in 1957 Priestley spoke of the play being offered in vain to Broadway. He was in America at the time of the Playhouse production and could not attend, and in his message he spoke of his regret at this and his confidence in the Playhouse. Certainly he was well served by the director and a company which included Ann Bell, Brian Blessed, James Cossins, Edward Hardwicke, Clive Swift and Michael Williams.

3 February 1960: *Concubine Imperial* by Maurice Collis who had worked in Burma for many years pursuing Oriental studies. The play was based on his book *The Motherly and the Auspicious*, the biography of Orchid, a young Chinese girl of lowly birth in 1835, who schemed her way into the Emperor's seraglio and the imperial court, forged ahead by devious means, including murder, until she controlled the throne, 'a She-Dragon gowned in silk', and ended her days as the Empress Dowager regarded with affection and understandable awe by millions of Chinese. This was a powerful enough subject for a drama, but the play was long and involved an ambitious production with a cast of twenty-two playing forty characters.

4 May 1960: *Strip the Willow* by Beverley Cross. The programme gave a quotation from *The Anonymous Lowlander* (1892): 'They danced a reel called Strip the Willow. It was all very wild and gay but I could see that the lean quartet – for all their whooping and laughing and in spite of their tartans and bonnets – were as serious and grim as the Four Horsemen of the Apocalypse.'

This cleverly gave a title for a witty comedy about three men and a girl isolated in a decaying folly on a hill top in western England after the fall of a nuclear bomb. It began with a game of strip poker and ended in a session of black magic invoking a strange devil.

5 June 1960: *Beautiful Dreamer* by Jack Pulman who was at that time successfully writing BBC Television plays. One of these, *All You Young Lovers*, was adapted for the stage as *Beautiful Dreamer*. It was a realistic piece on parent/teenager problems concerning the romance of a boy and girl in conflict with their suburban families.

6 September 1960: *A Cry of Players* by the American author William Gibson whose play *Two for the See-Saw* had been produced at the Playhouse in 1959; and an immediate contrast was twenty characters in the former against two in the latter. *A Cry of Players* was about Will Shakespeare, the strains of his domestic life, the awakening of his affinity with the theatre and the emergence of his genius.

7 November 1960: *The Survivors* by Irwin Shaw and Peter Viertel was premiered. Another American play, this time a vigorous 'Western' with a serious background of the Civil War and a family feud with a neighbour, it showed the futility of violence as a means of solution. It is interesting that this production was directed by Stuart Burge who became Theatre Director at the new Playhouse in 1969.

8 March 1961: *Celebration* by Willis Hall and Keith Waterhouse. This comedy about a wedding and a funeral became very well known and widely played. (It was revived at the Playhouse in 1986.) It achieved 89 per cent box office for its opening run at the old Playhouse, though the fact that this still resulted in a small loss on the production was an example of how difficult the financing of the theatre had become. However, there was more revenue to come from *Celebration* when within a few weeks a management made a proposition to transfer it to London complete with the same cast for a payment of fees, expenses and box office percentage. Naturally everyone wished to perform in London, and also the prestige and publicity for the Playhouse were considerable, so the deal was agreed, but there remained an unusual and urgent problem of replacing the whole company in Nottingham.

The production and transfer of *Celebration* was nearly a swan song for Val May. Very shortly after the event he was invited to interview for the post of Director of Productions at the Bristol Old Vic and in due course was appointed. In his last two years at Nottingham, during the time of those eight premieres, there were several other highlights, broadly in four groups:

James Cossins, Jeremy Kemp, Gabrielle Hamilton and company in *Celebration* (Hall and Waterhouse)

1. Four Shakespeares: *Midsummer Night's Dream, Much Ado About Nothing, Richard III*, and *The Merchant of Venice*. André Van Gyseghem directed the last of these, for a second time at the Playhouse, having included the play in his first season in 1948. *Richard III* had the largest cast ever assembled in the old theatre.

2. Five other 'standards': *An Ideal Husband* (directed by Michael Elliott), *The School for Scandal, The Beggar's Opera, The Clandestine Marriage* and *The Doctor's Dilemma*.

3. Two important modern plays: John Osborne's *The Entertainer* and *A Passage to India*, the E.M. Forster novel dramatized by Santha Rama Rau.

4. Two lively revues devised and directed by Val May: *You, Me and the Gatepost* and *Second Post*.

Through this work Val was very well supported by Colin George and several guest directors. Graham Barlow was in the Playhouse tradition of designers giving sustained quality in difficult conditions. The actor who probably had the most opportunities at the time was Robert Lang who played, for example, Oberon (his make-up and Ann Bell's as Titania were the most

Robert Lang, James Cossins, Michael Williams, Rhoda Lewis and Ann Bell in *The Entertainer* (Osborne)

effective one can recall in any *Dream*); Benedick; Richard III; Archie Rice (*The Entertainer*); Dr Aziz (*A Passage to India*): Sgt Major Tommy Lodge in *Celebration*.

And so Val May's departure in June 1961 closed another Playhouse era. He had made an impact of much style, built solid programmes of innovation and variety, maintained the high standard of company and staff, and taken part in the planning of the new theatre's technical requirements. In a farewell statement he expressed his regret at leaving Nottingham where he had been 'most impressed by the personal welcome given to him; by the tremendously stimulating sense of theatre of the Board in guiding policy and also for allowing him to undertake occasional productions outside Nottingham which, whilst possibly helping the Playhouse, had been of great assistance in furthering his own career.'

He left Nottingham with mutual respect and affection. As late as seven years after, this regard was shown by his giving some very valuable help. We follow the careers of all who have worked at the Playhouse and were not surprised at the distinction of his work for many years at Bristol, and the award of his CBE in 1969.

CHAPTER FIVE

FRANK DUNLOP, 1961–64

When in the latter part of 1961 the construction of a new Playhouse building became at last a settled matter, the remaining period in the old theatre was influenced greatly by the bright prospects ahead. Examples of accelerating development during 1961 to 1963 were substantial increases in Arts Council annual grants; donations of £10,000 from the Arts Council and £5,500 from the Gulbenkian Trust both specifically for use on equipment and furnishings in the new theatre; invitations for the company to visit Malta for a season at the Manoel Theatre and for a British Council-sponsored tour of West Africa. Another important feature was the decision to adopt a three-weekly policy. Above all, in those two years some of the programming and casting reached very impressive heights, so the plain old building had a dazzling end to its days as a theatre. In retrospect the record of plays and players looks on paper like a National Theatre in miniature.

Frank Dunlop

The experience of appointing a successor to Val May as Director of Productions gave an indication of how great interest was in the new possibilities at Nottingham. In anticipation of this the post was not advertised but the list of applicants included some well-known names. The board's choice was Frank Dunlop who was thirty-four and a freelance producer, then working in London at the Mermaid Theatre. He studied at the Old Vic School and had worked as an actor, designer, electrician and teacher, becoming a producer for the Midland Theatre Company and the Bristol Old Vic. He was an artist of great energy with a distinct administrative flair which seemed a strong formula for direction of a new theatre. His influence, and the pattern of his plans for the Playhouse, soon showed in the third production of his first season, *Macbeth* directed by Peter Dews. The company was led by John Neville, making his first appearance at the Playhouse, and it included Edgar Wreford, George Selway, Christopher Hancock and Margaret Tyzack. The setting and costumes were by Patrick Robertson and Rosemary Vercoe, commencing their association with Nottingham. This was followed by a James Saunders double bill, *Alas, Poor Fred* and *A Slight Accident* with a cast led by Frank Finlay.

The next play was Robert Bolt's *A Man for All Seasons*, directed by Colin George. Sir Thomas More was played by John Neville with Peter Dews and Margaret Tyzack. This production and the recent *Macbeth* were taken to Malta, and the two made an impressive season of a quality worthy to represent Britain at any theatre venue.

Harold Pinter's *The Caretaker* was directed by John Neville, and in an interesting change he played Aston himself in a repeat production two months later. Two plays were done for the Christmas 1961 season: an adaptation of *Great Expectations* with Donald Sutherland and Hugh Sullivan, and *Rookery Nook* with Charmian Eyre, Joan Heal and Graham Crowden (making a happy return.)

In February/March 1962 Frank Dunlop directed two major productions, *The Taming of the Shrew* with John Neville and Joan Heal, and Farquhar's *The Recruiting Officer* featuring an elegant Plume by Edgar Wreford and a rich performance of Sergeant Kite by Leonard Rossiter described as 'a combination of Sergeant Bilko and the aitch-dropping Tony Hancock'.

Perhaps the standard of plays led to a puzzled and mixed reception for *Maria Marten – The Murder in the Red Barn*, the Victorian melodrama based on a notorious killing in a Suffolk village 160 years ago. This version had twenty musical numbers by George Hall who co-directed with Frank Dunlop. Eric Thompson played the murderer, Corder, and Anne Stallybrass, Maria. The Playhouse even displayed the alleged murder weapons, a brace of pistols

Hugh Sullivan, George Innes, George Selway, Anthony Valentine, John Neville and Christopher Hancock in *A Man for all Seasons* (Bolt)

and a butcher's knife, loaned by a Bury St Edmunds museum! But this spree of hiss and horror did not find enough of the required sense of humour in its audiences.

In contrast was Ibsen's *An Enemy of the People* in a translation by Michael Meyer, directed by Allan Davis. John Stratton played Dr Stockmann and Alan MacNaughton the mayor. The pollution of municipal baths in a small Norwegian town sounds a prosaic issue, but from it Ibsen's characters illustrated, comically but faithfully, human weaknesses of avarice, deception, hypocrisy; and Ibsen said of this play: 'Writing it has given me a lot of fun.' At any rate the first-night audience expressed its approval by a standing ovation.

John Stratton, who in 1958 was the original McCann in Pinter's *The Birthday Party*, stayed to play the part in a Playhouse production with Alan MacNaughton as Goldberg and again the acting was memorable. For the 300th Playhouse production, in May 1962, Frank Dunlop directed, with grace and a suitable Gallic quality, Jean Giraudoux's *The Enchanted* which was described by Louis Jouvel (for whose company the play was written) as 'the biography of a moment in the life of a young girl when she turns from girlhood to womanhood'. At the Playhouse Jean Marsh played Isabel and the company included George Benson, Ronald Hines and Colin George.

Shortly after, Colin George was appointed Assistant Artistic Director at Sheffield Playhouse where in due course he became Director. His last production in Nottingham was Anouilh's *The Rehearsal* and he finally took his leave in the following play, *You Never Can Tell*, in which he played Valentine. Colin had been a wonderful support and comfort and the Playhouse was grateful for his three and a half distinguished years as actor and producer, and finally as Associate Director. Every demand on him was met cheerfully, whether major or minor. For instance, he had directed the annual Nottinghamshire Schools Tour which in 1962 was *Macbeth*, and a message was received that the actor playing the porter had sprained an ankle (Oh, that *Macbeth* – shades of John Harrison's production in 1952!) and Colin immediately rushed to the north of the county to substitute in time for performance. Colin's departure and his career advancement were not unexpected. He received recognition of the reputation he had made by his work in Nottingham when he was invited in January 1962 to direct Paul Daneman's *Richard III* at the Old Vic. During his time at Sheffield he had the experience of being involved in the coming of the new theatre there, The Crucible.

The work in schools had continued, and a *Times Educational Supplement* report in February 1962 stated that from 1949 to that time Nottinghamshire pupils from 20 collective and 30 modern schools had made 112,144 attendances at Nottingham Playhouse. They had seen a wide range of 74 plays at a cost to the authority of £16,260. There had been a conference of heads of schools and colleges participating in the scheme, representatives of the Playhouse, and the Director of Education. The report continued:

> *Proposals for the future included a variety of new activities in addition to the normal school visits to the Theatre. It is hoped to arrange visits to the schools by members of the Playhouse company to give talks and demonstrations and to arrange for school parties to go backstage at the Playhouse and to visit the Theatre's workshop. The Theatre hopes to make available to schools films and tape recordings of rehearsals. An experimental Jazz and Poetry session for schools is planned. It is also hoped to extend the choice of school plays and to arrange for parties to visit plays not included in the schools list.*

These paragraphs contain the germ of the very different theatre activity which is presented for schools today by many specialist professional groups (usually part of the staff of a main theatre) whose work is now called Theatre in Education (TIE). The basic change is that in the fifteen years of the first Playhouse there functioned one of the earliest professional children's theatres providing normal repertory performances for organized schools' audiences coming to *us*, but now there is a reversal and the TIE group performs specially written and study-related material *in* schools, and has close liaison with the education authority and schools staffs.

The production of Peter Ustinov's *The Empty Chair* was another example of strong casting at that time: Timothy Bateson, Peter Blythe, Patricia Burke, Barbara Leigh-Hunt, Jean Marsh, John Neville, Bryan Pringle and Job Stewart. After playing two leads at the Chichester Festival Theatre, which at that time was used by Laurence Olivier as a pre-National Theatre phase, John Neville (who had been appointed an Associate Producer at the Playhouse in December 1961) returned to play in *The Empty Chair*; direct *Twelfth Night*;

John Neville and Daniel Massey in *The Three Musketeers* (Dumas)

Barbara Leigh-Hunt and Daniel Massey in *The Three Musketeers* (Dumas)

as D'Artagnan to have a Christmas swashbuckle with Daniel Massey as Athos in an adaptation of *The Three Musketeers*; to play Macbeth and lead the company when it was taken with *Twelfth Night* on the tour of West Africa from January to March 1963. This concentration of work confirmed John Neville's status with Nottingham Playhouse on a permanent basis, which was an important event for Nottingham and regional theatre generally. It was also a remarkable decision by one of Britain's most distinguished actors.

After early experiences in repertory, particularly for three seasons at the Bristol Old Vic, John Neville started in 1953 his famous connection with the London Old Vic where his successes became legendary. During five years from 1954 he played there a host of major Shakespearean roles: Richard II, Orlando, Mark Antony, Romeo, Hamlet, Angelo, Aguecheek, and on a unique occasion alternated with Richard Burton the parts of Othello and Iago. This was an experienced and renowned actor established among the profession's leaders, and presumably one likely to have continued success. But it seemed in 1961 that he had become unhappy with a theatre structure in which the emphasis and trappings of stardom were disproportionately placed in London. Interviewed in January 1962 he was reported as saying that the appeal of working in Nottingham was 'to get away from the pernicious idea that only the best should be in London while the provinces can put up with any old thing'.

To a theatre worker in the regions these sentiments were welcome and sympathetic, though at the same time it might be claimed that many years of repertory in the principal centres such as Bristol, Birmingham, Manchester, Liverpool, and Nottingham itself, had produced work among 'the best' if the criteria were the fostering of new playwrights and actors, and providing regular opportunities for audiences to see some great plays. An article by Peter Ustinov in 1955 said: 'certain provincial audiences are by now quicker on the uptake, more sensitive, more critical, and more capable of listening than the audiences of the metropolis.' But, of course, in the case of eminent actors there is the difficulty that the investment required to mount their stage appearances is normally viable only in London. With new theatre buildings, increased subsidy from the Arts Council and local authorities, and outstanding professional commitment as had emerged in Nottingham from Frank Dunlop, John Neville and their predecessors, the regions reduced the 'quality gap', but the situation remains and is enough of a fact of life to compel acceptance of it. The great difference in costs between London and the regions can work to the latter's advantage if the theatre director's record and reputation are good, for he may contrive to provide from his budget the production of an interesting play with a great leading part which, offered to a star, might be irresistible, even at a fraction of normal salary, because the opportunity would be unlikely to arise from a commercial management in London. Perhaps also it was attractive to relax in a refuge away from pressures, and indulge in a little old-fashioned 'art for art's sake'.

But the specious aspect of this may have been an example of the very thing which John Neville felt in 1962 to be 'pernicious'. A new factor since he made the comment was the coming of the National Theatre. Early interpretations of the 'national' content incorporated certain ideals which might have met some of his criticism. *The History of the National Theatre* by John Elsom and Nicholas Tomalin recalled Peter Hall's policy in a statement he issued on 13 May 1974 at his first conference as Sole Director. In the policy's 'central considerations' the National Theatre was to be

> *a unique facility for the British theatre as a whole, not just as a*
> *home for the National Theatre company staging only work which*

*represents the tastes of its Director and his associates. It should as
well regularly provide a temporary home for other companies or
groups – regional, foreign, alternative theatre – who have something
they would like to show in National Theatre environment; . . . work
of the National Theatre company should be taken regularly to the
regions, and also seen abroad as often as can be managed, possibly
on an exchange basis.*

On several other occasions at that time Peter Hall stated his ideas for taking
the National's work to the regions. His proposals to divide the company into
independent groups would facilitate this, and he designated the Lyttleton
auditorium to receive return visits. This would develop the touring policy
which had been followed while the National company was still at the Old Vic
when, for instance, in 1974/5 it did forty-one weeks of touring, but not
without problems of staging adaptation, as Elsom and Tomalin example: 'For
Peter Hall's production of *The Tempest* to visit the Bristol Hippodrome it was
necessary to book that theatre for an extra week in order to install the flying
equipment used at the Old Vic – a very expensive addition to the costs of an
eight-performance run.' It is intriguing to mention here their further comment:
'In return, the Old Vic received the Nottingham Playhouse production of
Trevor Griffiths's *The Comedians*, which afterwards went to Wyndham's
Theatre under joint National Theatre and Nottingham Playhouse
management.'

So there are many hard economic reasons why close reciprocal links with
regional theatres have not materialized, and now the National Theatre might
claim that its basic work in London is difficult enough to fund without
incurring the cost of comprehensive touring.

Whatever opinion might be held on the general application of John Neville's
1962 comment, it was unusual at Nottingham Playhouse to feel that one was
being given anything inferior. Frank Dunlop's excellent direction of the theatre
during the first building's final phase, together with excitement in anticipating
the new theatre, generated a lively atmosphere which fortunately had little
disruption. It was a matter of dovetailing a closure and an opening, though it
transpired that the time between the two was longer than planned because an
opportunity arose to sell the Goldsmith Street building in August 1963, and
the expected completion of the new theatre by the following September was
delayed by bad weather for a further two months.

After the 1962 Christmas season there were commitments to two tours; a
production of *The Diary of Anne Frank* for the annual Schools Tour in

Nottinghamshire, and the visit to West Africa, the first by any professional theatre company, arranged after long negotiation with the British Council who obtained a special government grant for the purpose. This tour departed on 6 January 1963, to Nigeria for five weeks, Ghana three weeks and Sierra Leone one week. The company of eighteen actors and technicians was led by John Neville, Paul Daneman and Judi Dench, and the plays were *Macbeth* and *Twelfth Night* both directed by Frank Dunlop, with *Arms and the Man* directed by John Neville. Seventy performances were given, in cinemas and open-air sports arenas, etc., but all the difficulties were ridden out on a massive wave of welcome and appreciation. The messages that came back to Nottingham, and the stories on return, showed that everyone had an unforgettable experience. The tour included also a touch of destiny. The business manager travelling with the company, Alfred Farrell, died while in Nigeria and, apart from the shock, this was a considerable adversity in unusual circumstances. There were the tasks of liaison with local officials; problems of frequent transportation for distances in unfamiliar territory and on arrival improvisations in organizing and staging performances. The British Council provided help for the rest of the tour by seconding one of their Nigerian representatives, Peter Stevens (who coincidentally had graduated from Nottingham University) and his quick response to the work required by the company was impressive. The idea grew that he could be a strong candidate for the post of administrator of the new theatre in Nottingham, and he came to the UK for interview with the board in May 1963, when he was duly appointed. His management of the new Playhouse was very efficient, and later in his career he joined the National Theatre as Peter Hall's personal assistant before becoming general administrator at the National.

Personnel having left to go on tour, plans had to be made at the end of 1962 for the last six months in the old theatre. A very happy and most apt arrangement was made with André Van Gyseghem, the first director from 1948 to 1951, to return as director of productions and form a company for the final season. This was indeed alpha and omega and Van was intrigued by the situation. He brought the old authoritative and precise mien but perhaps there had been some mellowing over thirteen years. Since leaving Nottingham Playhouse he had been occupied as a freelance director but more as an actor, having joined the Old Vic company and later the Royal Shakespeare Company. He was very proud of the Playhouse progress since his foundation work, and especially of achieving a new theatre.

He put together an interesting last season with a range of classics old and modern; and even new work within the short period. His associate producer was Ronald Magill who directed the first two plays: Peter Ustinov's *Photo Finish* (the first repertory production) and Thomas Dekker's *The Shoemaker's Holiday*, and later *Billy Liar*. Van Gyseghem directed the remaining six plays, starting with John Osborne's *Epitaph for George Dillon* and then *Cymbeline*. The latter was designed by Anthony Waller which really resurrected the old team! In the company were Alun Armstrong, Golda Casimir, Richard Gale, Tom Gill, Jane Knowles, Viola Lyel, Michael Meacham, Moira Redmond, and Van himself took the lead in his production of a new play called *A Zodiac in the Establishment* by Bridget Boland whose work he valued greatly.

This curiously titled piece was a fantasy about an alchemist who in 1356 stumbled upon the elixir of life and has since wandered through the centuries until here he is working in a government physics establishment and lamenting that modern science has become the tool of politicians and money-makers instead of burgeoning under the aegis of altruistic philosophers. Thus disillusioned, and after so long on earth, he is not surprisingly now seeking to escape via an elixir of death. One notice declared it to be 'one of the most

Michael Meacham, Ellen Shean, Viola Lyell, Moira Redmond and Alfred Hoffman in *A Month in the Country* (Turgenev)

luminous plays ever to have its world premiere in Goldsmith Street', but *The Times* thought 'Miss Boland's story languishes because she has not given it a sufficiently interesting and intimately studied context'.

The penultimate production was Emlyn Williams's handsome adaptation of Turgenev's *A Month in the Country* of which the company gave a beautiful account. But Van Gyseghem kept all his theatrical flair for the last play in the old building by choosing the one with which we had started the adventure fifteen years before, Shaw's *Man and Superman*. Nothing could have been more fitting. It seemed to make a statement: 'This is how we came into this place and how we endeavoured to live in it – uncompromising in using energies and resources on quality plays, whatever their kind, and this is how we leave it.'

Earlier it was suggested that the first words of *Man and Superman* encapsulated our feelings at the opening on 8 November 1948. The play's last words were equally apt at the end on 13 July 1963 – 'Go on talking – Talking!' And so, indeed, we did when we began another life in a fine new home. Perhaps the final Goldsmith Street programme expressed it well:

> *The closure of a Theatre has become a commonplace, but on this occasion, the 322nd and last production, there is more cause for rejoicing than for a wake. Not often, these days, is a Theatre closed voluntarily so that, at one bold stroke, all its faults and defects can be instantly remedied with a fresh start in a new building. But it is a trend to be followed by other cities and towns and Nottingham may be justifiably proud of having set the pace. Nevertheless, in those who have given and those who have enjoyed shows in the old Theatre, a store of affection has accumulated. We at the Playhouse know that this will be common ground which will give the new Nottingham Playhouse what every new Theatre needs and few theatres recently built have had – a loyal and established audience. For the few months until the new building is complete, the Playhouse says 'au revoir'.*

CHAPTER SIX

JOHN NEVILLE, 1963–68

The new Nottingham Playhouse was handed over to the Trust on 19 October 1963 and opened on 11 December following. The period since closing the old theatre in July 1963 was longer than had been anticipated but was hardly sufficient for the mass of preliminary work. The monthly board meetings had longer agendas than usual and the executive committee was involved daily on such matters as transacting the sale of the old building and negotiating a lease for the new theatre from the city. Initial capital had to be found and budgets made for work on a far larger scale than before. A major task was the public appeal for funds. Its result and implications, discussed later, were disappointing and perhaps one had been too optimistic, like enthusiasts expecting too much from those not sharing their special interest. Yet the community was not being asked to support a starry-eyed ideal, but something

Exterior – new theatre

tangible designed for its pleasure, seen growing for months and now near completion. The names of its three distinguished artistic directors-to-be were known, and the prospects were exciting, at any rate to some of us. In a 1982 report the House of Commons Education, Science and Arts Committee recorded a comment made ironically by one of its witnesses, Mr P. Brinson: 'The Arts are an extra, they were an extra at most of our schools, they were something which happened on wet days perhaps . . . I am afraid we carry these attitudes with us.'

However, at the theatre we were sustained by absorption in the immediate responsibility of arrangements for the approaching opening. Two of the artistic directors were working in London on their last engagements before arriving for their full commitment to Nottingham. In June 1963 at the Mermaid Theatre John Neville had played the title part in *Alfie* by Bill Naughton, and again when the production transferred to the Duchess Theatre in July. In early August Frank Dunlop was directing, also at the Mermaid, Brecht's *Schweyk in the Second World War*. Both were in constant touch and when necessary made within-the-day visits until they were totally in Nottingham. They had met the third Artistic Director, Peter Ustinov, to agree the titles, direction, and some casting, of the first three plays which were to be: *Coriolanus*, *The Importance of Being Earnest*, and a new play by Ustinov, *The Life in my Hands*. The ensuing opening dates for these were 11 and 18 December and 8 January 1964, after which they were played in alternative sequence, so commencing the policy of repertoire which had been decided, and this was itself an innovation for regional theatre (apart, of course, from the special case of the Shakespeare Theatre at Stratford-upon-Avon).

It was a coup to have obtained, in Frank Dunlop's words, 'the greatest of international directors' for the opening production. Sir Tyrone Guthrie asked to direct *Coriolanus*, and one assumes the choice may have been influenced by the presence at the Playhouse of John Neville, one of the actors of that time equipped to play that part. So, a star director and a star actor, even if this is not among Shakespeare's greatest plays. Harley Granville-Barker said it lacked their 'transcendant vitality and metaphysical power' but 'here we have a play of action dealing with men of action; and in none that Shakespeare wrote do action and character better supplement and balance each other.' Hazlitt thought that in it 'Shakespeare has shown himself well-versed in history and state affairs'. And it may be that the happenings in *Coriolanus* are appropriate for transposition to some modern political situations. There is a charge against the language of the play that it has much rhetoric and too little of the poetical power of the great tragedies. But there are splendid moments like the

John Neville

Coriolanus 'You common cry of curs' parting speech at the Forum, having in its last line one of the most haunting in Shakespeare: 'There is a world elsewhere.'

The company included Dorothy Reynolds as Volumnia, Leo McKern as Menenius, James Cairncross as Cominius, and Ian McKellen as Aufidius. One recalls the closing scene, at the death of Coriolanus, when Aufidius shows the veneration he has for his enemy ('My rage is gone; And I am struck with sorrow'). In this production Aufidius knelt over the body and gave a strange unforgettable howl of grief which chilled the blood, and stirred an instinct that one was seeing a young actor destined for fame. John Neville, impressively uniformed and plumed, played Coriolanus splendidly, and put a mark of authority on those first hours on the new stage.

However, the production did not entirely escape whipping. There were mixed feelings about Tyrone Guthrie's hectic treatment of the first act, which one critic said was 'an anthology of Guthrionics – all effect and no causes – which dazzles the eye and dazes the ear without ever contacting the mind'. Bamber Gascoigne in the *Observer* said: 'Guthrie's first act is a very severe embarrassment. Other directors look for stage business to reinforce the words. Guthrie increasingly treats it as a welcome substitute. Any piece of foolery can be popped in as long as it tides us over a batch of boring old lines.' But all

John Neville and Dorothy Reynolds in *Coriolanus* (Shakespeare)

agreed that in the second and third acts Sir Tyrone had 'a change of heart and allowed the turmoil to die down'.

No one had reservations about the new building and the experience of being in it. Mr Gascoigne thought 'merely to stand here is a pleasure'.

Although *Coriolanus* received some general critical disapproval of the first act, the balance was restored by one distinguished voice, T.C. Worsley of the *Financial Times*, expressing praise and satisfaction. As the opening play at Nottingham Playhouse it was of particular importance to us, and it seems fair to quote the final paragraph of Mr Worsley's notice:

> *Whatever complaints there may be against Guthrie's handling of the early scenes, no one could deny that they are managed with a consummate artistry, the stage pictures, composed in vivid action, are immensely satisfying even at their most turbulent; and this mounting of the tension up to a full long-held dying close is a most original and daring stroke. To my mind it succeeds triumphantly. At*

*the end of the second act I had noted that this production, with sets
by Patrick Robertson and costumes by Rosemary Vercoe, was
visually the most marvellous I could ever hope to see, in spite of the
comparatively small resources at Sir Tyrone's command. By the end
of the last act I was swearing that this was the most marvellous
Coriolanus in every conceivable way that I should ever hope to see.
For, given the chance as they were in the last act, John Neville, Leo
McKern, Ian McKellen and Dorothy Reynolds delivered the poetry
in a manner worthy of its direction. This production would honour
London. London must come to Nottingham to see it.*

The occasion of the theatre's launch was described as a 'Gala Preview',
consisting of excerpts from *Coriolanus*, preceded by the civic formalities of
opening. It was realized that the latter would leave insufficient time for a full
performance of the play, and the first of those took place on the following
night, 12 December 1963. It had been arranged some time previously that
Princess Margaret, Countess of Snowdon, would be present at the opening,

Auditorium – new theatre

but this became impossible and instead the ceremony was headed by the Earl of Snowdon. He was clearly delighted with the theatre and his speech set an enthusiastic key-note.

The city gave an official reception which, alas, went awry at the end. When the theatre proceedings were finished, the many guests transferred to the Council House and commenced to partake of the buffet, inevitably much before the arrival of the company, who had no doubt experienced considerable elation after the curtain fall, and then had to change and travel to the venue, where they would expect to be suitably heralded and cosseted. But the early revelries were already entrenched, and disappointment climaxed when even the remaining provisions appeared to consist of inadequate hospitality, something which was strongly denied by the authorities. Understandably there was an excited reaction from the company. Sir Tyrone was for leaving the Council House to seek sandwiches elsewhere, and, instead of everyone enjoying a celebration, a dreadful situation of confrontation (even physical!) developed and the reception ended very unhappily.

The following day's press was awful to behold. For its headline a local newspaper appeared to have rummaged in its stock for the largest type it had ever bought, and the reports were most painful. There were two or three turbulent weeks of charge and counter-charge on the matter, and it was all a great pity for of course no reception ungraciousness had been intended, and the trouble could have been avoided easily by some thoughtful organization. Another unfortunate and quite incorrect aspect was the impression that the city valued its Playhouse lightly, whereas it had been a great achievement building the new theatre, representing an important and entirely new involvement by the city, a partnership which has continued and grown. As for those first-night blues, the storm settled in its cup, and energies were directed to where it mattered, the formidable task of conducting the new theatre.

Perhaps one should not leave the ill-fated civic reception buffet without recalling a welcome sense of humour in a sly reference to the happenings by Emrys Bryson in his review of the second production, *The Importance of Being Earnest*. In a Nottingham newspaper he said that in the opening scene John Neville and Michael Crawford, as Jack and Algernon, had 'unlike last week – plenty of muffins, tea cake and cucumber sandwiches to go at'.

This is an opportunity to mention the work of Mr Bryson, a doyen among regional theatre critics, who has delighted us with his expert and witty notices of productions. Nottingham Playhouse has been fortunate in having during its growth the benefits of his stimulating criticism, not of course by any means

Michael Crawford, George Selway, John Neville in *The Importance of Being Earnest* (Wilde)

always favourable, but providing regular constructive comment and, if there was medicine to take, a little sugar to help it go down.

He thought the production of *The Importance* was done with 'style if not panache' and he recognized Angela Baddeley's naturally warm and gentle personality in his note on her performance, saying 'she makes a pugnacious but rather friendly little Lady Bracknell, suiting her style to a less galleon-like portrayal than the usual.'

There were no complaints about controversial production treatment in the case of *The Importance of Being Earnest*, which was done in a conventional style enabling us to enjoy again its wit and theatrical finesse.

The remaining plays in the first season combined to state the new theatre's general policy: a base of Shakespeare and later classics, with a balance of contemporary or entirely new work.

Its wide range, presented by a company bedecked with many well-known players, in Britain's latest and very exciting theatre, and from the foundation of an already high reputation, made up a formula which could hardly fail. The local impact was great but soon it was national also. Mr Worsley's charge that London must come to Nottingham was soon heeded and the London trains brought playgoers regularly. The parked coaches displayed their origins: Leeds, Birmingham, Bradford, Doncaster, Leicester, Lincoln, Derby, even occasionally Newcastle-upon-Tyne. The first five plays, in their order, played to percentage capacities of 78.2, 99.1, 87.7, 93.9 and 91.6.

An example of the repertoire structure over two weeks was:

Monday, Tuesday	*The Importance of Being Earnest*
Wednesday, Thursday	*The Life in my Hands*
Friday	*Coriolanus*
Saturday matinée	*Coriolanus*
Saturday evening	*The Life in my Hands*
Monday, Tuesday	*Semi-Detached*
Wednesday, Thursday	*The Importance of Being Earnest*
Friday	*The Life in my Hands*
Saturday matinée	*Coriolanus*
Saturday evening	*Coriolanus*

The opening date for the theatre, being so late in the year, left no time to prepare a show specifically for Christmas, but *The Importance of Being Earnest*, having commenced on 18 December, functioned successfully as the seasonal production. This must have been to the liking of one board member of that time whose firm view was that the Playhouse should do its normal work through Christmas and leave pantomime and the like to the city's large commercial house, the Theatre Royal, which traditionally had such a show featuring popular names of the comedy and musical stage. This opinion did not prevail in following years during which many Christmas plays and pantomimes have been produced at the Playhouse.

The Life in my Hands, following early in the New Year, was an important part of the theatre's launching. Any theatre would be eager at the prospect of presenting the world premiere of a new work by Peter Ustinov. This play was written for the Playhouse and the opportunity came from his involvement as a co-Artistic Director. A further bounty was his wish to forego virtually all the royalties on this production, and the whole made a very generous contribution to the theatre's opening.

The play had a very fine cast headed by Leo McKern and Ian McKellen, with George Selway, Dorothy Reynolds, Yvonne Coulette, James Cairncross

Peter Ustinov

and Christopher Hancock. The guest director was Denis Carey who for five years was director of the Bristol Old Vic and later of the Shakespeare Theatre, Stratford, Connecticut; and in 1955 had directed the London production of Ustinov's famous comedy, *Romanoff and Juliet*.

The Life in my Hands was about capital punishment, was *against* capital punishment, the author being committed to the view that hanging, or any form of execution, has never been and never will be a deterrent to murder. Mr Ustinov said that his manuscript carried a note:

> *This play takes place nowhere and everywhere. It is not a comment on any particular society, but on society in general. Consequently it should not be thought of as a kind of detective story, in which the quirks of a particular legal system are exploited, but rather as a story with a broad and general application. Laws vary, but men are men everywhere; circumstances differ, but the rituals which men have invented for the dispensation of justice have a painful uniformity, as indeed does death.*

The production's programme also carried a piece by the author, developing his views on the subject, in which the point was made that 'when the world

Ian McKellen and Leo McKern in *The Life in my Hands* (Ustinov)

started filling up men began to suspect that life was perhaps valuable, not to say divine'.

New humanitarian concepts, from Wilberforce to the International Red Cross, and the advance in psychological understanding of the depths in man's nature, were forces in 'rationalizing the motives which lead to crime'. There were also the pressures of escalating populations and crises in their food problems. After saying that 'It is not reckless speculation to say that the assassination of President Kennedy caused greater sorrow more rapidly and in a form more concentrated than any event in history', Mr Ustinov concluded his note:

> Curiously enough, we have evolved sufficiently to consider a man
> capable of the crime of assassination as sick rather than mad, just as
> we consider those who cannot express themselves without swastikas
> on their arms or hoods over their heads as melancholy fools whose
> malady was sparked by some imbalance in their domestic lives. It is
> perhaps true that this kind of solicitude has its own dangers, and

*that we may become sentimental, soft, and squeamish in our
dispensation of justice once every act of folly is seen to have an
abstract, but nevertheless understandable motivation. And yet, is it
not more in keeping with our dignity as human beings to err on the
side of tolerance, that greatest of strengths forced to masquerade as
weakness among unthinking, timorous people, than to indulge as a
society in acts of revenge which we would be the first to condemn in
an individual? The imagination leaps forward like the hare; reality
crawls forward like the tortoise. If Aesop's estimation of their
relative chances is correct, there is reason for hope. A man who
takes life is miserable, and sick. A society which takes life as a
punishment is lazy and retrogressive, and in that its blood is cold
and temper even, it is often criminal to boot. Life is a thing of
incalculable value, we each have one in our hands, no more.*

So the issue was deeply felt by the author. The critic Herbert Kretzmer made
it clear in his notice that he was in sympathy: 'Mr Ustinov's passions in this
respect parallel my own.' But in his judgement, the play's story and
characterization did not achieve its purpose. 'But,' said Emrys Bryson, 'with
courage, skill, wit, pertinent cynicism and above all, his vast sense of
compassion, Peter Ustinov makes us stop for a while and wonder.' I recall a
letter from a friend about his 'most absorbing evening in the theatre for a long
time'.

The play and its background have been discussed here at some length as an
example of theatrical presentation of ideas in living form, and of materializing
within a few weeks Lord Snowdon's hope on the opening night, for Playhouse
productions to have 'not only artistic and commercial triumphs, but fierce
arguments in the foyer, in the buses and pubs and newspapers . . . and that
acclamation and protest will thunder round its head.'

After the first productions had made their impact, the season continued to
take shape. Of the remaining seven plays, five were new and several of an
adventurous kind. There was a rare opportunity to see the work of Calderon,
the great Spanish dramatist and poet of the seventeenth century. He was an
important influence in European drama and wrote some two hundred plays of
which about a hundred survive. The Playhouse presented one of the best
known, *El Alcalde de Zalamea*, titled for this occasion *The Mayor of
Zalamea*, a strong passionate drama newly adapted by David Brett, the
Playhouse's resident writer at the time. It was John Neville's first production at
the new theatre. In the preceding new play, *The Bashful Genius*, by Harold

Callen, he had given a graphic impersonation of Bernard Shaw, red-bearded and looking incredibly like him. This was directed by Frank Dunlop who staged also an adaptation, again by David Brett, of Alan Sillitoe's novel of Nottingham, *Saturday Night and Sunday Morning*. This had been a project of Frank Dunlop's for about two years but did not materialize in the old theatre. Now, with Ian McKellen in the lead, and Frank Dunlop's driving direction, this turbulent and sometimes bawdy piece about the streets and factories of Nottingham gave some of its citizens a shock. The revival in 1987 had audiences of 81.6 per cent capacity and was still effective in human terms in spite of considerable changes in the background social factors over twenty-three years. There was one unexpected reaction from older people who had seen both productions. An unsavoury incident in the story, shown openly and explicitly in the recent version, was declared to be less horrifying than on the first occasion which used a screen, and the happenings behind it were conveyed in such a way that the imagination exceeded the reality.

Two world premieres were an adaptation by Eleanor Parry of Muriel Spark's novel, *Memento Mori*, and the first professional staging in over four hundred years of *Sir Thomas More*, an enigmatical piece about the famous Lord Chancellor who was born in 1478, beheaded by Henry VIII in 1535 and declared a saint in 1935. (We had admired John Neville's portrait of him in the production of Robert Bolt's *A Man for All Seasons*, done in the old theatre.) From its centuries of confinement to the page only, it is obvious that *The Booke of Sir Thomas More*, which is the title of the manuscript of the Elizabethan play extant in the British Museum, is not a dramatic masterpiece, but it has some interesting features. Its date is thought to be *c.* 1600, that is only sixty to seventy years after its actual stormy events, and close enough to them politically for the life of More to be a delicate subject. It had a strange composite authorship of Henry Chettle, Thomas Dekker, Thomas Heywood, Anthony Munday and, *possibly* William Shakespeare. It is the latter point which has given the play a special place, because of the theory that a surviving specimen of Shakespeare's handwriting is similar to that of a contribution which he may have made to the play, in three pages of revision, with a Shakespearian ring about them. There has long been a scholars' issue, attempting to prove or disprove that the hand which penned those pages was the one which wrote the known six authentic signatures of William Shakespeare. Emrys Bryson said: 'Only a theatre like the Playhouse could do a literary curiosity like *Sir Thomas More* . . . and it is right that it should have been done.' Certainly the attendance figure of 71.8 per cent was excellent for such a play.

Ian McKellen, in his last part with the company, was splendid as More. We are gratified to have been a stepping-stone in the career of such a fine actor. Once again Mr Bryson put it well: 'After a season in which he has done anything from Calderon to Sillitoe, 25-year old Ian McKellen proves that as Sir Thomas More he is indeed a man for all seasons. Gravely spry, courteously dignified, he gives both role and production an authority remarkable for such a young man.'

Similarly Frank Dunlop's direction of *Sir Thomas More* was his swan song at Nottingham Playhouse. Sadly, he had for personal reasons resigned his place among the theatre's artistic directors. He had been a dynamic part of the Playhouse since his arrival in 1961. We owed much to his enthusiasm and vision when plans for working in the new theatre were being formed. Once more a departed theatre director went on to distinguished achievements. Frank Dunlop did many important freelance productions in Britain and abroad, and in 1967 joined the National Theatre as Associate Director, becoming Administrative Director from 1968 to 1971. He was a founder director of the Young Vic in 1969, and had a leading position in the international arts, as Artistic Director of the Edinburgh Festival.

In addition to the play *about* Bernard Shaw (*The Bashful Genius*) the remaining production of the season was appropriately one by him, *Arms and the Man*, directed by Richard Digby Day, a 23-year-old ex-RADA student attached to the Playhouse for a year on an ABC Television scheme. He was praised for his production and thought to have 'a gentle and sensitive touch, and a nice way with the rhythm of a play'. He had also been joint director with John Neville on *The Mayor of Zalamea* and with Frank Dunlop on *The Bashful Genius* and *Sir Thomas More*. (After fifteen years he returned to become Artistic Director of the Playhouse in 1980.) He has a flair for devising and compiling anthologies for rehearsed readings and four of his programmes were done in the first season: *Marlowe's Mighty Line*, *Anniversary 64*, *Byron – His Very Self and Voice*, and *Sweet Mr. Shakespeare*. The last of these, with John Neville and June Ritchie among the readers, was taken to Stratford-upon-Avon as the first official event in the town's quatercentenary celebrations. These readings illustrated the policy of providing the widest possible range of activity in the new building. There were other memorable Sunday evenings: poetry and jazz with two bands and readings by John Neville and Judi Dench; a visit by Joyce Grenfell and William Blezard; and a special highlight when Sir John Gielgud gave two performances of his Shakespeare recital *The Ages of Man*, which seemed to put a seal on the new Playhouse stage.

An instance of the first season's variety was a Victorian style music hall, produced by Master of Ceremonies Ronald Magill. The company included Bill Fraser, Joan Heal, and Bill Maynard; and John Neville contributed a happy rendering of 'Waiting at the Church'. Business was 100 per cent for this occasion. It had been a week's romp, but presentation, costuming and design were in the characteristic house style already established. In its old home the Playhouse gained a reputation for its imaginative staging, in conditions and dimensions requiring constant ingenuity. The new theatre's comparatively prodigious stage space and facilities were used impressively by the resident designers Patrick Robertson and Rosemary Vercoe and their assistant Richard Pickett. Guest designers in the early months were Carl Toms and Richard Negri.

During the company's summer break there was a programme of tours: the Manchester Library Theatre production of *Next Time I'll Sing to You* by James Saunders, the Western Theatre Ballet, James Bridie's last play *Meeting at Night* and two productions from the Prospect Company, *The Soldier's Fortune* by Thomas Otway and Shaw's *You Never Can Tell*.

The statistics for the first season, in its repertoire format, showed a total attendance for 190 performances in 29 weeks of 139,567, representing 83.3 per cent capacity. There were also 20 schools' matinées. But the figures cannot convey the impact of the new life which had been brought to this hitherto placid corner of the city. Here had been placed one of the most important new theatres in Europe, on its way to joining Robin Hood in the world's awareness of Nottingham!

However, this growth rapidly tested the building's physical resources. It was always known that the site was limited, but on it the architect, Peter Moro, had achieved a playhouse of about 750 capacity, with effective space in forecourt and foyers, to an exhilarating design. Ideally an area and budget of at least half as much again would have been required to provide adequate facilities for the scale of work which the Playhouse quickly undertook and developed over the years. Of course, compared with previous conditions an enormous euphoric leap had been made which sustained the first years, though some problems needed an early solution. In fact before the theatre opened the administrator was reporting that 'he was expected to accommodate in three 10' by 8' and one 10' by 12' offices, three Theatre Directors, one Administrator, one House Manager, one Head of Publicity, one Accounts Clerk and three typists, together with their office furniture and equipment'. Additional rooms were made by partitioning, and for several years neighbouring buildings were rented and adapted as offices. Storage for the costume department also soon outgrew its quarters and had already encroached on the rehearsal room.

Housing rehearsals has remained a major difficulty to this day. A studio theatre, which would have relieved the situation and also widened the range by making possible experimental work, could not be provided in the plans. An upper foyer bar area, later named the Siddons Room, was adapted for occasional studio-type productions, and the search goes on for the means to acquire a small auxiliary theatre.

In the background there were some upsetting happenings during the summer of 1964. The rearrangements needed following Frank Dunlop's departure were unexpected in such a short time. Also looming was the spectre of disappointing response to the public appeal for funds to meet the Theatre Trust's pledge to the corporation of £60,000 towards building the theatre. This commitment related to the difference between the building cost and the maximum amount the corporation was prepared to find, so one assumes that without it the project would have been abandoned.

The appeal had been launched in September 1963 with the sponsorship of the Lord Mayor of Nottingham and the Chairman of the Nottinghamshire County Council. It was pursued energetically by personal contact, interviewing, displays, brochures, extensive mailing, and much co-operation from the press, but the final amount raised, including covenants, was £24,950, only 42½ per cent of the minimum target.

Therefore the Theatre Trust had the problem of raising the remaining £35,000, which was far beyond its resources. In June 1964 representatives of the Trust board met the corporation's General Purposes Committee to discuss a settlement. The proposition put to the city was a cash sum of £37,000, being the appeal proceeds plus £12,000 from capital and revenue reserves, and the balance of £23,000 to be paid over twenty years by an increase of £1,150 per annum on the rent of £26,000 already fixed. (In tandem with the latter the corporation had agreed an annual grant of £13,000.) The corporation felt the offer was inadequate and after examining the Trust's accounts asked for a cash sum of £42,000 and £18,000 spread over rent, with an understanding that when the Trust's next annual budget was compiled the financial situation would be reviewed by the city. This was the formula finally adopted, but its effect was disturbing. Generating the cash required immediately reduced further the Trust's reserves, leaving working capital dangerously low in the opinion of several board members, particularly the Chairman, Mr B.L. Hallward, who felt strongly that the theatre's future had been put in serious jeopardy and, as the circumstances were generally intolerable to him, he resigned on 7 August 1964.

Indeed, everything did depend on productions continuing to prosper. The Nottinghamshire County Council had made a grant of £7,500 per annum, for three years; the Arts Council grant was to be increased to £20,000 for 1965/6, but survival would come only from a thriving box office, and so it did, reaching 80 per cent capacity over the next season, 1964/5. Making this happen needed a considerable and continuous artistic and administrative effort. Absorption of its fruits, for basic livelihood purposes only, eventually led to certain frustrations which overflowed in 1968.

The new Chairman of Nottingham Theatre Trust Ltd was Mr C.T. Forsyth, CBE. As Managing Secretary of the Nottingham Co-operative Society he had been influential in its several major benefactions to the city, including an Arts Theatre and an educational centre. The constant material support given by the Society to the Playhouse in its early years has been referred to and, in addition to the experience Cyril Forsyth brought to the Theatre Trust board, there was an aptness in him now becoming its leader. He was, as Richard Eyre suggests in his Memoir, a colourful character. From time to time Nottingham was a place of disputes on local public issues and on one of those occasions a political weekly referred to Cyril Forsyth as 'the city's éminence grise', which amused and delighted him. The comment was perhaps not without substance, but below the worldly exterior there was much warmth. As Chairman he once had to tell a well-liked Playhouse employee that his appointment must end, and this grieved him greatly. Years later he would say the incident was one of the most painful in his life.

Some re-organization took place also in the artistic direction. Ronald Magill and Colin George had been appointed associate producers and the latter directed the first play of the 1964/5 season, *The Merchant of Venice*. Bernard Shaw described this as a 'safe' play, and it was considered by Granville Barker to be 'as smooth and successful as anything Shakespeare ever wrote'. He thought it was 'a fairy tale with no more reality in Shylock's bond and the Lord of Belmont's will than in Jack and the Beanstalk'.

But as well as the moonlit gardens and sweet music there is the hard commercial Venetian Rialto, and if the play is a fable it is one with a good deal of moralizing. Certainly it is one of Shakespeare's most popular plays, with every ingredient – dramatic confrontations; verse ringing and lyrical; opportunities to please the eye by set and costume; strong acting parts, the main one being so famous as to be capable of carrying a production by the single interest of seeing the latest challenger's attempt.

During the play our reactions may alternate, but what does Shylock arouse finally, loathing or pity? We need not sympathize about the monetary failure of his bond; a period of trading would replace the ducats lost over that, and even rebuild the forfeited estate. Far worse would be the religious shame, and the life-time hurt from Jessica's betrayal, and here it seems Shakespeare may have felt the girl's character needed cover so, to make him more ignoble, he weights Shylock's concern, at the discovery, towards ducats rather than daughter. But there is no doubt about the stab over Leah's turquoise. Again, satisfaction from Shylock's defeat at the trial is surely embarrassed by the antics of Gratiano and company. No gentle rain of mercy comes Shylock's way; for him it does not season justice. Hazlitt said 'the appeal to the Jew's mercy, as if there were any common principle of right or wrong between them, is the blindest prejudice'.

Shylock has had countless interpretations, and in this Playhouse production the dignified portrayal by that splendid and much-lamented actor, Alistair Sim, smouldered rather than raged. Played in that way, and say that Shakespeare had shaped the part to include for Shylock traces of that element it lacks, a sense of Jewish humour, the Christians in *The Merchant of Venice* would really be impaired, in spite of the pound of flesh.

So here was this rich play, still giving pleasure, and sparking discussion. How satisfying that there were six schools matinées of such a production. Over the twenty-seven public performances the attendance was 92 per cent.

John Neville and Gemma Jones in *Alfie* (Naughton)

Among the fine Playhouse performances given by John Neville between 1963 and 1968 were four which illustrated the impressive range of his art: *Richard II*, Willy Loman in *Death of a Salesman*, More in *A Man for All Seasons*, and the title part in Bill Naughton's *Alfie* which followed *The Merchant of Venice*. With *Alfie* he had said *au revoir* to the London stage where during its run at the Duchess Theatre it was the performance to see. One might visualize a particular actor's attributes being compatible with Richard, More and Loman, but Alfie was a mutation, a sport among roles. A ruthless libertine; a Cockney Casanova; a downer of 'birds' as eager to shoot as a grouse moor gun on 12 August. At times John fastened on to his audience in a Max Miller style of leering confidentiality. This was Alfie's repellent side which, unrelieved, might have become tedious for the audience and unsatisfying for the actor, so the character is rounded by a softness beneath the shell. Inevitably one of his amours results in a baby which he visits, takes toys, and enjoys as thoroughly as any 'legitimate' father. These occasions are his happiest, but his obsession for no permanent entanglements keeps him philandering. He will not admit where love really lies, and is left with nothing. So disapproval of his immorality is tempered with pity for the futility of his life. All this was conjured expertly by John Neville, in a swift moving production, making full use of the revolving stage, by the same director as in London, Donald McWhinnie. Gemma Jones (who in recent weeks had played Portia) was another member of the original company, again arousing pathos as Gilda, the mother of Alfie's child.

Donald McWhinnie returned to direct a new play by Pauline Macaulay, called *The Creeper*, a thriller of an unusual and sinister kind. The company included Peter Woodthorpe and Peter Blythe whose effectively contrasted parts were summarized by Mr Bryson as 'Mr. Woodthorpe cool and controlled, yet with the exact fraction of unease beneath the gloss; and Mr. Blythe choking, fumbling, poignant and suddenly frightening'. The play, this time with Eric Portman in the lead, was transferred successfully to London, at the St Martin's where it was reviewed as a 'small masterpiece in mystery plays'.

Later in the season Mr McWhinnie directed the world premiere in English (translation by Lucienne Hill) of Jean Anouilh's *The Cavern* (*La Grotte*) which also went to London, at the Strand Theatre, with Alec McCowen. Gemma Jones repeated her Nottingham performance in which she was considered to show 'enormous harrowing eloquence'. Only a virtuoso playwright like Anouilh could attempt the teasing exercise he set himself through the part of 'The Author' in *The Cavern*. The actor enters to address the audience and suggests ironically that the set of characters and their situation about to appear make up a dish unlikely to be enjoyed. He is concerned that he has lost his skill in manipulating the events. This resembles the act of the self-deprecating juggler who charms and amuses us by the device of tricks going wrong, when we know that his ability is in fact brilliant, as with Mr Anouilh who presently reveals his real powers. The opening strategem is perhaps self-conscious, but also beguiling, and *The Cavern* develops into a potent example of Anouilh's blend of human innocence and evil. There were extremes too in audience reaction to the play: 'We were really shocked and embarrassed by the filth and the language . . . we hope never to go again', and 'I enjoyed it more than anything I have yet seen at the Playhouse, and we have seen some great productions'. When the new theatre was an innovation in the city, local newspaper correspondence columns were apt to erupt with that kind of invigorating controversy, which was heartening evidence of a caring audience. Many times in those early years when 'argument thundered round our heads' we recalled Lord Snowdon's words.

The whoosh of one theatrical firework faded disappointingly. This was a 'political extravaganza' called *Listen to the Knocking Bird*, by Claud Cockburn (programme note: 'like many of his generation was born in Peking, China. The Russo-Japanese war broke out immediately') and John Wells ('early interest in theatre at age 4 when taken to a production of *The Merchant of Venice* performed by local infants').

The script by these two *Private Eye* stalwarts was based ('loosely') on Aristophanes' *The Knights*. With music by John Addison, and Sean Kenny involved in the design, there was anticipation of a witty product; in the authors' words 'raffishly astringent'. The opening was certainly timed usefully, a few days before the 1964 General Election.

One critic felt that the trouble about parodying politicians is that they do it so much better themselves. And, indeed, our collaborators Wells and Cockburn themselves said: 'the amazing thing is that one day you write a line which you think that no-one on the political scene and in his right senses could possibly utter. Next day it stares at you in cold print on the news-stand.'

The satire of *Knocking Bird* cloaked a concern about tarnished values in modern life. Many of its ideas and gags were very funny but, as can happen in *Private Eye* itself, the humour was uneven; occasionally at schoolboy graffiti level, and there was an end-of-term rag feeling. So in spite of ingenious production by John Neville, and some gallant performances, this was comparatively unsuccessful and the audience fell to 53 per cent.

Donald McWhinnie completed a trio within the season when his production of Samuel Beckett's *Endgame* for the Royal Shakespeare Company came for two nights. The company was Patrick Magee, Jack MacGowran, Patsy Byrne and a Playhouse 'old boy', Bryan Pringle. The last two, as Nell and Nagg, occupied two dustbins from which their heads emerged from time to time. The other characters, Hamm and Clov, have a relationship which has been likened to Lear and his Fool, but the latters' world, enigmatical enough as it may be, seems crystal clear compared with that peopled by Beckett's characters striving for reason within their grotesque situation. Mr MacGowran himself said in a BBC interview: 'The grave error, I think, of most people approaching Mr Beckett's work is that they seek for meanings that are not contained in the text, they seek symbols, they seek hidden, subtle meanings that aren't there at all. . . .' In his book *The Theatre of the Absurd*, Martin Esslin makes a parallel comment: 'In the theatre, or at least in Beckett's theatre, it is possible to bypass the stage of conceptual thinking altogether, as an abstract painting bypasses the stage of the recognition of natural objects.' All this seemed to work much better with *Waiting for Godot* than *Endgame*.

Perhaps this Royal Shakespeare Company visit, prestigious as it was for the Playhouse, proved particularly testing for our audience, one of whom wrote, 'People like me need entertainment which leaves not quite such a nasty taste in the mouth!' In fact the programme balance over the whole season was very sound, and general satisfaction was restored when the twenty-six performances of the Christmas show produced, literally, 100 per cent audience. This was Stevenson's *Treasure Island*, adapted and directed by Ronald Magill. It had a pleasant feature in that Griffith Jones joined his daughter Gemma, already in the company, to play Long John Silver, and shoulder a live macaw.

This was followed by John Neville's *Richard II* which he also directed, assisted by Michael Rudman who had come to the Playhouse as an ABC Television trainee director. In the Old Vic season of 1955/6 John had a famous success as Richard II, a part which is said to be unpopular with actors, and it cannot be easy to sustain an audience's pity amidst so much self-pity. But Richard's progress to disaster is mitigated for us by the superb poetry which gives the actor means to retain some majesty during the ignoble story.

Ten years of life and experience can have an influence on the interpretation of such a difficult part. Perhaps the Playhouse version in 1965 was more humane than at the Old Vic. Emrys Bryson put it thus: 'Richard grows in stature as a man while he crumbles as a king.' Another of his distinctive comments was on Ronald Magill's John of Gaunt which 'rings with honesty like a silver shilling on a stone floor'. A strong Bolingbroke is necessary for the balance of *Richard II* and Michael Craig played the part with suitable

John Neville, Michael Craig and company in *Richard II* (Shakespeare)

presence and authority. It was said that *Richard II* had not been performed professionally in Nottingham for thirty-seven years, so the production was an event, and one of our most successful. Additional performances were given, and demand was so great that the production had to be brought back into the repertoire for two further weeks later in the year.

In March 1965, after a visit from Bill Fraser in a new comedy called *Collapse of Stout Party*, by Trevor Peacock, came a landmark, the first Chekhov in the new theatre. *The Cherry Orchard* was directed by Denis Carey and designed by Stephen Doncaster. The company was led by Angela Baddeley, warm, gay, tragic, impulsively generous as Madame Ranevsky; Norman Rodway brassy, ruefully tactless as Lopakhin; and Peter Howell fussy, irresponsible, drifting as Gayev. All brilliant characterizations, with which the whole company blended to form the capricious gathering on the stage.

It could be said that Nottingham Playhouse has done its duty by *The Cherry Orchard*. Apart from the production being discussed, we have staged this wonderful play on three other occasions so far: by our own companies in 1954 and 1977, and the Prospect Theatre touring visit in 1967. They all stirred one's thoughts on Chekhov's statement about his play. In a letter to a leading actress of the Moscow Art Theatre came the well-known comment: 'My play has turned out to be not a drama but a comedy and in places even a farce.' Also he wrote to his wife: 'The last act will be merry and frivolous. In fact the whole play will be merry and frivolous.'

The style of the Playhouse 1965 production was not melancholy; there had been a sympathetic affection for the characters and certainly many of their actions were frivolous, but the last act did not send us home feeling merry. Moved, concerned, yes; and how could one ridicule these lost confused people?

In fact Chekhov's assertions were questioned even before the first performance in 1904 at the Moscow Art Theatre. On reading the script the two directors there told him, after saying it was the finest thing he'd ever written, 'it has a lot of tears and a certain amount of coarseness' and 'it was wrong to have called it a comedy for it was a tragedy regardless of what escape into a better life you might indicate in the last act.'

In his turn, Chekhov had reservations about that Moscow Art Theatre first production, saying, for instance, that the actor playing Firs gave an 'abominable' performance. But even if he had wished to influence the development of the play and its theme, his health prevented him being active at the theatre, and he died in Germany only six months after *The Cherry Orchard* opened.

Are not Trofimov's two long speeches ('All Russia is our orchard . . .') at the end of Act II the heart of the play, and revolutionary for the Russia of the time? The Russian censor thought so and cut two passages, which Chekhov revised accordingly for the production, but ensured that the original was retained in his manuscript.

James Agate summed up the play in his review of J.B. Fagan's production in 1925: '*The Cherry Orchard* is an imperishable masterpiece, which will remain as long as men have eyes to see, ears to hear, and the will to comprehend beauty.'

Denis Carey directed also the next play, Ben Jonson's *Volpone*, designed by Patrick Robertson and Rosemary Vercoe whose sets and costumes were described as 'cascading with rich fantasy'. The name part was played by Hugh Manning and Mosca by Antony Webb. The attendant toadies were Christopher Hancock as the advocate Voltore (The Vulture), John Tordoff as a senile Corbaccio (the Raven) and John Neville as the greedy merchant Corvino (the Crow) brilliantly sustaining a bird-like walk and cawing voice.

Hugh Manning and Gemma Jones
in *Volpone* (Jonson)

The mocking fun of this parade of baseness, in present-day terms black comedy (but with more retribution than now), was played with much gusto; a riotous display of villainy receiving its come-uppance. In his lifetime Jonson was (and obviously has remained) overshadowed by Shakespeare, but his verse in *Volpone* matches the play's frenzied action, and can also be exotic:

> Thy baths shall be the juice of July flowers,
> Spirits of roses, and of violets,
> The milk of unicorns, and panthers' breath,
> Gathered in bags, and mix'd with Cretan wines;
> Our drink shall be prepared with gold and amber,
> Which we will take until my roof whirl round
> With the vertigo; . . .

T.S. Eliot suggested that Jonson was no less a dramatic poet than Marlowe and Webster, though his poetry was 'on the surface'.

John Neville had to be decidedly mobile during some performances of *Volpone*. Simultaneously he was making a film at Shepperton Studios as Sherlock Holmes in *A Study in Terror*. After a morning's filming he was flown to Nottingham Airport and, having changed during the journey, emerged from the aeroplane as Corvino and was whisked by car to the Playhouse in time for a schools matinée. There is a photograph of him in costume outside the theatre on arrival, surrounded by children, calmly signing their autograph books. There was another performance of *Volpone* in the evening and he returned to Shepperton the next morning for more filming.

John had been awarded the OBE in the 1965 Birthday Honours and while filming was under way on location in Osterley Park, the cast gave a champagne lunch celebration. A press report said: 'They noticed an unfamiliar figure cheerfully helping himself to the wine. He turned to them and remarked "Say what you like about these ancestral homes – this is the best bobsworth I've ever had".'

The remaining two productions of the Playhouse 1964/5 season were a new play called *The Elephant's Foot* by William Trevor, directed and acted by Alastair Sim, with Roger Livesey, Ursula Jeans and Richard Kay, and a revival of J.B. Priestley's always popular *When We Are Married*.

During the summer recess four visiting companies were, first, the Ludlow Festival with *Hamlet* directed by Colin George, led by Emrys James and Margaret Rawlings. (Patrick Robertson had a multiple design exercise: first for the open-air production at Ludlow; second, for the Playhouse visit; then to fit

Alastair Sim, Roger Livesey, Ursula Jeans in *The Elephant's Foot* (Trevor)

the miniature Georgian Theatre at Richmond, Yorkshire; and finally a setting for Sheffield Playhouse.) Next was the Prospect production of an adaptation by Lance Sieveking and Richard Cottrell of E.M. Forster's novel *Howard's End*, directed by Toby Robertson and starring Eleanor Bron. There was also a return visit from the Western Ballet Company and, finally, a new London-bound comedy by Keith Waterhouse and Willis Hall called *Say Who You Are*, with Ian Carmichael, Lana Morris, Patrick Cargill and Jan Holden.

An important development during July 1965 was the appearance of the Playhouse's first Arts Festival, lasting eight days. The organizing of it required a considerable effort from a company and staff already heavily involved with the repertoire programme. There was no financial provision for it in the budget, so appeals for sponsorship were made, not in vain, to local industry. In spite of those limitations the festival was a success, in a carnival atmosphere. Army trumpeters were obtained to sound a fanfare at the opening by Lord Goodman, Arts Council Chairman (who took the opportunity to praise the Playhouse and John Neville).

On the first night there was the production of a lively show about Nottingham called *'Owd Yer Tight* by Emrys Bryson; followed by a late night performance by Larry Adler. In the evenings entertainment continued with performances of *When We Are Married* and a revue, *Changing Gear*, directed by Michael Rudman; a recital by the Alfred Deller Consort, and a final concert by John Dankworth and his orchestra, with Cleo Laine singing. During the day in the theatre foyers there were exhibitions; readings of their work by poets including Hugh MacDiarmid; Playhouse Youth Workshop contributions; and in the theatre a matinée visit by the Royal Ballet Demonstration Group. Tickets for some of the events were inclusive of buffet and wine, and refreshment tables with bright umbrellas were set out on the forecourt outside the restaurant and bars. It was all rather like an eight-day party and the town loved it, clamouring for a second festival while the first was still in progress. In fact the Playhouse had its festival for three years, thus pioneering the idea and laying the foundation for the city to inaugurate its annual festival, which is now among the best.

The national standing of the Playhouse grew rapidly and was strengthened by the inclusion in the 1965/6 company of Judi Dench, Alan Howard, Harold Innocent, John Shrapnel and Edward Woodward.

The first production of the season was *Measure for Measure*, directed by John Neville and Michael Rudman. The audience could prepare itself from the programme statement that 'the action takes place in Vienna and the time is the present'. But there were those whose faces fell when the opening scene revealed a contemporary cocktail party in progress; smooth jazz in the background and guests modishly attired. Presently the Duke of Vienna departs, bowler-hatted, carrying his airline luggage and leaving in charge his deputy Angelo, black-shirted and hearted. One could read the thoughts: 'Another modern dress Shakespeare! It will never work with *Measure for Measure*, of all things. How can you transpose the morality?' And, of course, it was not acceptable to everyone. About the modern setting a reviewer made the jibe that we wonder whether Claudio is talking of astrology or car hire when he says:

> So long that nineteen zodiacs have gone round
> And none of them been worn; . . .

In spite of the sniping, most of the near-capacity audiences enjoyed the experiment. This production of the tragi-comedy had a tremendous atmosphere of seedy corruption; a Harry Lime ambience which seemed an updated link to the play's Viennese setting. There were two hilariously raffish comic gems from Edward Woodward and Harold Innocent flashily dressed as Lucio and Pompey.

This may have intensified a modern audience's difficulty with *Measure for Measure*; the uncompromising puritan and religious stance as against the 'measure' of human life, in this case the lady's brother, though the situation for him is not evenly balanced because his offence does incur the death penalty under the state's law however pitiless its content. The twist is that Angelo, the judge applying this law rigorously, finds his cold-blooded detachment tormented by burning lust for the supplicant herself, the beautiful and innocent Isabella. So the play is not simply a question of moral absolutes but asks fascinating questions about human frailty and the vulnerability of judgements within the necessity of social order: 'Judge not, etc.; Who keeps the keepers?'

During the production the Playhouse arranged a forum, 'Measure for Measure and Modern Morality'. Included on the panel were the then Bishop of Southwell and Director of Education for Derbyshire; John Neville and the Chairman of the Theatre Trust. There appears to be no record of its discussion or conclusions but it is certain there were many differences.

About the acting in the production there was unanimity. Alan Howard had perhaps the hardest work in reconciling Angelo's two sides, despotism and hypocrisy, and he was fine in conveying the torture of the character's guilt. Judi Dench has said that 'of the productions [of *Measure for Measure*] I have been involved in probably the most interesting was a modern dress one at Nottingham Playhouse . . . the challenge of the whole production was terrific and because it was in modern dress the audience was able to identify more quickly with the characters. I'm talking principally about a young audience who may never have seen the play before.' And then this dry anecdote: 'As Isabella I had to come bursting in through the door after-hours at this night club in a white nun's costume. I asked John Neville how on earth I was to do this. He replied that I was to come on like any nun would come on after-hours in a night club.'

Judi Dench and Edward Woodward then had a sparkling time in Ronald Magill's production of Noël Coward's *Private Lives*. During the second act fracas everything in sight seemed to be overturned or thrown. In the romantic calmer moments their singing was itself an example of the play's line on 'cheap music' being strangely potent.

John Neville's *Richard II* returned for fifteen more performances, all to capacity audiences, and it appeared that this production could have had an unlimited run. Among some interesting cast changes were Alan Howard as Bolingbroke and Harold Innocent as Northumberland.

The Christmas season was thirty-four performances of Ronald Magill's adaptation of *A Christmas Carol* directed by Donald McWhinnie. It had an

Judi Dench and Martin Friend in *Private Lives* (Coward)

Wilfred Brambell and John Tordoff in *A Christmas Carol* (Dickens)

excellent study of Scrooge by Wilfrid Brambell, hinting in the early scenes at a less pitiless character than usual, and more convincing for that.

Judi Dench had three further parts during her time at the Playhouse: Margery in *The Country Wife*, Barbara in a new play by Pauline Macaulay, *The Astrakhan Coat*, and finally *St Joan* directed by John Neville. A critic greeted that occasion by saying that Judi Dench had the distinction of being the first of many Shaw St Joans who 'would certainly perform in the new Nottingham Playhouse'. In fact there have been no successors, which is perhaps astonishing artistically, but not surprising financially in view of the costs, especially in the difficult economics of the arts in the late eighties.

In his Preface to the play Shaw says the facts in Joan's case were accounted for by 'a combination of inept youth and academic ignorance with great natural capacity, push, courage, devotion, originality and oddity'. The actress has to handle this complex characterization which Shaw duly brought to the part, together with his balance between warmth for the heroine and understanding for those she often irritated. Also she has to merge with

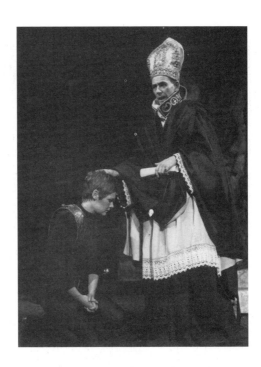

Judi Dench and Christopher Hancock
in *St Joan* (Shaw)

different acting styles inevitably met in the playing of strong and diverse male
parts surrounding her, as was the case in this production. Broadly, there are
two stage Joans: the ethereal teenager proceeding with her banner of
spirituality before, which makes the early scenes seem less plausible and the
trial unbearably cruel. That gentle and sweet actress Celia Johnson played
such a part with the Old Vic Company in 1947 and her performance was
poignant. The other Joan is the shrewd and sturdy peasant, femininity
overridden to the extent that she sleeps securely alongside her soldiers and
Poulengey would 'as soon think of the Blessed Virgin herself in that way, as of
this girl'. This Amazon-like reading was the approach of the first of Shaw's St
Joans, Sybil Thorndike, in 1924. This Joan marched to her goal with blazing
courage and strength carried through to the trial, which made the conclusion
very moving. Of that performance James Agate said: 'The part is one which no
actress who is a leading lady only and not artist would look at. But Miss
Thorndike is a noble artist, and did nobly.'

Judi Dench was, of course, entirely the artist in her interpretation. The
youthfulness of her Joan stays in the memory and this feature was stressed in
The Times notice: 'She gives to Shaw's relentless but superbly innocent saint a
touching and unusual quality of a daring child.' There was something of the
tomboy; a commonsense sturdiness nearer to the soldier than the artist; a

John Shrapnel and Judi Dench in *St Joan* (Shaw)

Judi Dench and Jimmy Thompson in *St Joan* (Shaw)

relaxed comradeship, effective, for instance, in the encounters with Dunois.
And a different acting strength for the frustration in the trial scene; piteous
bewilderment at denouncement of the beloved voices; her own voice speaking
Joan's farewell: 'His ways are not your ways. He wills that I go through the
fire to His bosom, for I am His child, and you are not fit that I should live
among you. That is my last word to you.'

The production in May 1966 of Marlowe's *Doctor Faustus* with John
Neville leading and Harold Innocent as Mephistopheles, had a special interest.
It was directed by André Van Gyseghem, the first Artistic Director of
Nottingham Playhouse when it commenced in 1948, and it was appropriate
that he should have had this opportunity of working in the new home of the
company he founded so splendidly. It seemed that Van, perhaps recalling years

Harold Innocent and John Neville in *Doctor Faustus* (Marlowe)

of coping with the limitations of the old, small stage, decided, with his Designer Stephen Doncaster, to try out all the considerable equipment and facilities now enjoyed by his later successors. In any case, the production's trappings were overwhelming for most critics: 'The revolving stage spins round the multiple set, and the lift which bears devils to and from hell moves so slowly as to drag the action down . . . somewhere in the middle of it John Neville appears to be a solidly real Faustus.' However, if all hell and damnation were to be literally let loose, this was the play for it to happen. The costumes of the Seven Deadly Sins were startling in their fantastic barbarity, and though the general comment was made that 'a powerful poem had been turned into a kind of pantomime', that is a familiar place for a demon king. It was an evening of magic, which Van enjoyed creating and in the process showed his Nottingham friends that he still had his theatrical flair and vigour.

During the 1965/6 season there was a range of work supplementary to the repertoire. Early in 1966 plans had been made with the British Council for a repeat of the Playhouse company's 1963 visit to West Africa, but political unrest there brought cancellation and instead arrangements were made for a tour to the Far East in February. The productions were *As You Like It* and

A Man for All Seasons directed by John Neville and Michael Rudman respectively. Thirty-two performances were given and the itinerary covered Bangkok, Penang, Kuala Lumpur, Borneo, Singapore and Manila. The company of twenty-five included Edgar Wreford, William Russell, Mary Yeomans, Terence Knapp and James Cairncross. Before departure the plays had a week in Nottingham and were taken to the Flora Robson Theatre, Newcastle-upon-Tyne.

The annual tour to Nottinghamshire schools was Goldini's *Mirandolina*, and in the season of visiting companies during the summer break was a Victorian music hall, brilliantly chaired by Mr John Moffatt, and supported by Miss Doris Hare, Mr Basil Hoskins, *et al*. Prospect productions brought two pieces, Anouilh's *Thieves' Carnival* and a compilation by Bill Dufton called *From China to Peru*, with a company including Timothy West, Julian Glover, Isla Blair and Sylvia Syms. Another distinguished visit was the Royal Lyceum Theatre Company of Edinburgh in *The Life of Galileo* by Bertolt Brecht, directed by Peter Dews. This version was the result of a collaboration between Brecht and Charles Laughton in California at the end of the Second World War, and the production was a profound experience. Tom Fleming was superb as Galileo and in the large cast were Brian Cox, Leo Sinden and Fulton Mackay.

Among several single-night visits were the Royal Shakespeare Company with their entertainment about English kings and queens, *The Hollow Crown*, devised and staged by John Barton; and Michael Macliammor in his famous evocation of Wilde, *The Importance of Being Oscar*.

Finally, the Playhouse organized its second Arts Festival for two weeks in July. A musical adaptation of *Moll Flanders*, together with *Doctor Faustus* and Chekhov's *The Proposal* were in repertoire in the theatre. A recital compiled and directed by Richard Eyre entitled *The Disciplines of War* was performed by John Neville and four members of the company, with songs by Jean Hart. This moving anthology was the first of the items taking up the festival's theme of war. It had been devised by Richard Eyre with much sensibility.

Indictment of nuclear war was contained in three showings of the film *The War Game*, made by Peter Watkins for the BBC but not used by them. A major event of the festival was a performance of Benjamin Britten's *War Requiem* by the Bournemouth Symphony Orchestra and a festival choir with Gwyneth Jones, John Mitchinson and Donald Bell as soloists, and conducted by Meredith Davies.

The lighter side of the festival included a return visit from Larry Adler; concerts by the New Jazz Orchestra and the Midland Sinfonia. There was a performance by John Neville and Vanessa Redgrave of *Poetry of Life*, a recital devised by John Carroll on Lord Byron's life, from his letters, journals and poems.

Again a new season (1966/7) opened with a Shakespeare, *Julius Caesar*, directed by Michael Rudman. Audiences at 100 per cent were obviously undaunted by a mixed reception from the critics. There was acclaim for Harold Innocent as Caesar, David Neal's Brutus and the Mark Antony of John Turner. In the repertoire *Julius Caesar* had an interesting pairing with *Antony and Cleopatra*, played by John Turner and Barbara Jefford and directed by John Neville. All scheduled performances of that production were sold out before opening and more were added. This time the reviewers were agreed, praising especially the realization of the poetry, among Shakespeare's most enchanting. It is poignant dramatically, and liberates all the passion a player may have within. Barbara Jefford, beautifully costumed by Rosemary Vercoe, created a definitive Cleopatra, described by Emrys Bryson as 'A package deal of shrew, kitten, tigress and wistful child. . . . Dignified in her white and golden robes, almost playful as she lets the asp wriggle into her bosom, Miss Jefford dies like a statue in the Great Pyramid, with a happy, proud surprise.'

However, it seems that some very well-known actresses of their time have emerged unsuccessfully from the challenge of Cleopatra. When Edith Evans

John Turner and Barbara Jefford in *Antony and Cleopatra* (Shakespeare)

did the part for the Old Vic in 1925 James Agate said: 'She has not enough passion and vulgarity for Cleopatra, or you may say she has too much fastidiousness. . . . I need not say that what brains and skill could do was achieved. But the actress was simply not suited.' In the same notice Agate said: 'The best Cleopatra I ever saw was Janet Achurch.' There is another side to that in Bernard Shaw's long review of Miss Achurch's performance in a Manchester production of *Antony and Cleopatra* in 1897. In discussing the right way to declaim Shakespeare he said: 'There must be beauty of tone, expressive inflection and infinite variety of *nuance*.' After saying that 'Miss Janet Achurch has a magnificent voice, and is as full of idea as to vocal effects as to everything else on the stage', he goes on: 'Of the hardihood of ear with which she carries out her original and often audacious conception of Shakespearian music I am too utterly unnerved to give any adequate description. The lacerating discord of her wailings is in my tormented ears as I write, reconciling me to the grave.' He concluded his notice: 'She has at last done something that is thoroughly wrong from beginning to end.' This was at about the time when Shaw ended his affair with Janet Achurch, whom he had met in 1889 when he was thirty-three and with whom he had for some eight years one of his actress-liaisons. (When he wrote *Candida* she was in his mind for the part.) Did some personal disillusion creep into his strictures on her Cleopatra?

The first premiere of the season was Charles Wood's *Fill The Stage With Happy Hours*, directed by Patrick Dromgoole. Alfred Burke (remembered from the early days in the Goldsmith Street theatre) played the seedy, despairing manager of a tatty repertory company in a dingy provincial theatre, acting his disillusion in a bitter, loveless relationship with his ex-actress wife now stationed behind the theatre bar, a part played brilliantly by Barbara Jefford. Both are reduced to angry, quarrelsome and melodramatic postures. The play was described by a critic as a 'very modern, full-length, over-long re-working of Terence Rattigan's *Harlequinade*'. Another was reminded of John Osborne's Archie Rice in *The Entertainer*. Alan Brien, in the *Sunday Telegraph*, thought the two main characters 'play ghastly games with each other which make those of Albee's George and Martha seem like Peter Pan and Wendy'. Though cleverly written, the play was too much of a theatrical in-piece, too introspective and narrow in its situations, to have general appeal, and this was reflected in an attendance figure of 50.4 per cent, low for the Playhouse in those days.

The year 1967 commenced with Arthur Miller's *Death of a Salesman*, directed by Michael Rudman, in which John Neville gave one of his finest

John Neville and Ronald Magill in *Death of a Salesman* (Miller)

Playhouse performances as Willy Loman. A play of this stature, in a production of such quality, amounted to a dramatic experience. The part of Loman so dominates the play that when the interpretation is true, the effect is overwhelming.

In his autobiography Arthur Miller recalls preparation for the original production in 1949. At first Lee Cobb went through rehearsals in an abstracted, only half-aware manner, to a puzzling degree. But suddenly, on about the twelfth day, a scene being rehearsed blazed into life, and henceforward the tragedy of Willy Loman was awesomely acted out. The author, director and other onlookers were electrified, and moved to tears as Lee Cobb released 'a magical capacity to imagine, to collect within himself every mote of life since Genesis and to let it pour forth. He stood up there like a giant moving the Rocky Mountains into position.'

One would need to have seen the performance to understand fully how that impression of great strength in Mr Miller's description became related to the story of the character's downfall. John Neville's Loman drew much compassion as we witnessed the last days of someone exhausted by long frustration, and now doomed in a hopeless situation. But this man's spirit and pride flickered, and he was not shabby. Still there was the effort to uphold a salesman's appearance when visiting customers. There is a photograph of John, showing his usual precise attention to detail, in a scene with Uncle Ben. The way the hair is cut and dressed; the use of a light moustache; the decent suit (which Linda has pressed?); the tie and good shirt with neat cuffs and links; the well-shaped hat before him on the table. The head is bowed, eyes closed, the expression one of despair; his clenched fists have crashed to the table. The production of this fine modern tragedy played to 93.4 per cent and John would wish to acknowledge the splendid support he had from the company (including Gillian Martell, John Shrapnel and Ronald Magill) under Michael Rudman, in a clever composite set by Ken Calder.

In the next production, called *Beware of the Dog*, directed by Noel Willman, John Neville made a leap in style, from the profundities of *Death of a Salesman* to what someone described as a 'non-musical revue'.

Chekhov wrote a number of short stories, his 'vaudevilles', eleven of which were adapted by Gabriel Arout, and translated by Yvonne Mitchell, into an entertainment of two acts. The first had five scenes which, though played with charm, were light-weight dramatic anecdotes, in fairness not unlike the insubstantial original sketches. The second act was a different matter, blended from three stories. A flirtation grows into a bitter-sweet, tender episode which must soon end poignantly; a situation echoed in Noël Coward's *Still Life/Brief Encounter*. John Neville and Ann Bell acted exquisitely and in the summer of 1967 the play had a London run at the St Martin's.

Also, and immediately after its Nottingham Playhouse performances in February, *Beware of the Dog* became the first production at the opening of Newcastle-on-Tyne Playhouse. In September 1966 Nottingham Theatre Trust had been asked by the Newcastle City Council to consider organizing the opening and running of the Flora Robson Playhouse which the city had acquired and wished to operate until the building of a new theatre. The scheme had the interest and blessing of the Arts Council and Northern Arts Association.

Maybe the success of the new Nottingham Playhouse had inspired Newcastle, and certainly it might have seemed a good reason to seek our advice and involvement. John Neville and Peter Stevens were interested in the proposition and in due course recommended that the Trust accept the commitment, for a term of up to two years or when Newcastle had formed its

Ann Bell and John Neville in *Beware of the Dog* (Arout)

own Theatre Trust. After the financial arrangements had been settled, the planning went forward and in quite a short time the Newcastle Playhouse had opened, in February 1967. *Beware of the Dog*, with its two glamorous leads, gave the new venture an enthusiastic start, playing to 86.7 per cent capacity. But this level of business was not maintained, and the next plays, *Measure for Measure* and *Arms and the Man*, attracted only 52.7 per cent and 47 per cent. Generally, support stayed at this moderate level and there were even worse experiences with, for instance, *Look Back in Anger* at 46 per cent and *Hobson's Choice* 28.5 per cent. The disappointing average figure for the first half-year was 35 per cent, in spite of the efforts of John Neville and the Nottingham administration. The long distance between the theatres caused some supervision problems, and perhaps also there had been an overestimation of the potential from an established theatre's association with another starting from scratch and in temporary accommodation. Nottingham had a unique success pattern. The building was new, exciting and already acclaimed. It had a famous actor as theatre director and, very importantly, there was the solid foundation of fifteen years repertory achievement. However, a Newcastle Theatre Trust was duly formed, and the Flora Robson Playhouse passed into its control in June 1968.

The season was supplemented by some interesting occasions. Max Adrian in his superb evocation of George Bernard Shaw; Ravi Shankar; Sonny Rollins and Ben Webster in a jazz evening presented in association with Ronnie Scott; the Ballet Rambert brought a week's programme including the premiere of Glen Tetley's *Ricecare*.

For the third Arts Festival in July John Player & Son gave a magnificent guarantee of £7,500. This was a measure of the success of the two previous festivals, and made possible events such as a lavish version of *The Damnation of Faust* by Berlioz; a world premiere of Robert Shaw's *The Man in the Glass Booth* with Donald Pleasance and directed by Harold Pinter; a jazz concert by John Dankworth, Cleo Laine and Benny Green. There was classical music from the Melos Ensemble, the Paganini Trio and the Midland Sinfonia; a garden party; a presentation by the Playhouse's Youth Workshop demonstrating an activity very important to John Neville, the regular Saturday morning sessions between young people and company members to discuss and practise drama.

After the festival the summer season of tours in 1967 contained two distinguished productions from the Prospect Company. First, *The Cherry Orchard*, in a new version by Richard Cottrell, directed by him, with Lila Kedrova as Madame Ranevsky and Patrick Wymark as Lopakhin and, second, an adaptation by Lance Sieveking and Richard Cottrell of E.M. Forster's novel *A Room With A View*, directed by Toby Robertson. The company included Timothy West, Fiona Walker and Hazel Hughes.

The main season, having presented *The Silver Tassie* and *The Miser* among plays in the repertoire, closed in June with a production by David Scase of *A Midsummer Night's Dream*. It ended also with a situation which itself seemed dream-like and unreal, making the play title wryly apt. This was the commencement of events which led to John Neville leaving Nottingham Playhouse.

On 27 April 1967 John Neville had announced to the board that he wished it to accept his resignation as Theatre Director in July 1968 or at such an earlier date as the board might prefer. After long discussion the board agreed that 'John Neville's resignation as Theatre Director of the Nottingham Playhouse to take effect in July 1968 be received with the deepest regret and in the hope that John Neville will reconsider his decision'. John had emphasized that he had no sense of bitterness or rancour towards the board, and he issued a statement which was entirely personal and not made jointly with the board:

> *This is the second year running that the Arts Council have not given us the amount of money required for this theatre to move forward.*

*If we are to mark time or stand still, I have come to the end of what
I can contribute. Nottingham Playhouse is the best in the country. A
lot of good work has been done here, but the amount of money we
are getting from the Arts Council will only just allow us to mark
time and I would find it heart-breaking to work in this theatre under
these conditions. I believe most firmly in the future of the Playhouse
and I believe passionately in its influential role in this region. The
attitude of the Arts Council is now well known, they are penalising
our success. Every other theatre of note in this country has been
given a considerable increase to allow forward movement. My
feelings are quite sincere. We have enjoyed a great deal of success
here, but our constant preoccupation is against becoming smug and
complacent about the high attendance figures. We consistently try to
find new approaches in presentation, and ways of widening our
audience. My future? I have no plans, I can say no more than that.*

The background figures to the situation were that the grant from the Arts
Council for the year in question was £50,000. The offer had first been
£45,000 (an increase of £3,000 on the previous year) plus a guarantee of
£5,000 against loss, with instructions not to budget for a loss, but after
representations from the Theatre Director and Administrator the structure was
changed to a straight amount of £50,000. But the administration still felt that
at least £57,000 was needed if the Playhouse was to expand its work, taking
plays to towns without theatres and doing more for schools.

The resignation was a theatrical sensation. It made headlines and simmered
for weeks in the national press. Weighty editorials appeared on the subject and
reporters descended on the city. Was it, they enquired, really the case that Mr
Neville had taken such a drastic step because of (one said 'a trivial') £7,000?
John answered this in an interview with Emrys Bryson, who put the question:

E.B. If the Arts Council agreed to make up the money to the full
£57,000 would you stay?
J.N. *I honestly believe that this is academic because once the Arts Council
have made their allocation I know from experience that nothing can be
done about it. And I find it difficult to believe in any case that they
would make up the full £57,000 since they have already allocated the
money they think is right in this particular instance.*
E.B. But suppose they really did pull out the stops and make up the full
money?

*J.N. It would obviously make a great difference but I would want
    further. What I'm after really is a massive reappraisal of allocation
    of money to the provinces as opposed to London.*

E.B. So it's not just a matter of £7,000 for the Nottingham Playhouse as such?

*J.N. No. I would want to know whether the sum that we ask for the
    following year was likely to fall short as we have fallen short the last
    two years, or are we going to come up against the same problem
    again. To be scrupulously fair to the Arts Council we are up against
    the fact that there isn't enough money around. Once the Covent
    Garden Opera House have taken theirs (£1,250,000 I think), the
    National Theatre have taken theirs and the Royal Shakespeare have
    taken theirs, there isn't enough to go round. And I believe that the
    scale of the operation that we are doing here at this theatre is of a
    size and an importance and a stature that warrants more money. . . .*

Other questions at the end of the interview were:

E.B. How far do you speak for the Board on all this?

*J.N. I must emphasise that all these views are personal and do not
    necessarily reflect the opinion of the Board.*

E.B. Why 15 months notice?

*J.N. I had planned next autumn's programme and had to act in all
    fairness. I wasn't exactly leaving in a fit of pique.*

E.B. How far is the Playhouse a one man band? How much do audiences
    come to see John Neville?

*J.N. It was a going concern before I came and is too well established to
    be much of a one-man show. In the six months that I didn't act we
    kept the same figures for attendance.*

As could be expected, the Arts Council disliked being continually referred to
unfavourably in the press publicity. It spoke of the regular increases in its annual
subsidy to Nottingham Playhouse and gave a reminder about its many other
clients needing support from its limited Treasury grant. It suggested that
Nottingham City Council should review its funding and rental policy for the
Playhouse. It was also extremely anxious, and made a special visit to a board
meeting to express its disquiet, that there should be no deterioration in the
excellent relationship it had enjoyed with Nottingham Theatre Trust during the
Playhouse's twenty years' existence. Obviously the board shared that concern and
gave assurances.

The weeks passed without any sign that the resignation would induce a commitment from any of the funding bodies to provide forthwith more money for the Playhouse. According to a press report, dated 8 August 1967, the subject was raised at a function in London attended by the Minister for the Arts, Jennie Lee, and by John Neville. Apparently Miss Lee insisted that the Playhouse should look to the City Council for any additional subsidy. She said: 'Look at the proportion of your money which is coming from London.' The report went on: 'The argument ended with Miss Lee forecasting that Mr. Neville would not go through with his resignation and Mr. Neville insisting that he would.'

Thus after three months the board had no evidence for supposing that John Neville's conditions on funding would be met, and had to assume that as things stood he still felt, as he had said in his resignation statement, that 'he had come to the end of what he could contribute'.

So the board was left with the prospect of continuing uncertainty regarding its key post. Also it must have been aware that making such an important new appointment, and allowing for a successor's own notice, could require months of time.

The board held a special meeting on 8 August 1967 to consider the matter and decided: 'In the best interests of both Mr. Neville and Nottingham Playhouse, the Board now agrees to accept the resignation of Mr. Neville as submitted by him to the Board at its meeting on 27th April 1967, with effect from July 1968.'

The chairman of the board then received a telegram from John Neville withdrawing his resignation. This necessitated a further special board meeting at which the decision to accept the resignation was confirmed.

The turbulence that occurred following John Neville's resignation was mild compared with the storm which raged in the city and beyond after its acceptance and withdrawal. Only when his successor had been named in the following December did the waters become calmer. The four months of polemic involved meetings, deputations, petitions, press articles, pros and cons letters; formation by the Playhouse Supporters Club of an Action Group which in due course sent representations to Westminster, Nottingham City Council and the board. For a time the issue was the main talking point in the town, and depth of feeling was shown by instances of friendships jeopardized by opposing views on the subject.

Not surprisingly there was a flood of support for John. To say he had charisma was more than coining a fashionable expression. He did have, to use a definition of the word, 'the personal quality capable of influencing large numbers of people'. He was, of course, a fine and famous actor and, as discussed in these pages, had worked hard in playing some heavy leading parts simultaneously with administrative duties. All this plus the effect and success of the new theatre had made a great impression, and for John a strong position of glamorous appeal, compared with the prosaic and background work of the board however necessary its function and experience.

John Neville himself said in a *Sunday Times* article, 'I am not known to be a contentious man nor are the members of the [Nottingham Playhouse] Board, which has always had the reputation of being one of the best in the country.' Again, in a statement on 'The Nottingham Fracas' to a House of Commons Estimates Committee (Grants For The Arts), the Arts Council had said,

> *The Council hold Mr. Neville in high esteem but at the same time recognize that the situation was concerned with resignation and not a dismissal and they recognized that the Board had over many years conducted the affairs of the Theatre with competence and had maintained a happy relationship with Mr. Neville's several predecessors who were men of considerable distinction and independence of spirit and certainly were not men who would have accepted a position where they were subjected to undue domination or interference.*

So, intrinsic in the Nottingham circumstances was something fundamental which could not be dispersed by fervent demonstrations. Local objectivity in the matter was not easy to find, but perhaps a Nottingham newspaper editorial in 1967 was a notable effort. It put the question 'What is the Playhouse controversy all about?' and said this deserved a 'dispassionate and reasoned answer' and 'In trying to give one, and in expressing a further opinion, we hope that the Playhouse will be helped towards a new era of harmony and good will. . . . Basically, of course, the issue is still a matter of whether the Board of the Nottingham Theatre Trust are justified in declining to allow John Neville, director of the Theatre for the past four-and-a-half years, to withdraw his resignation, which was submitted on the grounds that the Arts Council grant was inadequate to finance future plans.' After further recapitulating of events the newspaper continued:

> *Unfortunately the matter goes deeper than a simple reversal of the decision to accept Mr Neville's resignation. In answering the points of difference Mr Neville made it clear that he had no intention of*

*staying on while the present Theatre Trust Board continued to have
charge of the administration. He is, as far as is known, still of this
frame of mind. In other words, the board must go – or a significant
part of it – for Mr Neville to stay. It is not simply a question of one
man's future but of the future of the Theatre itself – in essence a
struggle for its control. Mr Neville is not taking an active part in this
struggle. It is the newly-constituted committee of the Playhouse
Club that is seeking, by the manipulation of public opinion, to force
a change of mind upon the board, a change that could only be
brought about by a split among the members and the resignation of
several individuals who were largely responsible for bringing the
present Playhouse into being after nursing its predecessor through
some difficult – although happier – times in Goldsmith Street. It is
being argued that the present Theatre Trust board, a properly
constituted and responsible body, do not effectively represent the
playgoers of Nottingham and that the Playhouse Club should have a
more decisive say in the administration of the Theatre. But to bring
this about by the present form of coercion would only result in
deep-seated discord that could well do irreparable harm to the
Theatre. The time for consideration of this issue is when the present
troubles have been resolved and the affairs of the Playhouse can be
discussed in a less emotionally-charged atmosphere. The merits of
Mr Neville as an actor and a director are widely recognised, but in
the present circumstances there is no real alternative to his leaving
the Theatre in July, 1968.*

The season 1967/8 opened with *Othello* and Eugene O'Neill's *A Long Day's
Journey Into Night*, directed by Noel Willman and Michael Rudman
respectively. The two plays were a mini-season in themselves, built round a
unique visit by the American actor Robert Ryan, known to us best as a
Hollywood film star. This project was described by Mr Ryan as originating
from working with John Neville on the film of *Billy Budd*. Mr Ryan contacted
John Neville, on hearing that the latter was Theatre Director in Nottingham,
to say he had a wish to do *A Long Day's Journey* and also at the back of his
mind was Shakespeare, and 'could he use me?' Apparently John Neville was
immediately for the O'Neill play and after some thought came to the
conclusion that 'Since the Moor is a foreigner in *Othello* anyway, the
American accent would not hurt. . . . He asked me to play Iago and we soon
went into rehearsal.'

Robert Ryan and John Neville in *Othello* (Shakespeare)

It was an interesting venture for the American, who it was said earned $250,000 from motion pictures in the previous year, and had now come to work in an English regional theatre for about $150 a week. But in the past he had played Romeo to Katherine Hepburn's Juliet in Stratford, Connecticut, and Antony there in 1960, and before that Coriolanus in New York, so he had roots in Shakespeare. Also he said: 'I would like to set up a truly repertory theatre in New York one day. I would need help, but I think we could get top talent to work with top talent at minimum salaries. I would do it and I know others would.'

Thus there was a traceable background to Mr Ryan's readiness to do classical stage work within Nottingham circumstances. All this was commendable to the Playhouse and in sympathy with the atmosphere there, especially coming from the 'nice guy' which Robert Ryan proved to be, though his pleasant personality was not perhaps the best natural basis for the tortured passions of Othello. So his performance had a composed calmness which presented a sitting target for Iago's villainy.

It was a different matter with the O'Neill play. Emrys Bryson commenced his review with 'Ah, this is better.' He continued: 'After more than three hours you come out of the Theatre in the knowledge that you have been seared in the flame' and, on Robert Ryan's performance as the father, James Tyrone: 'Robert Ryan here shrugs himself into a role that is tailormade for him, and is most impressive. He has a quiet gravity as the head of this disturbed household, a gentle humour and a subtly clear way of laying bare the puzzled suffering of the man. With superb strokes he conveys both fatherly strength and human weakness, coupled with disappointment and sorrow, the stony face suddenly made young as he recalls younger glories.' In that production the Playhouse's Gillian Martell gave a wonderful account of the mother, Mary Tyrone.

The next play, John Arden's *The Workhouse Donkey*, a complex lampoon of municipal politics, was directed with zest by John Neville and Alan Dossor, but some critics felt that the hilarity ran out of steam after an hour or so, and the play 'crumbled into incoherence', in spite of an assumption that its themes might have greater impact in a venue further north than the place of its first production four years earlier, at the Chichester Festival, where it had been directed by Stuart Burge.

In Willard Stoker's production of Charles Dyer's *Staircase* there were fine performances by John Neville and Ronald Magill as the homosexual barbers, Charles and Harry; the one sharp and taunting, the other homely and patient, but linked to each other in shared loneliness, and in some self-mockery. Charles has a description of themselves as 'two frail old twits'. The clash of the contrasting personalities, acting out their problems, held our interest and compassion. The author had a programme comment on the play and the significance of its title:

> All life is a kind of blackmail. It is very lonely and that is a problem
> for the young and a tragedy for the old. And out of this loneliness
> springs this blackmail – we tend to climb up on our friends as much
> as they will allow us to. It is not social climbing, but emotional
> climbing; we use them. In this respect one of the characters uses the
> other very much as a staircase. Charles uses Harry, he climbs up

using Harry as an escalator between emotional flops. Their
relationship is not homosexual; they are not practising, physical
homosexuals, that is.

The production was brought back into the repertoire for a week late in the season, which meant that the part of Charles was John Neville's last at the Playhouse.

A revival of *A Midsummer Night's Dream* played through the Christmas period and *All's Well That Ends Well* came at the end of January. Thus, with *Othello*, the season included three Shakespeares, and they had an average attendance of 86 per cent.

A seasonal highlight which we considered important was a production of *Boots With Strawberry Jam*, a new musical on the life and loves of Bernard Shaw, by John Dankworth and Benny Green, directed by Wendy Toye, with settings and costumes by Patrick Robertson and Rosemary Vercoe. It was in

Cleo Laine and John Neville in *Boots with Strawberry Jam* (Dankworth & Green)

two acts, the first based on Ellen Terry and the second on Mrs Patrick Campbell, both played by Cleo Laine, with John Neville as G.B.S.

The show was first called *Our Dear Bernard*, and the changed title sprang from a quote in a letter to Shaw from Mrs Pat in 1912:

> *My Stella used to sing a song which I told her was silly, and she declared was funny – your last letter reminds me more of it than your others –*

> He's mad, mad, mad,
> He's clean gone off his nut,
> He cleans his boots with strawberry jam,
> He eats his hat whenever he can,
> He's mad, mad, mad.

In a skilful note accompanying the production, Benny Green wrote of Shaw's courtships by mail and referred to 'the correspondence with Ellen Terry, in which two people exchanged the tenderest love letters for several years without ever actually coming face to face. . . . For a man like Shaw the postal love affair was the perfect arrangement, giving him the chance to practise his literary style while absolving him from any obligation to translate words into deeds.'

That is a practical view, but it is a fairly hard assessment. The correspondence between Shaw and Ellen Terry commenced in 1892. Four years later, when he was forty and she forty-eight, the letters became loving and more frequent, at one point every three or four days. There were lulls over the years and the letters ceased in 1922. Even at the beginning Ellen was herself saying: 'I think I'd rather never meet you – in the flesh. You are such a Great Dear as you are.' Shaw said:

> *Ellen and I lived within twenty minutes of each other's doorstep, and yet lived in different worlds. . . . We both felt instinctively that a meeting might spoil it, and would certainly alter it and bring it into conflict with other personal relationships. And so I hardly ever saw her, except across the footlights, until the inevitable moment at last arrived when we had to meet daily at the rehearsals of the play I wrote for her, Captain Brassbound's Conversion. . . . After the play was disposed of our meetings were few, and all accidental. One of these chance meetings was on a summer day in the country near*

*Elstree, where I came upon a crowd of people at work on a cinema
film. Ellen Terry was there, acting the heroine. She was
astonishingly beautiful. She had passed through that middle phase,
so trying to handsome women, of matronly amplitude, and was
again tall and slender, with a new delicacy and intensity in her
saddened expression. She was always a little shy in speaking to me,
for talking, hampered by material circumstances, is awkward and
unsatisfactory after the perfect freedom of writing between people
who can write. She asked me why I did not give her some work in
the theatre. 'I do not expect leading parts' she said: 'I am too old. I
am quite willing to play a charwoman.' . . . 'What would become of
the play?' I said. 'Imagine a scene in which the part of a canal barge
was played by a battleship! What would happen to my play, or to
anyone else's, if whenever the charwoman appeared the audience
forgot the hero and heroine and could think of nothing but the
wonderful things the charwoman was going to say and do?' . . . It
was unanswerable; and we both, I think, felt rather inclined to
cry. . . . She became a legend in her old age; but of that I have
nothing to say; for we did not meet, and except for a few broken
letters, did not write; and she never was old to me. . . . Let those
who complain that it was all on paper remember that only on paper
has humanity yet achieved glory, beauty, truth, knowledge, virtue
and abiding love.*

'She never was old to me!' The last time I was at Smallhythe I thought of the words, and felt that in Shaw's heart Ellen Terry had a place which never died.

Interest in the musical's subject, author, composer and star leads brought all the critics. Several disliked the 'episodic plot line' and mentioned underdevelopment of relationships between characters too caricatured. On the latter point one notice was unhappy at the 'diminishing' of every major being presented, for example Irving, Wells, the Webbs. Perhaps this approach was too serious.

However, in spite of doubt on the concept, the show had 'witty exuberance and fresh invention, and few repertory theatres had the technical resources and ability to cope with a couple of dozen major scene changes and the same total of musical numbers'.

There was certainly agreement about John Neville's expertise as G.B.S. and Cleo Laine's performance as Ellen Terry and Mrs Patrick Campbell. Obviously her singing was a most effective feature, and also we were impressed by her acting ability. One would have expected her range of skills and her personality to have been used more in musical theatre.

The Dankworths returned to the Playhouse quite soon after the Shaw musical, in a concert directed by John Dankworth entitled *Facade and Followers*, cleverly programmed, and an outstanding occasion among Playhouse Sunday shows. Mr Dankworth led a six-piece band in a performance of the Sitwell/Walton *Facade*; the poems were read by Cleo Laine and Annie Ross. Then John Dankworth's version of *Sweeney Agonistes – Fragments of an Aristophanic Melodrama* by T.S. Eliot. This had been performed only once before, at the Eliot Memorial Concert in June 1965. The same two lady readers were amusing as Dusty and Doris. This programme ended with a group of Eliot's poems from *Old Possum's Book of Practical Cats*, set to music by Iwan Williams, who led the four-piece band. The readings were by Terence Knapp ('The Naming of Cats' and 'The Ad-dressing of Cats'); John Neville ('Gus: the Theatre Cat'); John Neville and Ursula Smith ('The Song of the Jellicles'); John Dankworth and Cleo Laine ('Mungojerrie and Rumpelteazer'); Ronald Magill ('Old Deuteronomy'). It is interesting that many years later Andrew Lloyd Webber was enormously successful with *Cats*, his long-running musical based on Eliot's poems.

In 1966 the Playhouse had hosted a touring company's *Galileo*, but in April 1969 it had its first own production of a Brecht play, *Mother Courage*, one of his best known, directed by Alan Dossor. With its large cast and setting of the German Thirty Years' War in the seventeenth century, Brecht created an epic story. The adventures of the well-named leading character take us into another world of suffering under the oppression of a futile war. Yet we have the human interest of her survival; her ingenuity and cunning; her spirit in the face of the loss of her children; the courage of the common people caught up in conflict. Wars have their songs and those in *Mother Courage* were drab compared with, say, the (no less poignant) liveliness of 'Tipperary' in the First World War.

A critic said: 'Hazel Hughes in the name part is the best I have seen in an English production; indomitable, bawdy and shrewd.' And indeed she had some of those qualities in her own personality. She played many parts at the first Playhouse and it was a pleasure to meet and again enjoy that sense of humour, earthiness and warmth. She liked to tell stories against herself. One of these came from her hilarious reminiscences of entertaining the Forces during the war. A fellow-artist in one such company was an actress and dancer named Hy Hazell, whose style was elegant, and very different from Hazel Hughes, who was delighted to relate that in the company they were known as High and Low Hazel. In her distressing terminal illness she was always brave, and her last letter described visits and flowers from great ones in the profession, such was the affection for her.

Of the last three productions in the 1967/8 season two were premieres, for which Michael Denison and Dulcie Gray came to lead the company. The plays were *Vacant Possession* by Maisie Mosco, directed by Donald McWhinnie, and *Confession at Night* by Aleksie Arbuzov, translated from the Russian by Ariadne Nicolaeff. The first was described by the author as 'a macabre comedy about the pattern of life; the awful truth with all the tears and laughter'. The author of the second play, Arbuzov, travelled from Russia to attend the first night. He had a success in London with a previous play called *The Promise*, but Harold Hobson in the *Sunday Times* dismissed *Confession* as a disappointment after promise, and generally the critics were unimpressed. The events of the play, dangers and defiance during German occupation of a small town in the Ukraine in 1944, should have excited and moved us, but the treatment of characters and situations was too superficial. Perhaps one difficulty was covering a large subject within one play.

After John Neville left the Playhouse in June 1968 he acted in London and at the festivals in Edinburgh and Chichester; he then worked in Canada at the National Arts Center, Ottawa and the Manitoba Theatre Center. In 1973 he was appointed Director of the Citadel Theatre, Edmonton, and later of the Neptune Theatre, Halifax, Nova Scotia. While he was in Halifax he was offered the post of Artistic Director of the most prestigious classical company in North America, at the Stratford Festival Theatre in Ontario, but declined, preferring at the time to complete the work of establishing the Neptune Theatre. However, when in 1985 the opportunity in Ontario occurred again, he accepted. After years of working with much success in Canada it was not surprising to read in an interview that he now looks upon that country as his home.

CHAPTER SEVEN

STUART BURGE, 1968–73

We have said that the controversy over John Neville's departure abated only when his successor had been found and named. There had been bitter forecasts that the Playhouse would now decline into a third-rate shadow of former glory; would find it impossible to find a new theatre director of any kind; and 'would probably sink into becoming a bingo hall'. Indeed, the point about no one wanting the position had been made by well-known members of the theatrical profession and, coming from such a quarter, caused some nervousness among local theatre-goers. The statement was rash and short of consideration, but no doubt came from the excited temper of the time.

It was unnecessary to show such panic for two reasons, one from the past and one relating to the future. The first was based on the curiously overlooked fact that Nottingham Playhouse had been in existence not for five years of the new building, but for twenty efficient years. The board was the same structure which had presided over the whole period, so was hardly without experience of theatrical affairs. It had appointed, and worked smoothly with, the several distinguished theatre directors who had successfully built the Playhouse's reputation. The second reason for confidence was contained within comments by the Director who had agreed to succeed John Neville. In a press interview he referred to the appeal of the Playhouse post as being 'the greatest theatrical opportunity outside the National Theatre and the Royal Shakespeare Theatre in London. . . . I find it the most exciting job one could have. It is a tremendous opportunity. I could have wished that I had taken it over in other circumstances, but it is not my business to look over the past.'

The new Theatre Director was Stuart Burge, a 49-year-old stage, film and television producer of great standing in the British theatre. It is only fair to say that when making the above statement he emphasized also that he had balanced the attraction of the appointment against the atmosphere in which he was to take over. It had been a difficult personal matter for Mr Burge, as he described:

> *I have taken a long time to make the decision. Before I took it I saw*
> *John, who is a good friend of mine. . . . I have investigated every*
> *possibility, and I have come to the conclusion that if John cannot*

Stuart Burge (right) with
Richard Eyre

stay on, it is right to accept. It seemed to me that there was no way
out of it. The offer from the Board was unanimous, but admittedly I
received letters from the supporters' group in outright terms. I
replied to them as best I could, and I have tried to explain my
situation, which is not nearly as difficult as John's. However one
had to make the decision and face the facts squarely. I feel that it
would be useless to delay any longer, and I knew it was unfair to
everybody to continue to delay, but the reason I had delayed so long
was to make sure that the position could not be changed. And I
knew that the offer was likely to be made elsewhere.

On one matter Mr Burge apparently felt assured. In an interview with the
publication *Plays and Players* he was reported as saying, 'Really I am in an
absurdly strong position. They [the Board] dare not have another row and if
anything must give the Director a freer hand than before. It is rather a
responsibility.' In fact, whatever the Neville controversy was about, it certainly
could not be the issue of the Theatre Director's artistic freedom. Total respect
for that had been a fundamental principle for the board since its formation in
1948, and the people best able to confirm that are the previous directors. I
would be confident, and content, with their verdict.

In spite of Stuart Burge's eulogy on the attractions of the job, the Playhouse was fortunate to secure him at a time when it was essential for the new director to have indisputable experience and ability with which to establish immediate authority. Stuart Burge's name in itself gave assurance to the public and profession that the Playhouse's future was in the safest of hands, and so it proved. He joined the Old Vic as an actor in 1936 and became stage manager for the European tours. Between 1939 and 1946 he was a member of the company at the Bristol Old Vic and Oxford Playhouse, and began his career as a director in 1948, having his first London productions in 1949/50. In 1952 he was appointed Director of the Queens Theatre, Hornchurch, where he directed over sixty productions. He began a distinguished freelance career with work at the Old Vic; Stratford, Ontario; the USA; and at the Chichester Festival Theatre on first productions of plays by John Arden and Christopher Fry. He also directed films including *Othello* (based on the National Theatre production), *The Mikado* and *Julius Caesar*.

The summer season of visitors in 1968 included Ballet Rambert, Phoenix Opera, Prospect Productions. The latter brought *The Beggar's Opera* directed by Toby Robertson and in the company were Peter Gilmore, Hy Hazell, Angela Richards, also former Nottingham Playhouse personalities in James Cossins as Mr Peachum, and the designer Voytek.

There were three months between John Neville's last production and Stuart Burge's debut in September 1968 with Shakespeare's *King John* (apparently no irony intended!). During the weeks of preparing this major production to launch his theatre directorship, Stuart was probably too busy to be much affected by any consequences remaining after John Neville's departure, but he and his new company must have been aware of an atmosphere of suspended judgement, both locally and further afield.

In fact *King John* came as the spearhead of a season which by any standards was superb for range of programme, quality of company, direction and design, and was one of the most distinguished ever at Nottingham Playhouse. Any doubts or reservations dispersed as quickly and quietly as morning mist.

The Times headline for its notice of *King John* was 'New regime gets off to a flying start' and proceeded to commend the production as 'strongly cast, well designed, and animated by a fresh approach to the play'. Among the reviewers there was considerable surprise at the choice, though several took the opportunity to redress the usual underrating and neglect of 'one of Shakespeare's most unjustifiably unpopular plays'.

Certainly critics from Hazlitt to Agate have been patronizing about it. The latter said: 'What a bad play this is!' It had 'one or two exquisite bits and

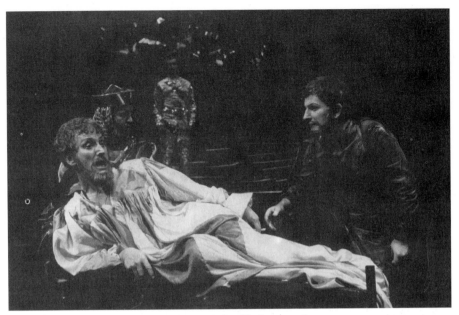

Barry Foster and T.P. McKenna in *King John* (Shakespeare)

some good declamatory stuff in it, made up of single lines which seldom flow into each other. This gives a disjointed, halting effect, and the resulting sum is not poetry. Such lines as:

> Which now the manage of two kingdoms must
> With fearful bloody issue arbitrate.

might also be parody, the second line being the perfect echo of Peter Quince.' Hazlitt in his *Characters of Shakespeare's Plays* says '*King John* is the last of the historical plays we shall have to speak of, and we are not sorry that it is.' He was troubled that the sheer horror of the play's events had 'a real truth in history'. He preferred such painful subjects to be illustrated by 'fictitious danger and fictitious distress'.

One wonders indeed whether dislike of the play has some of its base in abhorrence of the king's character; villainous and vacillating; murderous and cowardly. Many of Shakespeare's characters have one or another of these attributes, and charge through regular revivals of their plays, but perhaps the aggregate in King John is hard to take. In this production Barry Foster played the part in an ingenious and original way, to combine within the royal personage evil intent and 'idiot laughter', even sinking into giggles on his deathbed. The play's other main part, Philip Faulconbridge, bastard son of King Richard I, was played finely by T.P. McKenna, taking his place at court powerfully and savouring his heroic speeches.

There is something very deeply felt in the Bastard's fiercely scornful tirade in the first scene of Act II: 'Mad world! mad kings! mad composition!' and the contempt towards 'Commodity, the bias of the world'. Perhaps for our time we might transpose this 'commodity' as 'corruption', and the speech's hatred of it has all the sound of an author's own conviction put into his character's mouth. Another interesting conjecture of Shakespeare's personal feelings creeping into *King John* was made in a piece by the former Playhouse actor, Emrys James, who played the name part during his splendid years with the Royal Shakespeare Company. (Who could ever forget his hauntingly moving Feste there in the *Twelfth Night* of 1970?) He notes that the date given to the play *King John* is 1596 and says: 'On 11th August 1596 the parish register of Stratford-on-Avon records the burial of Hamnet Shakespeare, son of William Shakespeare. . . . I find it difficult to believe that the loss of that twelve-and-a-half year old boy in 1596 is not echoed in the lament of Constance for her son:

CONSTANCE:	There was not such a gracious creature born,
	But now will canker-sorrow eat my bud,
	And chase the native beauty from his cheek,
	And he will look as hollow as a ghost,
	As dim and meagre as an ague's fit;
	And so he'll die; and, rising up again,
	When I shall meet him in the court of heaven,
	I shall not know him; therefore never, never
	Must I behold my pretty Arthur more.

●　　●　　●　　●　　●

KING PHILIP:	You are as fond of grief as of your child.
CONSTANCE:	Grief fills the room up of my absent child,
	Lies in his bed, walks up and down with me,
	Puts on his pretty looks, repeats his words,
	Remembers me of all his gracious parts,
	Stuffs out his vacant garments with his form;

●　　●　　●　　●　　●

> O Lord! my boy, my Arthur, my fair son!
> My life, my joy, my food, my all the world!
> My widow-comfort, and my sorrows' cure!'

Emrys James's conjecture about this and Shakespeare's young son Hamnet was made also by the theatre critic and scholar, Ivor Brown, who suggested there is 'an authentic death-bed vision' in the words 'As dim and meagre as an ague's fit'. Is there an echo of Lear and Cordelia in Constance's 'never, never'? How well did Shakespeare understand grief.

A further significance has been suggested about the play's date, being only eight years after the defeat of the Spanish Armada. This maybe was close enough to fire the speech with which the Bastard ends *King John*, words which were a rallying cry nearly three hundred and fifty years later, in the Second World War:

> Come the three corners of the world in arms,
> And we shall shock them; naught shall make us rue
> If England to itself do rest but true.

Finally we should mention Stuart Burge's staging of *King John*, which for some was over-stylized, and felt by one critic to show a Guthrie influence. The set was a tiered structure with a multi-purpose revolve, in which the action flowed, and the bright colours of the costumes – red and gold for the English, blue and silver for the French – made glittering patterns. One thought of a pack of cards come to life. The critic B.A. Young said: 'The slow-motion choreographic battle at Angiers that brings down the curtain for the interval is brilliantly conceived.'

It was all a theatrical fling of great vitality. If such light and life could be injected into this dark and cold-shouldered play, the future looked bright for Nottingham Playhouse.

Original ideas in production continued with the second play, *The School for Scandal*. Stuart Burge had persuaded Jonathan Miller to direct. It seemed in fact that Dr Miller was intrigued by the opportunity to put into practice some strong views on the conventions of this play's usual stage presentations. He described his approach in a stimulating programme note which commenced:

> The School for Scandal *is one of those plays which has suffered the crushing misfortune of becoming a classic. Whatever the author's original intentions might have been, they have long since been*

smothered beneath layers of theatrical varnish, piously applied by
successive generations of actors and producers. The play, in other
words, has become fossilized – it preserves its original shape, to be
sure, but its substance has been replaced by the dead materials of
thoughtless convention. In the last sixty years or so The School for
Scandal *has become an idealised phantasy of the eighteenth century; a*
model of how we would like to imagine that period – 'Lud,' lorgnettes
and lace handkerchiefs. In this production I have tried to re-animate
Sheridan's original play by trying to restore some of the original
character of late Georgian England, instead of the high Versailles camp
and all the familiar, glazed artificialities of Shaftesbury Avenue. Pat
Robertson, Rosemary Vercoe and I have come back to Hogarth and
Gilray in an effort to give back some blood to a production that was
otherwise dying from anaemia. . . . The eighteenth century saw the
development of caricature as a special convention, both in the graphic
arts and in the drama. Many of the scenes in Sheridan's plays are like
Gilray cartoons come to life and throughout this production I have
tried to preserve the bulging, warty vitality of this particular idiom.

So this was an experience of the play unlike any other hitherto served to the
Playhouse audiences, some of which raised eyebrows at the robust characterization
and occasional coarse stage business. But it had a strong persuasion that we were
looking at real eighteenth-century people, not marionettes. The company appeared
to enjoy the 'liberation' and there were strong performances from Ronald Magill,
T.P. McKenna, Cherith Mellor, Moira Redmond, the latter as Lady Sneerwell
unrecognizable in a grotesque, witty make-up.

In 1896 there had been an impressive production of *The School for Scandal* at
the Lyceum Theatre. The company included many stars of their day, including
Fred Terry as Charles Surface, Forbes-Robertson as Joseph Surface and Mrs
Patrick Campbell as Lady Teazle. This was at the time when Bernard Shaw was
drama critic for the Saturday Review and he used the occasion to write a lengthy
notice which incorporated a dissertation on the changes in morality since the
play's first appearance in 1777. Shaw's review fills eight pages (drama critics note
– those were the days!) and short extracts cannot do justice to Shaw's case but
here is a sample in order to give the flavour and to set something alongside
Jonathan Miller's views:

Compare the gentlemen of Sheridan's time with the gentlemen of to-
day (1896). What a change in all that is distinctively gentlemanly! –

the dress, the hair, the watch-chain, the manners, the point of
honour, the meals, the ablutions, and so on! Yet strip the twain, and
they are as like as two eggs; maroon them on Juan Fernandez, and
what difference will there be between their habits and those of
Robinson Crusoe? Nevertheless, men do change, not only in what
they think and what they do, but in what they are.

The third play of Stuart Burge's first season continued to suggest that the Playhouse's new regime favoured the unusual, the experimental and the stimulating. The rarely performed Shakespeare and its unconventional treatment; the Sheridan classic with a very new look indeed from an exciting, unorthodox director with ideas about interpretation, in this instance stripping down the veneer to show the real wood; and now a new play, large-scale and controversial, described as 'a Gothic comedy seeking to explore the outer limits of humour'. During November 1968 these three productions running in repertoire formed a display at the time unsurpassed in Britain.

For several weeks before rehearsals started *The Ruling Class* was making headlines on the matter of who was to play the huge leading role. It seemed a scoop when this was agreed with the Canadian-born stage and film star Christopher Plummer, then filming in Spain, but he had to withdraw and the part was taken over, to the delight of his friends in Nottingham, by Derek Godfrey, a star of the Old Vic and Royal Shakespeare Company, and early in his career a favourite member of the old Playhouse company.

The Ruling Class, by Peter Barnes and directed by Stuart Burge, was a wildly comic diatribe, against the aristocracy in particular. Of John Napier's fine settings no one who saw it will forget his burlesque of the House of Lords chamber, gilded and cobwebbed, peopled with caricatures of petrified lords. On the first night every national critic attended, and it was one of those occasions to put a theatre on the map if it was not already there.

The nature of the play kindled in practically every review the extremes of praise and castigation. From 'shockingly one-sided' to 'far and away the most exciting thing I have seen at Nottingham'. From 'flabby bladder of undisciplined writing' to 'the maddening thing is that much of the material is very good and funny'. From 'simply the best new play I've seen this year' to 'let me qualify hastily that it is also a thoroughly bad one, and far too long'. From 'most of the time it is hilarious creating surrealist situations of inspired lunacy' to 'three hours of obscurity, however brilliant, can be too much'. And a plaintive little letter in a newspaper: ' "Will someone please explain?" asks Dinsdale Gurney in *The Ruling Class* at the Playhouse. I wish someone would. Playgoer.'

Vivienne Martin, Derek Godfrey, Ronald Magill in *The Ruling Class* (Barnes)

In spite of its mixed reception *The Ruling Class* was not a 'nine days wonder' to be seen no more after the Playhouse run. It was transferred to London, at the Piccadilly Theatre, again with Derek Godfrey in the lead, and later made into a film with Peter O'Toole.

The next play in the repertoire was *The Seagull*, directed by Jonathan Miller. Again he was praised for a clear reading. Approval was expressed beautifully by Emrys Bryson:

> *Instead of the usual heavily ominous atmosphere and pregnant*
> *pauses, the philosophising by melancholy people who seem to know*
> *that they're in a play, it brings human beings to warm, solid life. . . .*
> *Like the placid, misty lake that is the centrepiece, its figures have*
> *depth and currents below the surface. But they are not people*
> *overwhelmed by tragedy. They have tragedy, and despair, but they*
> *have them in different shades, fragmented with fun and hope and*
> *love as well. In short, they are ordinary human beings.*

However, every audience for a Chekhov play will have those who have little sympathy with his characters, who will seem, as someone said, to be part of 'a static picture of frustrated people continuing to be frustrated', and one duly heard such a reaction on this occasion, despite Dr Miller's unequivocal interpretation.

Those critics are in the company of the ones who attended the play's first night in St Petersburg in October 1896. They hissed, and after only the first act congregated in the bar, saying: 'Where is there any action? Where are there any recognisable types? It's all so watery – He's lost his talent – He's written himself out.' These comments were reflected in their reviews, and Chekhov was deeply hurt and distressed.

Some of the responsibility for the catastrophe lay with Chekhov himself. He had been unusually perfunctory over the casting, and disappointed without remedying at rehearsals. Also he made an error of judgement when he allowed a leading actress to use *The Seagull*'s opening performance as her benefit night. This Madame Levkeyeva had a following from her work in broad farces, and these supporters, having filled the theatre expecting similar fare, were predictably displeased with *The Seagull*!

The St Petersburg intelligentsia who had been crowded out at the first night were a different, and approving, audience on the second night, after which the actress playing Nina sat down at midnight and rushed a note to Chekhov: 'I've just returned from the theatre, dear Anton Pavlovich. Victory is ours. The play is a complete, unanimous success, just as it ought to be, just as it had to be. How I'd like to see you now, but what I'd like even more is for you to be present and hear the cry of "Author" . . . I clasp your hand.' This must have given comfort to Chekhov, at a time when he needed it, for the incident was one of the most painful of his life. But those unfavourable notices had done damage and the theatre management took the play off after only five performances. Although productions of the play appeared around the country from time to time, *The Seagull* was not properly and permanently established until the famous production by Stanislavsky at the Moscow Art Theatre (or the People's Theatre as it was called then) in December 1898, two years after that disastrous opening. Illustrations of the ornate stage settings and of the company at rehearsal are somewhat forbidding to present-day eyes, as indeed would probably be the case with pictures of English Victorian stage work. One particularly interesting photograph shows Chekhov reading the play to the whole company, in rather a posed group, but the intense absorption shows genuinely enough, and we can take it Chekhov was determined to ensure that this time the interpretations would be just as he intended.

Chekhov did not see the production at that time. He had become ill in Yalta and by the time he was able to return to Moscow the season was over, the company disbanded and the theatre let for the summer. But according to

Stanislavsky (in his *My Life in Art*) Chekhov demanded to see his play and a special performance was given in another theatre. It must have been a strange experience. A nervous, unsettled company playing to Chekhov and 'about ten other spectators', and it is not surprising that the impression was 'only middling'. Apparently Chekhov was not pleased with some of the acting and production features. Stanislavsky himself, having played the writer, Trigorin, in 'the most elegant of costumes – white trousers, white vest, white hat, slippers, and a handsome make-up' was no doubt deflated by disapproval of his stunning appearance and the author's comment 'you need torn shoes and checked trousers'. However, when Stanislavsky followed this direction in later productions he realized its wisdom, and seems to have agreed that a famous writer of natural good looks and in bohemian garb was a more romantic proposition for playing Trigorin than as a stuffy vision in immaculate, total white.

One cannot say whether the Playhouse production of *The Seagull* unfolded to Stuart Burge's liking, and critics had been doubtful about some of the casting. Theatre directors face many worries and they have often been heard to bemoan their lot, though foremost among the compensations must be the power to decide on a great play and plan its presentation. Regional theatre is a main place where such authority may be exercised by an artist from the profession (almost in the manner of the actor-managers of the last century) as distinct from the operations of impresarios and speculators. But the opportunities do become much fewer, due to squeezing of grants, the increased dominance of financial controllers and the consigning of theatres to the mercy of 'market forces'. So perhaps it would be appropriate to change tense and say *was* a main place.

However, in 1969 the times were still golden. *Macbeth* with Barry Foster and T.P. McKenna (disliked by some critics from 'a poor sequel to the brilliant *King John*' to 'Stuart Burge can be forgiven for dropping a little chaff among the corn, as he has undoubtedly done with *Macbeth*.'); *The Entertainer*, played by Denis Quilley, about which there was no dissatisfaction, but delight to have that fine actor in the company again, and to hear his fine singing voice. Later he took over the *Macbeth* from Barry Foster who had departed to films. A very accomplished production by T.P. McKenna of *The Playboy of the Western World* (which Irving Wardle in *The Times* thought 'has a good deal more life than the Abbey's own recent version') and another Irish piece, *The Hostage*.

A few weeks later Mr Wardle wrote of 'one of the most staggering examples of grotesque comedy I have ever seen'. This was Leonard Rossiter's performance as Hitler (Ui) in a production by Michael Blakemore of Brecht's

The Resistible Rise of Arturo Ui, which appeared previously at Edinburgh. In July the Nottingham version transferred to London at the Saville Theatre.

In his Notes on the play Brecht said: 'The great political criminals must by all means be exposed, and preferably to ridicule, for they are not so much great political criminals as the perpetrators of great political crimes, which is altogether different . . . [and] the small-time bum who has been allowed by our rulers to become a big-time bum deserves no place of honour in the annals either of bumming or history.'

This story of Chicago gangsters Arturo Ui and his fellow thugs, and their progress from petty to massive terror, was an allegory of the horrors of Hitler and his pack of monsters. Brecht's writing and Rossiter's acting (the cold, mean look; the flat, menacing voice) brilliantly pulled out the tragic implications.

Satire and truth were equally savage, and firmly compatible. The production was a major contribution to what was on offer in the British theatre at the time. And Leonard Rossiter's Ui is one of Nottingham Playhouse's unforgettable performances, among such as Michael Aldridge's Othello, Jean Forbes-Robertson's Viola, John Neville's Richard II, Barbara Jefford's Cleopatra, Michael Hordern's Lear, and Imelda Staunton's Piaf.

During 1969 many fringe activities continued at the Playhouse. The theatre was in use frequently on Sundays, serving all interests. There was an alliance with the Australian Music Association to present an opera, *The Growing Castle* by Malcolm Williamson, directed by the composer; jazz from Humphrey Lyttelton, Marion Montgomery and the Roland Kirk Quartet; the Band of the Royal Marines; concerts by the Scaffold and from Valentine Levko of the Bolshoi Opera. One remembers with particular pleasure a delightful occasion with Lilli Malandraki and Donald Swann which they called *An Evening in Crete*.

The Playhouse 1969 Arts Festival ran from 21 June to 8 July. Some local business sponsorship was found and there were links in that year with Nottingham University, but the demands on resources, human and financial, were huge and the Theatre Trust chairman took an opportunity at the opening reception to say that if an annual festival in Nottingham was to continue, the city and the county authorities must become involved. In fact it was the last year of the festival being based and run at the Playhouse and, the foundation having been well laid, the event became an annual civic feature.

The year 1969 was a choice one for our finale. All the arts had distinguished representation in the theatre or adjoining concert hall. To illustrate the quality, there was the Royal Philharmonic Orchestra with Pierre Fournier as soloist; a recital by Dame Sybil Thorndike; a jazz concert by John Dankworth, Cleo Laine and Richard Rodney Bennett; the Phoenix Opera Company in *The Marriage of Figaro*; guitar playing by Paco Pena. In the theatre two productions alternated, Brendan Behan's *The Hostage*, and a production by Michael Blakemore of *Widowers' Houses* with a company including Frank Middlemass, Nicola Pagett, Robin Ellis, Anthony Newlands and Penelope Wilton. Every day the Playhouse forecourt bustled with brass bands, steel bands, folk singers and dancers, jazz groups, poets and, above all, crowds of people enjoying the atmosphere, eating and drinking at the open-air tables. The Playhouse Club held a garden party in the university grounds. It was with some style that the festival torch was passed to the local councils.

After all that, the Playhouse had a summer season of four visiting companies. A new comedy by Keith Waterhouse and Willis Hall called *Children's Day* with Prunella Scales and Gerald Flood; the Ballet Rambert; another new play, *Zoo, Zoo, Widdershins, Zoo* by Kevin Laffan with Lynn Redgrave and produced by our former Theatre Director, Frank Dunlop; Ibsen's *The Wild Duck* by the Scottish Actors Company including Brian Cox, Robin Bailey and Anna Calder-Marshall. This last production, en route for the Edinburgh Festival, had its opening at the Playhouse and the setting was built in our workshops.

The next season took the Playhouse to the end of 1969, a little over a year since the arrival of Stuart Burge. The plays were *The Hero Rises Up* by John Arden and Margaret D'Arcy; *The Alchemist* by Ben Jonson; *King Lear* played by Michael Hordern and directed by Jonathan Miller; *The Demonstration*, a new play by David Caute; *Huckleberry Finn* adapted from Mark Twain's book. These five productions were presented within three months (making a total of nineteen for the year) and amounted to an incredible volume of high-standard work in the period.

The Hero Rises Up had a showing in London in the previous year, at the Roundhouse with, according to all accounts, woeful effects. This new production, directed by Bill Hays, played at the Edinburgh Festival before opening at the Playhouse and was obviously an entirely different matter. The play, about Admiral Lord Nelson, was concerned not so much with the naval victories as with features of his private life and character. We see, of course, the infatuation with the florid Lady Hamilton and his heartlessness towards the poignant Lady Nelson, and generally a low marking for morality, although that weakness is hardly unusual in men of great exploits in war, politics and other areas. Like the rest of us they have frailties and certainly their adoring contemporary public would cheer the virtuoso deeds and overlook the commonly experienced failings. The show's approach was suggested when the curtain rose and we saw the Trafalgar Column collapsing to the ground! And the use of music, ballads and *Threepenny Opera*-style songs was a clever idea. Also, as could be expected from the accomplished authors, there were some fine scenes even if they sat rather uncomfortably within the format of a musical satire, produced, in one critic's view, as '90 per cent hilarious buffoonery'. It was excellently acted by Robin Parkinson as Nelson, Peter Whitbread, Donald Gee and David Dodimead. Thelma Ruby did some show-stealing with her songs as the coquettish Lady Hamilton.

Coincidentally there was a naval theme in a Playhouse Children's Theatre tour at that time (to sixty secondary and comprehensive schools within six weeks) of a show called *Weevils in my Biscuit* by Charles Savage who had come from directing the youth organization at Exeter. The programme was described as 'following the progress of an expedition and the remarkable state of affairs which existed in Nelson's time, with press gangs, floggings, weevily biscuits, and all'.

The Alchemist, in a version by Peter Barnes, was directed vigorously by Stuart Burge (just back from directing a film of *Julius Caesar*) in a brilliant setting by Trevor Pitt. In fact the opening scene was done at a pace which

David Dodimead, Frank Middlemass in *The Alchemist* (Jonson)

might have caused confusion in those unfamiliar with the story and goings-on. But Jonson, in arguably his best play, was served well by a fine company playing the assortment of fantastic characters. Even Shaw, no lover of Jacobean dramatists, agreed about the medley, but added an acid rider: 'There is much variety in a dust-heap, even when the rag-picker is done with it; but we throw it indiscriminately into the "destructor" for all that.' G.B.S. at his most peevish! There is a lasting memory of Frank Middlemass as Sir Epicure Mammon. Professor Harry Levin has a phrase: 'The fat knight is a Falstaff who has suddenly begun to babble like a Faustus.' If we add 'and lust like a Casanova' perhaps we catch a flavour of Frank's skill in the part.

Ever since the announcement during the summer of the Hordern/Miller *King Lear* there had been eager anticipation of what was recognized as a major feature of the coming British theatre season. Sir Michael started rehearsals in Nottingham on his fifty-eighth birthday and remarked ruefully, 'I shall not be celebrating my birthday at all. I shall just be working on the play – which terrifies me.' Probably this is the effect which the part of Lear has had on most of those who have played it. Consider the actor doing research before starting rehearsals; he encounters: (a) Hazlitt: 'The Lear of Shakespeare cannot be acted. The contemptible machinery with which they mimic the storm which he goes out in, is not more inadequate to represent the horrors of the real elements than any actor can be to represent Lear.' (b) Lamb: 'Lear is essentially impossible to be represented on the stage.' (c) A.C. Bradley: 'Lear is too large for the stage.'

But our actor has comfort from the wise Harley Granville-Barker, practitioner as well as text analyst: '*King Lear*, it is said, cannot be acted. The whole scheme and method of its writing is a contrivance for its effective acting. . . . All the magnificent art of this is directed to one end; the play's acting in a theatre.'

So the academic factor may be resolved, but what of the practical hurdles? The development of equipment in present-day theatre may add to the problems of Lears in the storm scenes. Wind machines, thunder contrivances, mists of stage smoke, lightning and every other kind of lighting effect. It is enough to crack a voice within the cheeks, and the endeavour to top all the bedlam leads to shouting. The force is picked up also for the sizeable anger in the play and in the end the casualties are the overwhelmed lines, whose beauty can be lost as though they are of little more importance than those of the hard-pressed sailors in the first moments of *The Tempest*. Compare this with the likely level of storm simulation for the first Lear at the Globe in about 1605. What his audience experienced foremost was the raging of the storm within

Peter Eyre, Michael Hordern, David
Dodimead in *King Lear*
(Shakespeare)

his mind, surely the important part of the analogy. Perhaps some performances
of *Lear* were recalled by its author when writing his Sonnet No. 23!

> As an unperfect actor on the stage,
> Who with his fear is put beside his part,
> Or some fierce thing replete with too much rage,
> Whose strength's abundance weakens his own heart.

Michael Hordern's Lear was not in the declamatory, heroic manner. Nor
was his appearance that of a gaunt ancient Druid of four score years. He had
about the age of that Nottingham birthday, plainly cloaked, looking to one
critic 'more like a farmer than a king'. A human person amidst those savage,
far-off times; a pathetic loss of depth in the rising waters; an inexorable decline
of kingship. The delivery of the five 'nevers' over his dead Cordelia was
heartbreaking, and made nonsense of that assertion of the part being
unplayable. That is a line being *heard*, while being written by a man of the
theatre first and, for the moment, poet second. It is the stuff of theatre and
knowing about the actor's means of driving at the heart of an audience.

Again Frank Middlemass gave a great performance and an original reading
of the Fool in, presumably, Jonathan Miller's concept. Irving Wardle in *The*

Times described it as 'the funniest Fool I have yet seen, an elderly, broken-down comic who uses his regal employer as a cross-talk stooge'. James Agate once said 'anyone who wants a comic Fool should go to the *Yeoman of the Guard*'. But the comedy of Frank Middlemass's Fool was the kind close to tragedy, with very moving effect.

The programme for this production of *King Lear* quoted in full Matthew Arnold's poem, *Dover Beach*. Reading it before the performance was appropriate to the play's poignant close in that same locale. This was an instance of good standard in Playhouse programmes, and they deserve mention. The format was simple, but the cover for each play had its own design, and editorial content was of much quality and interest. Savants such as G.R. Hibberd, Nigel Alexander and D.R.S. Welland would contribute regularly on the plays and their significance. The director of the production might discuss his interpretation, or quote his rehearsal notes to the company. During the first years in the new building programmes were provided free, an urbane innovation which, alas, had to be sacrificed eventually to economic pressures.

The Demonstration by David Caute was a new play, lengthy in cast and for some people too long at nearly three hours. The title came from a situation of student revolt. It had an authoritative air which was not surprising as Mr Caute was at the time Reader in Social and Political Theory at Brunel University, having been a Fellow of All Souls at the age of twenty-three and made history by resigning on political grounds.

The play had a complicated structure, handled with skill; not only a play within a play, which has been done before, but a further play within (like Chinese boxes, one critic said) and an interaction of reality and fantasy. Marius Goring, who gave the play much strength, was a professor of drama whose students reject the play he has set for them, and demand that it is replaced by one of their own with the theme of revolt. A real-life situation is superimposed and the outcome is rather like returning to square one.

Stuart Burge and the company contrived a realistic impression of student commotion and Harold Hobson in the *Sunday Times* said: 'Far away in distant Nottingham they create the authentic atmosphere of the London School of Economics, or Brunel.' In the same notice he also referred to the Playhouse as being 'the most interesting Theatre in the country', a tribute which was probably sparked by the Playhouse continuing to include in its programme new work of importance.

In February 1970 the Playhouse was invited by the National Theatre to take its productions of *The Alchemist* and *King Lear* to the Old Vic for one week.

The *Daily Mail* said: 'The National Theatre has lent its ground to an away team. The guests, the Nottingham Playhouse Company, must be very near the top of the repertory league's Division One.' However, continuing the analogy, the critics kicked the ball around rather wildly and neither production scored many goals. Of the two *The Alchemist* fared better. There were reservations about Michael Hordern's Lear, which we had found so moving in Nottingham. Reviewers generally recognized the departure from that 'ranting and raving' which the part can engender, though one said it had led to 'little majesty in this Lear'. But nothing marred our pride in the distinction of our company appearing at the National Theatre.

While everyone was away in London we were able to stage a week of the English Stage Company's production of Chekhov's *Uncle Vanya* directed by Anthony Page and acted by a wonderful cast which included Paul Scofield, Colin Blakeley, Ralph Michael, Anna Calder-Marshall and Gwen Ffrangcon Davies. It was felt that this performance ranked with the consummate production directed by Laurence Olivier at Chichester in 1962. Kenneth Tynan said in 1958: 'In *Uncle Vanya* Chekhov created one of the most improbable and least playable heroes in dramatic literature. Everything about him is either negative or ridiculous.' In 1899 one Russian theatre director wrote to another: 'I am told *Uncle Vanya* is a success in your theatre. If this is true you have performed a veritable miracle.'

In bringing D.H. Lawrence's play, *The Daughter-in-Law*, into the repertoire, Stuart Burge corrected the strange disregard of Lawrence's plays, set in the district where he was born, so close to Nottingham and therefore likely to be interesting to the region's Playhouse, but this was the first of his plays to be produced here. Stuart directed it himself and with his company caught the atmosphere, situation and speech of the mining people of Eastwood. Such realism in locale is vital for Lawrence's dramas and the difficulty in achieving it may be a reason for their neglect. We continued to redress the matter during the next five seasons by producing Lawrence's other main plays, *A Collier's Friday Night* and *The Widowing of Mrs Holroyd*.

Lawrence wrote: 'I enjoy so much writing my plays – they come so quick and exciting from the pen.' And when he sent *The Daughter-in-Law* for a friend's opinion his own comment was: 'It is neither a comedy nor a tragedy – just ordinary. It is quite objective, as far as that term goes, and though no doubt, like most of my stuff, it wants weeding out a bit, yet I think the whole thing is there, laid out properly, planned and progressive.'

The Playhouse's main offerings in the Nottingham Festival of 1970 were two world premieres: *A Yard of Sun* by Christopher Fry and a musical adaptation of Walter Greenwood's *Love on the Dole*. The former was a comedy described as the 'summer' segment of the author's concept of a cycle of plays following the seasons. The others had appeared intermittently over about sixteen years, and their standing at the time may be judged by the names of the leads: *The Lady's Not for Burning* (John Gielgud and Richard Burton); *Venus Observed* (Laurence Olivier) and *The Dark is Light Enough* (Edith Evans). These were linked seasonally to spring, autumn, winter.

Christopher Fry's plays gave elegance to the repertoire of the fifties and were much in favour – almost a vogue. They had true originality and a distinctive style. We had ourselves produced three during the early years at our first theatre. But their popularity declined when the turn in the theatre came from the influence of the new dramatists (Osborne, Pinter, Wesker, etc.) and Fry's plays were seen less and less. So after a very long time since the last play there was great interest in the coming of *A Yard of Sun*. In fact even before our production appeared in July the National Theatre booked it for a week in August.

The time of the play is 1946; the scene is Italy, the crumbling courtyard of an old palazzo in Siena; and generally the theme is the effect the war has had on a little community, on one family in particular, their experiences, the changes in individuals and how they are adjusting to life after war. This is shown mainly through four characters: Angelino Bruno and his three sons, Roberto, Luigi and Edmondo. These were played by, respectively, Frank Middlemass, John Shrapnel, Michael Burrell and Robert East. Roberto the wealthy opportunist who has been abroad racketeering his way through the war; Luigi the ex-Fascist and Edmondo the idealist doctor who fought with the partisans. The re-uniting of these widely different characters created emotive clashes, but to some the verse form left the outcome blurred; the design obscured by decoration. One critic put it: 'No issue is being squarely faced.' Perhaps this is unfair to Mr Fry who did not set out to give us panaceas. An absolute delight, on which everyone agreed, and termed 'masterly', was Robin Archer's setting and Nick Chelton's lighting for this production. The buildings of the courtyard glowed in the hot Italian sun; one felt that here was Shakespeare's eternal summer.

The second premiere of the festival, a musical version of *Love on the Dole*, also had distinguished settings. The designer, Patrick Robertson, used back projection very effectively and reminded us of Lowry paintings. The *Guardian* review by Gareth Lloyd Evans said: 'Among the finest evocations of period I have ever seen in a Theatre.' The show was choreographed and directed brilliantly by Gillian Lynne. The leading part of Sally was played and sung by Angela Richards.

Walter Greenwood's novel, and the play adaptation by Ronald Gow, on what life was like for some people during the Depression in the thirties, had become virtually social documents of their time. There was critical comment that the musical medium was unsuitable for such a story. For example, an incident of a young apprentice being too ill-paid to afford a pair of long trousers was treated as a cue for a joke and song. But the story's popularity in its previous forms was based on its truth and immense heart, and those qualities were not smothered by the music. In any case, around the time of *Love on the Dole* was there not a song book which contained:

> Sing me a song with a social significance,
> There's nothing else that will do!

In a programme note Mr Greenwood, after maintaining that the message of *Love on the Dole* was as valid in the seventies as it was in the thirties, said: 'It is my belief that the present musical version will underline the humanity and warmth of its characters and in entertaining its audience carry the message even more poignantly.'

Early in the new season, 1970/1, came a further world premiere, *Lulu*, sub-titled 'a sex tragedy'. It was adapted very skilfully by Peter Barnes (who also co-directed with Stuart Burge) from two plays by Frank Wedekind (1864–1918), a German journalist/dramatist/actor little known in Britain. He was a rebel often involved in hostile politics and once imprisoned in Munich for attacks on royalty. He formed a theatrical company to present his own plays which had characters and sexual themes expressing Wedekind's revolt against what he saw as a hypocritical, stifling environment. *Lulu* was an example of this. Fine direction and a superb performance by Julia Foster in the name part gave us a prime production. Julia looked beautiful; fresh, cool, undaunted, though still a part of the sensuality swirling around her. A triumph in a most difficult part.

At the time Julia Foster made a comment on the playing of Lulu which has also general interest relating to the art of acting:

> *Lulu was a woman who captivated everyone who came in her path.*
> *This affected the audience, but most of all, it affected me. It widened*
> *my mind, made me realise things about myself I'd never suspected.*
> *Lulu's on stage practically all the time and that in itself is pretty*
> *terrifying. With a part like that, if it's a flop, you know exactly*
> *who's to blame. It gave me a tremendous sense of . . . 'power' is the*

Julia Foster in *Lulu* (Wedekind)

only word I can think of. The sense of being able to 'carry' an
evening. It was frightening, but at the same time exhilarating.

The production of *Lulu* had a sensational success. At the end of the
Playhouse run in December 1971 it opened at the Royal Court Theatre in
London to acclaim and capacity business, after which it transferred to the
Apollo Theatre. In the meantime our production of *Hamlet*, with Alan Bates,
Celia Johnson and directed by Anthony Page, had entered the Playhouse
repertoire and in due course also transferred to London at the Cambridge
Theatre which was used at that time by the National Theatre. All this was
prestigious, and welcomed by the company, but left the home stage somewhat
deserted. However, the solution was with good touring products available at
that time, particularly from the Prospect Theatre Touring Company directed
by Toby Robertson. We already had a close contact with them by being
something of a regular staging post for their productions en route to the
Edinburgh Festival which was a feature of their work. Our workshops had
constructed stage scenery for them, including the two plays visiting us at that
season, which were the tenth and eleventh Prospect productions to appear at

the Playhouse: Charles Macklin's *The Man of the World* directed by John David with a company including Russell Hunter, Geoffrey Chater, Tim Pigott-Smith, Faith Brook and Susan Fleetwood. They were also in the second play, an important first production, directed by Robert Chetwyn, of Ian McKellen's *Hamlet*.

Mr McKellen's career had thrived during the seven years since his time with our company which opened the new Playhouse. He had become renowned for performances of Edward II and Richard II. The critics had been enthralled with his work, bestowing epithets such as: 'the new Olivier from Wigan' (his home town). His fame as already one of the finest Shakespearian actors was such that his Hamlet performances at the Playhouse were sold out weeks before the opening.

Other visiting companies at that time were Oxford Playhouse with *The Merry Wives of Windsor*; the Royal Shakespeare Company with *Old Times* (Pinter); the Scottish Actors Company with *The Douglas Cause* (W.D. Home); and the Cambridge Company with *Hay Fever* (Coward).

At the time of our first production of *Waiting for Godot* by Samuel Beckett, reaction to the play was still in turmoil. Fifteen years on, the dust had settled and, although it will always be nonsense to many people, *Waiting for Godot* now had its place in dramatic literature. There is no plot in the play; only a repeated situation, that Godot will not appear, and indeed the programme has already revealed that such is the case. Little happens and what is said is mostly inconsequential, so we seem to be in a dramatic vacuum, but Beckett skilfully sustains a sense of expectancy via the handling of the dialogue and by the mystery of Godot. 'Who is Godot?' Beckett was asked, and he replied, 'If I know I would have said so in the play. . . . If the subject of my plays could be discussed in philosophical terms there would be no reason for me writing them. They are self-explanatory.'

That advice has been ineffective in restricting discussion on the play's intent, and each new production stimulates more debate. Some of this is sparked by the virtuoso acting which the play seems to inspire. This was certainly true on this occasion. The performances of Peter O'Toole, Donal McCann, Frank Middlemass and Niall Toibin were exceptional and full of moving experience. There was something beautiful and eerie in the quiet, tentative appearances of the Boy (Mr Godot's child?), for a moment unnoticed by the grubby prating tramps. Against them he had a fresh, pure, spiritual look, giving his message, answering their questions courteously and clearly. When he has gone, pathos and hopelessness return. Vladimir and Estragon settle down for another wait and, with cross-talk, quarrelling and making up, and funny business with hats and boots, remind us of two broken clowns in a music hall act. Perhaps this is

Donal McCann, Niall Toibin, Peter O'Toole in *Waiting for Godot* (Beckett)

how Beckett saw us; filling in time, waiting? Harold Hobson summed up in the *Sunday Times*: 'Until *Waiting for Godot* closes next Saturday it makes Nottingham Playhouse the theatrical capital of England.'

The opening production of the 1971/2 season was Shakespeare's *Richard III*, directed by Peter McEnery, with Leonard Rossiter as Richard, in a very untraditional style. In his programme note Nigel Alexander said Shakespeare's early histories formed a chronicle but *Richard III* is 'an ironic drama shaped out of historical events. . . . The picture of the king is necessarily a dramatic caricature with "machiavellian" overtones rather than a historical portrait.' (Mr Alexander made a witty reference to 'the resistible rise of Richard', a subtle touch relating Leonard Rossiter's Richard to his memorable performance in Brecht's *The Resistible Rise of Arturo Ui*.)

This production was a bold attempt at a different outlook on the play. It was not a matter of joining controversy on Richard III's character as shown in Shakespeare's play, although he took some obvious liberties, such as Mr Alexander's point on 'the presence of Margaret, commenting on the events of 1485 in England, when the queen had died in France in 1482'. Also, Professor G.M. Trevelyan tells us,

There is no clear evidence that [Richard] was more responsible for
the deaths of Henry VI and Clarence than the rest of the Yorkist
party, nor, prior to his usurpation of the throne, was his record as
treacherous as that of his brother Clarence or as bloody as that of
his brother Edward. But the glittering bait of the crown ensnared his
soul; he murdered his two nephews under trust, and the
disappearance of the Princes in the Tower, following the violence of
the usurpation, lost him the loyalty of the common people.

Shakespeare's text may overload Richard with infamies but the murder of the
princes is in all conscience enough to establish villainy. So if this production had
in its approach elements of fantasy, perhaps this is no more than accepting myths
in a 'realistic' form presenting a fiendish murder campaign (against brother, child
nephews, confederates) and bizarre consequences (e.g. immediate wooing of a
victim's widow). Such ingredients seem nearer to melodrama and the modern idea
of black comedy and give grounds for the unusual treatment in Peter McEnery's
interpretation, which commenced with Richard in jester-like, knee-breeches
costume of blue and yellow striped satin, tassels on cap, munching an apple,
dispensing a knowing wink. He reminded us of Andy Pandy or Noddy or, as
several critics perceived, a wolfish Mr Punch. It was even suggested that Punch's
familiar cry 'That's the way to do it!' when he, like Richard, struck down his prey,
might serve as a sub-title on this occasion. The idea of puppetry was sustained by
a group of giant, wax-faced dummies in various guises; funeral cortege, aldermen,
citizens, and finally as soldiers suffocating Richard at his death. The manipulation
seemed to be a comment in itself.

The substantial attendance figure of 69 per cent confirmed our audience's
interest in the production. Inevitably there were differences among the
reviewers, and one particular flurry occurred when the *Guardian* critic left the
theatre after only half an hour. His notice took the form of an open letter to
Stuart Burge, first apologizing to his host, the Theatre Director, for leaving and
then giving his reasons. Here is an excerpt: 'I could appreciate that Mr.
McEnery's intention was, perhaps to cut through a traditional naturalistic
production. . . . For me what emerged was yet another demonstration of the
contemporary principle that the director's whim is more important than the
playwright's realisation.' Stuart Burge was thus given the opportunity to
respond openly in a letter to the *Guardian*'s editor:

It has been our policy here to do each classic for today, attempting
to clear away the cobwebs of 'tradition' which have nothing to do

with the original. The text is searched for its original intention and, on the whole, very faithful versions are presented, with especial attention to the rhythm and value of the language. Sir, give us a critic who likes being in the theatre in this day and age, and not one who seems to prefer the classics, dusty with traditional comment, safely embalmed on the library shelf.

Stuart Burge directed *The Tempest* which, at the end of its Playhouse run, was paired with our production of Harold Pinter's *The Homecoming*, in a tour of northern France under the auspices of the British Council, a first occasion of its kind to that area. The departure was quite impressive; the company set off in a large coach, preceded by a pantechnicon carrying the scenery, costumes and properties, to the cheers of the envious stay-at-homes.

At about this time Mr Burge discussed the theatre directorship. He reminded the board that when he took the position in 1968 it was understood that he would stay for about three years. He was now in a fourth year and he

The Tempest (Shakespeare)

wished to have an absence of several months to direct a series for BBC Television. This was agreed, and a temporary arrangement was made with Mr David William to act as a joint Theatre Director while Mr Burge was away.

Stuart returned at the beginning of 1973 and in February directed Maxim Gorky's play *Yegor Bulichov and the Others*, the first production of Moura Budberg's translation, entitled *The White Raven*. He also directed Ben Jonson's *The Devil is an Ass* presented with Marston's *The Malcontent* directed by Jonathan Miller, as a Jacobean season.

Mr Burge was now into another year and it was not surprising that, in September 1973, a further joint theatre directorship appeared, with Richard Eyre, who was the outright recommendation of Stuart Burge. This joint situation continued until March 1974, when it was announced that Mr Eyre had been appointed Theatre Director of the Playhouse.

Stuart Burge's five years as Director were vital and will always be esteemed at the Playhouse. He returned to freelance work and has done many distinguished productions in films and television. In 1974 he was awarded the CBE.

CHAPTER EIGHT

RICHARD EYRE, 1973–78

Richard Eyre commenced his career as a Director in 1965 when he was Assistant Director at the Phoenix, Leicester. In the following year he became Associate Director at the Royal Lyceum Theatre, Edinburgh, and, from 1970 to 1972, Director of Productions. He won awards for best productions in Scotland in 1969, 1970 and 1971, and worked also at the Everyman Theatre, Liverpool.

He had in effect been in charge of productions at the Playhouse during the joint arrangement, apart, perhaps, from Stuart Burge's involvement in the Jacobean plays. Richard had demonstrated his quality earlier in a wonderful production of O'Casey's *The Plough and the Stars*, in which the company was mainly Irish and included Donal McCann as Fluther Good. (He had co-starred with Peter O'Toole in *Waiting for Godot* in our 1970/1 season.) The native-born players created an exciting realism which made the performance a true

Richard Eyre

experience. The company had a unity from the strong Irish ambience, and this must have been a bonus for a director. But also one of Richard Eyre's strengths was his flair for moulding a company style; a feeling that a group of players had been working together for months. The actors were his passionate concern, and this, added to his special interest in contemporary dramatists, made a basis for one of our liveliest regimes.

Vigorous it was, into the deep end with a group of five: *Brassneck*, *Soft or a Girl*, *Three Sisters*, *The Taming of the Shrew*, *The Crucible*.

Brassneck was a premiere, a new play by Howard Brenton and David Hare, directed by the latter who at the time was at the Playhouse as resident dramatist. The play (Harold Hobson's review was headed 'bold as brass') concerned the rise and fall of a brazen family in a Midlands town, ruthlessly exploiting sins and failings in the community; corruption, selfishness, vanity, graft and greed. It was assumed the deplorable situations represented the economic and social systems around us, and thus the play was political comment, but not one-sided; the authors' disgust extended to Left and Right.

Left to right: Griffith Jones, Liz Whiting, Bob Hescott, Roger Sloman, James Warrior, Jonathan Pryce, Myles Hayle, Jane Wymark, Ralph Nossek and Bill Dean in *Brassneck* (Brenton and Hare)

We saw some unpleasant people, in a bizarre range of activities employing on stage unusual features, for example, a 17-hand horse called Little John, a vintage vehicle, a golf course bunker, a Masonic lodge and its rites, a Pope in full vestment, a night club, a wedding cake from which emerged an exotic dancer who reached full nudity via mayoral robes, masonic apron (an intriguing touch) and an old school tie. This may give an idea of the play's startling nature. It was very effective as a trumpet fanfare for a new leadership.

Brassneck was certainly exuberant, ebulliantly directed by David Hare, and it had splendid acting including an introduction to the stunning talents of Jonathan Pryce. The critics were quick to react to what they saw as the blazing of a trail, and referred to 'an esoteric influence' in recent programme building. Emrys Bryson, after insisting that artistic standards at the Playhouse had not fallen though attendance figures had, said: 'There are many (and a lot of them 'regulars') who felt a wave of indifference about such academic curiosities as an obscure Gorki play or a Ben Jonson comedy so rare as to lie unstaged for three centuries.'

It is interesting that the attendance figure for *Brassneck* was 61.2 per cent and, although the comparison with the appeal of the Gorki play, 37.9 per cent, was firmly valid, the Ben Jonson achieved a very respectable 72.8 per cent, although it was far too early in Richard Eyre's time for those figures to have significance.

Mr Bryson's comments had general implications and his article (September 1973) referred also to widespread lower audience levels 'through a mixture of reasons – ranging from the impact of colour television to the embarrassments of inflation. . . . The fall-off is not peculiar to Nottingham. The whole country – Birmingham, Liverpool, Bristol, all with differing techniques and ideas – has experienced this undertow.'

Soft or a Girl was a musical by John McGrath, first presented at the Liverpool Everyman and re-worked for Nottingham. The show had a similar outlook to the previous production but with less clamorous treatment, and it was not *Brassneck* to music. It had its own charm, perhaps prompted by a dozen songs, also written by John McGrath, and excellently performed by a group called Petticoat and Vine. This came from the title number:

What can be	The lad's
The matter with him	Gone mad
His hair's so long	What's happened
His waist's so slim	To the world
He sings sweet songs	He's round

| His clothes fit tight | The bend |
| And he won't fight | Is he soft or a girl? |

We saw two old soldiers placed a generation forward in time and heard their observations on the 'new world' they had fought for, in this case the new Nottingham. This gave opportunities for caustic comment and spirited response. Modern youth replies to the above scornful lyric:

Who needs fighting	We don't care
Who needs wars	If we're plain or purl
If men were dogs	We don't care
They'd walk on all fours.	If we're soft or a girl.

The situation also pilloried changed local conditions, such as concrete blocks, polluted river, traffic chaos, but the device became stretched, and limited its effectiveness.

Arthur Miller said *The Crucible* is by far the most frequently produced of his plays, so it is surprising that Richard Eyre's presentation of it appears to have been the first by our own company at Nottingham Playhouse, though it was done again in 1982 by Richard Digby Day. Apparently it invariably plays to good business (84.5 per cent and 69.5 per cent here) and has a fascination for theatre-goers.

Apart from being one of the most powerful of modern plays, it acquired an extra significance as a parallel to the procedures in American politics in 1953 of the House Un-American Activities Committee chaired in a paranoid manner by Senator Joseph McCarthy. The committee's persecutions resembled *The Crucible*'s witch-hunting betrayal of associates. Having decided to write *The Crucible*, was Arthur Miller's treatment of the play influenced by his disgust at the methods of McCarthyism? The critic Kenneth Tynan thought that in this play Mr Miller was 'imprisoned by his convictions' and said: 'In *Death of a Salesman* he observed mankind in detached, dispassionate surview: in *The Crucible* he takes sides. And the strength of his convictions breeds the ultimate weakness of his play. . . . He presents the judge as a motiveless monster, which is as if Shaw had omitted the Inquisitor's speech from the trial scene of *St Joan*.'

As though he anticipated such opinion, Mr Miller has a passage in a brilliant essay (introducing a publication of his *Collected Plays*):

A play cannot be equated with a political philosophy. . . . I do not believe that any work of art can help but be diminished by its adherence at any cost to a political programme, including its author's. . . . Doubtless an author's politics must be an element, and even an important one, in the germination of his art, but if it is art he has created it must by definition bond itself to his opinions or even his hopes.

The *Crucible*'s force as a work of art is paramount, and Mr Miller says it becomes more successful 'as more time elapses from the headline "McCarthyism" which it was supposed to be about'.

Other major dramatists have been uncomfortable with the title of iconoclast. Shaw wrote his famous exposition, *The Quintessence of Ibsenism*, welcoming Ibsen as a fellow assailant on antiquated beliefs. Alongside the evaluation of Ibsen's plays as having, in general terms, a social purpose, there is a doubt. The Director of a Playhouse production of *A Doll's House*, John Fillinger, said: 'Ibsen's plays have suffered from labels attached to them by admirers and detractors alike. . . . *A Doll's House* is no more about "Women's Lib." than *An Enemy of the People* is about public hygiene.'

The great dramatist himself said, when addressing the Women's Rights League in 1898: 'Whatever I have written has been without any conscious thought of making propaganda.' Yet in his preliminary notes for *A Doll's House* in 1878 (a pioneering date for re-considering the status of women) Ibsen wrote:

A woman cannot be herself in contemporary society. It is an exclusively male society with laws drafted by men, and with counsel and judges who judge feminine conduct from the male point of view. The wife in the play ends up quite bewildered and not knowing right from wrong; her natural instincts on one side and her faith in authority on the other leave her completely confused. She has committed a crime, and she is proud of it, because she did it for love of her husband and to save his life. But the husband, with his conventional views of honour, stands on the side of the law and looks at the affair with male eyes.

In the play, when the danger of Nora's crime being exposed is suddenly lifted, her husband's exultation is for his own rescue only, and he assumes that Nora, broken and dazed by his attack and rejection, will return immediately to her role as the plaything in the doll's house. For two and a half hours the play is a straightforward drama of familiar construction, until Ibsen explodes the bomb of a completely changed Nora, shocked into bitter reaction, and total rejection of her present life: 'I must stand quite alone, if I am to understand myself and everything about me. It is for that reason that I cannot remain with you any longer.' So she departs to find herself. Shaw made his legendary comment: 'The slam of the door behind Nora is more momentous than the cannon of Waterloo.'

Did the ending of *A Doll's House* uncover the nugget of Ibsen's intent to concur, however indirectly, with the emancipation of women? Maybe in terms of propaganda Nora's transformation was unlikely for the character we had known hitherto, and conviction would have been helped by signposts of latent strength earlier in the play.

One of Richard Eyre's outstanding productions was *A Streetcar Named Desire* by Tennessee Williams, in 1975. Everything about it was of the highest standard. Watching this play is a taut, nerve-wracking experience. The pathetic Blanche is doomed, in spite of the flutters of hope and the clutching at dreams. Her crushing is inescapable, and even our compassion is depressing. But here is the classic up-lift of tragedy; after coming through the fire of it there is a

Zoë Wanamaker and Mark McManus in *A Streetcar Named Desire* (Williams)

sense of satisfaction. We have known the truth of the dramatist's profound observation. Gemma Jones returned to the Playhouse to play and look the part of Blanche superbly. Also in a fine company were Mark McManus and Zoë Wanamaker, and the whole production, as one critic put it, 'hit you between the eyes'.

Early in 1976 the Playhouse commenced a season of comedy. The repertoire was *Entertaining Mr Sloane, Pygmalion* and *The Servant of Two Masters*, blended with a week of Old Time music hall and a visit from the London Contemporary Dance Theatre.

André Van Gyseghem, our first Theatre Director, thought Bernard Shaw's *Pygmalion* was one of the best comedies of the twentieth century, and he was quick to stage a production of it in the opening year of Nottingham Playhouse. It had another showing in 1957 and, apart from anything else, a revival was now surely irresistible in order to take the opportunity, while she was still with the company, of Zoë Wanamaker playing Eliza. She was duly superb, both as

William Russell, Zoë Wanamaker and Ralph Michael in *Pygmalion* (Shaw)

the flower-girl and in blossoming to the new Eliza. Once again Emrys Bryson put it well: 'With her husky voice and that wonderful kittenish face that can make her look first like a cat bedraggled from the rain and then one that's been given a saucer of cream, she gives us an Eliza to cherish.' Richard Eyre's fine production had William Russell as Higgins and Ralph Michael as Colonel Pickering.

The classical legend is that Pygmalion fell in love with the sculpture he had created and Aphrodite endowed the statue with life, into the flesh and blood of Galatea. Shaw sub-titled his play 'A Romance' but he teased on the Higgins/Eliza relationship leaving a pleasant surmise on its outcome. In the play's last moments Eliza 'sweeps out disdainfully' but Higgins, left alone, 'chuckles and disports himself in a highly self-satisfied manner'.

Of course in his long and very entertaining prose sequel Shaw gives the answer: 'What is Eliza fairly sure to do when she is placed between Freddy and Higgins? Will she look forward to a lifetime of fetching Higgins's slippers or to a lifetime of Freddy fetching hers? There can be no doubt about the answer. Unless Freddy is biologically repulsive to her, and Higgins biologically attractive to a degree that overwhelms all her other instincts, she will, if she marries either of them, marry Freddy. And that is just what Eliza did.'

The Playhouse's main contribution to the Nottingham Festival of 1976 was Richard Eyre's production of Ben Jonson's *Bartholomew Fair*. The choice was appropriate for a city with a tradition of one of Britain's largest annual fairs, the Goose Fair. Audiences met the fairground setting immediately on entering the theatre and saw a foyer exhibition of items lent by the Lady Bangor Fairground Collection of Wookey Hole, Somerset. A roundabout cockerel and horses, authentic carvings, gold cherubs and pillars incorporated into the scenery, steam organ music from the loudspeakers, strings of coloured lights, sand on the stage, a puppet show, a company of thirty-eight. Ken Campbell and his Road Show had been drafted in, and among those playing Jonson's raffish characters were Sylveste McCoy, Arthur Kohn, Andy Andrews, Pat Keen, Carolyn Pickles and Ralph Nossek.

It was a boisterous, noisy affair, in one critic's words 'a certain relentless gaiety for two-and-a-half hours'. One wonders about the stamina of those at the original four-hour presentation in Jonson's time. Richard had access to ideally suited actors without whom it would not have been possible to contemplate doing the piece. During the interval they mingled with the audience in foyers and on the forecourt where Sylveste as the 'cut-purse' did a little make-believe pocket picking and Whit the pimp 'offered' his ladies of easy virtue. The production achieved an atmosphere of a festival within the festival.

Bartholomew Fair (Jonson)

There was a distinguished company for the splendid *Othello* in 1976 including Daniel Massey in the name part, Timothy West as Iago and Alison Steadman as Desdemona. Notoriously Iago is a show-stealer, a factor intrinsic in the play because the Moor's astonishing gullibility makes such demands on our patience. (A.P. Herbert's zany character Topsy, writing to her friend Trix, says '. . . . and then the black man sees *another* girl giving the young man his wife's handkerchief *instead* of saying Hi that's my wife's property how did you get it he *merely* goes off and murders his wife, my dear *too* uncalled for.')

The smooth progress of Iago's scheming is somewhat incredible too and sometimes to make sense one needs to conjecture about the characters' background. There is a secondary jealousy in Iago's envy of Cassio's appointment as lieutenant? Stanislavsky, in his instructions for the Moscow Art Theatre's production of the play, enters into some speculation. He submits, reasonably, that in the governing high society of Venice in which Othello has to mix, the cultured Cassio would be more useful to the general as his aide

Daniel Massey and Timothy West in *Othello* (Shakespeare)

than the rough-spun battlefield comrade, Iago. Stanislavsky suggests even that Iago may suspect his wife Emilia of infidelity with Othello during the time she may have spent housekeeping for the general in his bachelor establishment before his life with Desdemona, but few productions have the rehearsal time for wandering in such byways. Richard Eyre's production had unfamiliar features. Timothy West's Iago was a development of a smiling villain. Its menace had a curiously humorous touch. His scoffing at Othello used mocking 'black-face talk'. Mr B.A. Young in his *Financial Times* review made the astute point that 'Iago was only 28 years old and he [Mr West] makes him young and playful by nature, a faceful of winks and grins which he shares generously with the audience.'

Daniel Massey looked splendidly handsome and dignified as Othello. In the earlier scenes his manner was aloof but later he became the baited animal. The pace of speaking was rapid which perhaps blurred some great lines, and the grotesque situation needs the poetry to carry it. Desdemona is rather a nagging

Alison Steadman, William Hoyland, Antony Sher in *Travesties* (Stoppard)

wife, for a new one, and Alison Steadman made her quite a doughty young woman, which is consistent enough with facing the world in a sensational marriage. The whole production was forceful and one of Richard's best. Aptly it had its reward with an attendance figure of 96.5 per cent.

Richard Eyre's last full season in Nottingham, that of 1976/7, had opened with the *Othello*, followed by Tom Stoppard's *Travesties*, a very testing piece for company, director (in this case Michael Joyce) and, it could be said, for audience. The date is 1917 and the situation revolves around an English amateur dramatic company's production of *The Importance of Being Earnest* in Zurich where at this time lived James Joyce, Lenin and the Dadaist Tristran Tzara. An unlikely involvement follows, in a mosaic of fact and fantasy; a display of verbal fireworks; an exercise for the literary-minded, summed up by the critic Gareth Lloyd Evans: 'Above all it forces you, with pleasure, to exert your mind. And that's a change.' It was not surprising to hear of a few customers not returning after the interval but, as the attendance figure was a comfortable 66 per cent for a sophisticated piece, the choice was justified and illustrated the audience confidence which had been built during the previous four years. The actors were stimulated into sparkling performances. Among them was Antony Sher, a newcomer who had played Gratiano in *Othello* and now had a lead, Henry Carr, in *Travesties*. The immediate impression was that we were looking at a future star and so, of course, it transpired. Antony Sher was born in South Africa and came to London to study drama. Eventually he was two years at the Everyman Theatre, Liverpool where he had invaluable opportunities in large parts. (Two of these were Buckingham in *Richard III* and the Fool in *King Lear*.) It is some fifteen years since his work in Nottingham but there remains the recollection of strong creativity in the acting, particularly in individuality of movement, a stamp which was on all the parts he played during the Playhouse connection of nearly a year. He had a natural gift for comedy, and indeed Richard was fortunate in the comedians who worked for him in Nottingham, among them Ken Campbell, Sylveste McCoy, originals with distinctive movement, and a certain unorthodox quality.

The next production was the ever-welcome *Hobson's Choice* by Harold Brighouse. Incredibly this great comedy could not find a first production in England in 1915 and instead appeared in New York where it was enormously successful. It opened in London a year later since when it has become a classic, with irresistible characterization in a warm, satisfying story in which the deserving triumph. A box-office 'banker' (84 per cent), and simultaneously so worthwhile.

One of Richard Eyre's most important productions at the Playhouse was in association with Trevor Griffiths in his version of *The Cherry Orchard*. Our previous showings of Chekhov's play had followed the familiar pattern of an elegaic evocation of a dying era in Russia; a nostalgic story of a way of life gone for ever. This has been the case in several translations and so the mood has become virtually traditional. On that basis productions have had charm and sweet sorrow, though as such have always been difficult to reconcile with Chekhov's own dictum about the play being a comedy.

Richard Eyre felt there was an ambiguity which left the situation unclear and also caused problems for actors. Hence the project to have a new concept of meaning and dialogue. Looking back it is surprising this had not been done before, but now there was great interest in the interpretation by such a distinguished modern dramatist as Mr Griffiths.

The new version was acclaimed as an acute and thoughtful reading. Characters were dissected to heighten understanding. For instance, in their reactions towards the imminent bankruptcy, and the forced sale of the Ranevsky estate with its precious orchard, they seemed more realistic, even if

Bridget Turner, Ralph Nossek, Dave Hill in *The Cherry Orchard* (Chekhov)

more calculating, and thus more credible. A different emphasis was given to the student Trofimov's character when the reason for him being banned from university is shown, not as a failure to pass the examinations, but because of his political activities, which makes his major speech in Act III more positive.

Thus writing and direction in this production had new stresses, but it was basically faithful. A discerning review by Benedict Nightingale in the *New Statesman* said of Mick Ford's superb performance as Trofimov,

> *Here's a callow, rather priggish young man, but one whose political analyses are substantially correct and whose enthusiasm for the future seems boundless. He leaps onto a wayside bench, a scrubbed, bony skinhead and, brandishing a Bolshevik fist, invites his shining girl-friend to reform nothing less than Mother Russia with him: an embryo Lenin, but not without humour, self-mockery and tenderness, the most forceful persuasive voice on offer, and a plausible person as well. I don't think Chekhov would have disowned him.*

Other approval of the text came from Irving Wardle in *The Times* when he referred to 'the many passages in which Griffiths and his director have sharpened up Chekhov's point to make it stick deeper. Again and again I was struck by passages that seemed totally unfamiliar. "From every tree in your orchard," Trofimov tells Anya, "there are people hanging." But no, it is there in the standard text, in a more muted form, usually passed over unnoticed.'

Chekhov would certainly have approved the humour brought into the production. Full use was made of the good fortune of having the skilful comedian, Antony Sher, in the cast , as Epikhovdov, the estate clerk, behaving with endearing clumsiness, a cross between Inspector Clouseau and Frank Spencer.

The felicitous Emrys Bryson summed up: 'At last we can see the wood for the cherry trees.' With this production Nottingham Playhouse achieved an influence on modern classic theatre.

In 1977, ten years after our previous production, Richard Eyre revived Arthur Miller's *Death of a Salesman*. Perhaps there was a compulsion from having at the time an intriguing candidate to play Willy Loman. In the

Comedians (Griffiths) with Jimmy Jewel

Comedians (Griffiths) with Jimmy Jewel

premiere of *Comedians* by Trevor Griffiths, Richard had Mr Jimmy Jewel in the key part of Eddie Waters, the professional comedian tutoring an evening class of young men seeking to become comics. This seemed inspired casting because, of course, Jimmy Jewel *was* a famous comedian for many years in his double act with Ben Warriss. After the end of that partnership he took leading parts in television comedy. The announcement of a principal straight acting role in an important new play sounded bold even allowing for a lifetime on the stage, and knowing all there was to know about timing and controlling an audience, until we remembered that those very qualities amounted to a consummate comedian acting his material, just as the tragedian does in a playhouse. Indeed, the actress May Agate once pronounced that 'you cannot be a comedian at all without tragic gifts'. When we recall Mr Jewel's lugubrious countenance alongside the jaunty chaff of Mr Warriss, there seems a very short step to his world-weary demeanour when confronted with his motley of student comedians.

The steps to Willy Loman are longer, and one notice of *Death of a Salesman* mentioned 'an occasional tendency to the over-dramatic gesture and a snarl when he should allow the man's deep exhaustion to silence his reactions'. But

David Beames, Jimmy Jewel, Malcolm Storry in *Death of a Salesman* (Miller)

the same critic continued, 'Jimmy Jewel turns in a performance that is quite haunting', and this was echoed in a chorus of enthusiastic acclaim.

Death of a Salesman is regularly staged in the UK, and sometimes becomes anglicized, but the situation and the characters are specifically of America and do not transpose satisfactorily. Richard Eyre's production was praised for its convincing American atmosphere. For instance, in addition to the very moving Willy Loman there was entirely faithful playing of his two sons, Biff and Happy, by Malcolm Storry and David Beames.

Richard Eyre left the Playhouse in 1978 and became producer of the BBC Television *Play for Today* series. He went, he said, 'with massive regrets' and it is clear from his memoir contained here that he had been very happy in Nottingham. The regard Richard expressed was indeed mutual, and we had much to admire. Nowadays (1993) we see his successful direction of the National Theatre and we feel that Nottingham was an important progression to the heights of theatre.

There would have been pleasure if Richard's last Playhouse production had been some kind of festive showpiece. Perhaps we had insufficient time for that, but there came a fitting plan that there should be a piece by the playwrights with whom Richard had worked so closely at the Playhouse: Trevor Griffiths, Howard Brenton, David Hare and Ken Campbell. Also it was pleasing that it should be a light-hearted valediction to Richard, in fact a satirical version of the BBC's *Any Questions*. However, this intention waned, as Richard described in a BBC *Kaleidoscope* broadcast in March 1978: 'Every couple of days I would ring up all the authors and I realized that really nothing was happening and there was an air of dissatisfaction with the subject, but the truth was that we'd actually played the subject out by talking about it, there really was nothing more in the subject.'

A new spur was needed urgently. Richard continued: 'I had an idea for *Candide*, I recently read *Candide*, I thought that a contemporary *Candide* or taking *Candide* as a beginning was an excellent starting point, a quest play and a play that involved Candidian ideas of character, interacting with many, many different worlds and that's really what happened. It went off from there and parts of the play were written separately and parts of it were written as a group. Trevor and Howard worked together on a number of scenes and that was truly participatory.'

So a concept emerged very different from the original burlesque: a polemical pilgrimage by a working-class hero named Ken Deed (!) who finds his baby daughter dead in her cot, and desolation complete with the disappearance of his distraught wife. He does not accept the medical verdict of cot death, but sets off in the belief that the cause came from milk powder baby food which, incorrectly mixed, can result in dehydration. (This he learns from a hospital nurse.) His travels and efforts to call attention to his tragedy, and to expose the danger, lead him into a number of macabre encounters. A depressing aspect is that nowhere does Ken, frenzied and deeply unhappy, find sympathy, understanding or simple help. Everyone he meets seem to be dark and dubious creatures: policeman taking bribes, doctor unfeeling, surgeon bungling operation, clergyman hypocritical, judge oppressive, business man depraved and licentious, prison governor cold and superficial, MP too busy to care. Even the scene where a film is being made is violent. Truly all occasions informed against poor Ken. But he is re-united with his wife and, when she becomes pregnant again, they resolve to call a boy Geronimo or a girl Boadicea, and to place their hopes in a new generation.

There were about twenty scenes, some very short. It required Richard's expert staging to cope with that, within John Gunter's clever set. While the four-handed authorship could well have succeeded with the revue first envisaged, it did not work smoothly with *Deeds*. The critics (and they came in full force for Richard's last production) made guesses about whose hand was responsible for a particular episode. The excellent opening scene of Ken Deed returning from work to the tragic situation in his home was felt to be the work of Trevor Griffiths, 'direct, naturalistic and unsettling'. They all seemed sure that Ken Campbell was the source of a very funny scene of a Hyde Park orator ranting at his audience. Especially revealing, they thought, was the remark to one bystander: 'You're not wearing that plastic mac, it's wearing you.'

In the theatre *Deeds* was hardly a success with an attendance of 25 per cent, whereas we would all have liked Richard's splendid years at Nottingham Playhouse to have been saluted with a 100 per cent bang. But his work is firmly and unforgettably part of our story.

During 1973 there was a major development at the Playhouse in the field of Theatre in Education. A specialist branch was formed called Roundabout, directed by Sue Birtwistle, with its separate company and staff. It had its own premises and transport, and personnel totalling about sixteen. Its financing came from an allocation earmarked for the purpose from the main house's Arts Council grant, and from earnings for services provided for the local authorities. Roundabout also performed very successful children's shows in the main house at Christmas-time.

Whereas the Playhouse's work for youth in the first years had been by regular visits to the theatre in school time, as described earlier, the process was now reversed and the material used to tour schools was quite different. There was liaison with schools and teachers and a range of techniques developed: subject research, commissioned writing, design, presentation, acting, dancing, mime and audience involvement methods acquired from the experience of performances for children. An important final feature was follow-up visiting to hear reactions and evaluate the impact of the work.

A few examples of work at the time were: *Square Roots* – a programme taking the form of a fantasy in which very young children explore the vision of shape and numbers. *Noun the Clown* – for top infants in which the children travel through the Land of Words in order to help a clown who has forgotten how to talk and smile, enabling the children to explore words and their uses. *What Next* – a half-day programme for ten to eleven year olds which allows the children to examine aspects of family and community life.

TIE work released much enthusiasm and many creative ideas which understandably overshadowed the old facility of visits to theatre performances as part of school life. Perhaps the ideal would be the organized practice of both activities. Thus progress might be made towards furthering the theatre as a familiar, standard experience, so redressing a little the concept of it being predominately a middle-class diversion.

Much Ado About Nothing (Shakespeare)

During the (approximately) four years of Richard Eyre's time as Theatre Director at the Playhouse there were about fifty productions, excluding various Christmas work. Analysis shows:

%		
12	Shakespeare	*Shrew, Othello, Twelfth Night, Much Ado, Henry IV, As You Like It*
12	Other classics	Jonson, Goldini, Marlowe, Goldsmith, Webster
22	New	*Comedians, Churchill Play, Brassneck, Touched, Bendigo,* etc.
27	Modern classics	Chekhov, Shaw, O'Casey, Gogol, etc.
27	Current	Stoppard, Orton, Miller, Ayckbourn, Nichols, Williams, etc.

This is brilliant programme building. The range is so comprehensive that, if we used a university analogy, attendance at every production would provide

Jonathan Pryce in *The Government Inspector* (Gogol, adapted by Adrian Mitchell)

materials for the practical side of a degree in theatre. In all categories the choices are among the best of their kind. You could enjoy equally O'Casey and Feydeau, *Travesties* and *The Government Inspector*. The outstanding features are the amounts of Shakespeare and of new work. The latter is nearly a quarter of the total, which represents a courageous policy both financially and in the nurturing of new dramatists, which had long been a Nottingham Playhouse purpose but not to this concentrated extent. It was especially striking because the new playwrights at the time were much fewer than, say, in the fifties when there was a large number of current dramatists at various stages of fame.

The mid-seventies saw the emergence of a group of playwrights, radical and innovative, resolved to give the theatre a proverbial 'shot in the arm', or a kick elsewhere perhaps. In London the work of some of these authors was put on at the Royal Court Theatre, and Nottingham Playhouse became another platform. The work was important and enlivened the country's theatre, but some playgoers were unhappy with such a proportion of political/sociological pieces, loosely described as anti-establishment. Of course others were stimulated but were insufficient in number to avoid some 'box-office blues'.

However, the solid classical base, and interest in the staging of currently successful plays, founded a substantial audience level for the four years of Richard's stay in Nottingham. Another factor in his popularity was the standard of company. In the memoir which he most generously spared the time to write for this book he gives the names of many players who worked for him early in their careers and who have since become theatre celebrities. The strength of the cast lists, and his continued commitment to new plays, were reasons why Richard Eyre sustained a feeling of freshness in Playhouse work. It is usual for the early stages of a regime to engender such an atmosphere, coming from the arrival of new personnel and different ideas in programming, but in his last season, after over four years at the Playhouse, Richard directed two premieres (*Touched*, by Stephen Lowe, *White Suit Blues* by Adrian Mitchell) and several other large productions (*Death of a Salesman*, *The Alchemist*). It was from this level of vitality that Nottingham Playhouse's first thirty years closed, with a long-established leading place in the British theatre. Those of us who were involved through the whole of the three decades had proud memories of what had been achieved, and bright confidence for the future.

Annually we see in the press an assortment of judgements from pundits and personalities on which plays, films, books, etc. they have enjoyed most during the year. How would one apply such an exercise to the best Playhouse experience over thirty years? It is, of course, a subjective, personal affair, and it may amuse Nottingham Playhouse enthusiasts to make their choice, remembering that one of the charms of theatre is satisfaction from its allied arts, for example, an effective stage scene using superb lighting. So the acting may have long faded but we never forget Robin Archer's glowing palazzo in old Siena, in Fry's *A Yard of Sun*, or in later years the magic of the setting by Robert Jones taking us to the enchanted world of *A Midsummer Night's Dream*. But my own most moving moment would be two lines from the beginning of *Twelfth Night*, spoken by the matchless Viola of Jean Forbes-Robertson in the old theatre. After the shipwreck and, as she thinks, the loss of her brother, she asks her companions what country they have reached. 'Illyria, lady.' Then gravely, without her tears, but compelling ours, she says:

> And what should I do in Illyria?
> My brother he is in Elysium.

NOTTINGHAM REVISITED
by Richard Eyre

If I were prone to believe in portents and omens, metaphors that carry some hint of what the future holds, my first sight of Nottingham Playhouse would have been depressing indeed. In the early sixties I was visiting Sheffield, as an improbable candidate for attachment to a steel company as a fledgling chemical engineer. I stayed with some friends of friends, and apart from seeing molten steel pour from the lip of a Bessemer converter, and a visit to an umbrella factory where the all-female workforce teased us with sexual banter that remains unrivalled in my experience, I remember nothing of my stay in Sheffield apart from a mild flirtation with my hosts' daughter in the back of a cinema. It was the trip to Nottingham that sticks in my mind.

I had expressed a keen interest in theatre, albeit that I had rarely attended a theatre performance outside the realm of pantomime. So we visited Nottingham Playhouse. At the edge of Wellington Circus (a name that I still find exciting – redolent of clowns, elephants, sawdust *and* the military) there was a large crater, the kind of hole that looked as though it might have been created by the bomb that breached the Moehne Dam. Concrete was being poured into holes which sprouted long, rusty, iron feelers. We watched the laying of the foundations for perhaps twenty minutes, and then bored, and somewhat dispirited, we drifted away.

When I returned to Nottingham Playhouse in 1965, the theatre had already opened, lost two of its trio of artistic directors, and had established a national reputation. In those days we were mercifully free of those sanctimonious terms like 'regional' and 'community' which always succeed in making you feel diminished wherever you come from. The theatrical megaliths of today – the National Theatre and the Royal Shakespeare Company – weren't the size of a Third World country, government hadn't been so remorselessly centralized, Mrs Thatcher hadn't become the high priestess of opportunism, and a theatre in Nottingham or Glasgow or Birmingham or Bristol had every chance of being (at least temporarily) the national focus of good theatre.

I came to see John Neville play Richard II, and it still remains one of the best Shakespearian performances I've ever seen. I wasn't at the matinée during which Judi Dench played one of the soldiers, dressed from top to toe in chain-mail, and the whole company, but for John Neville, were convulsed, 'corpsed', shuddering hopelessly on stage as if infected by collective frenzy. This was the anarchic side of John's company, the wild, larky, raffish side that, combined with their brio and skill, made for a heady atmosphere on-stage and off. I was working as an actor at the Phoenix Theatre, Leicester, and I was drawn to the Playhouse as often as I could manage.

John unwittingly returned the compliment by coming to see my first professional production at Leicester, *The Knack*. To my surprise within two days of seeing the production, John wrote to me and offered me a job directing a schools' production of Goldini's play *La Locandiera*, which was to tour Nottinghamshire under the title *Mirandolina*. I remember little of the production, and I'm not sure it was highly regarded by the schoolchildren of Ollerton, Mansfield and Retford. The play ended with the (theoretically touching) reconciliation between the mistress of the inn, and her manservant, which was invariably underscored by shouts of 'Go on, have 'er' from the youthful audience.

John was sufficiently encouraged by this production to ask me to be Assistant Director on a tour of *As You Like It* and *A Man for All Seasons* which was destined to tour Sierra Leone, Ghana and Nigeria for the British Council. The Biafran War put paid to that plan, and we were transferred to South-East Asia, touring Malaysia, Borneo, Singapore and the Philippines. I fell in love with the East, and with travelling, and perhaps even with love itself, and after the tour was over returned from Manila the slow way – via Hong Kong, Cambodia, Thailand, India, Egypt and Greece. It was, as they say, the time of my life.

I worked sporadically for the Playhouse on my return, and then, for many years, I lost touch. I became Assistant Director at Leicester, then Clive Perry's Associate Director in Edinburgh at the Royal Lyceum Theatre. I lived in Edinburgh for nearly six years, and it was there that I met Sue Birtwistle. By a happy accident the two of us were sought out, independently, by Stuart Burge – she to start a Theatre-in-Education company attached to the Playhouse, and me to be his successor at the Playhouse. Unlike most fiction, this particular plot worked out rather well: Sue started the Roundabout Company; I became the Artistic Director of the Playhouse; we got married, had a daughter (who has just done her A levels), and we lived happily ever after. Mostly.

Nottingham was a thrilling place to be in the early seventies. I was lucky enough to work with several of a new generation of playwrights who were young, ambitious, cocky and keen to repudiate the old avant-garde and establish a new one. Together with a clutch of talented young(ish) writers, we embraced (or tried to) new forms of staging, vivid use of language, of music, of design. Of one thing we were certain, that the hub of the theatrical universe was Nottingham, not London. 'What we will do,' I would intone sanctimoniously, 'will be *our* work, not a watered-down version of what's happening in London.' And sometimes, perhaps, we succeeded.

Memory is often merciful, and never more so than in the theatre. Only the highlights remain, the rest – the unhappiness, the failures, the misjudgements – are washed away like silt, leaving the glinting ore behind. I remember many productions fondly in vivid detail – *The Taming of the Shrew*, *Brassneck*, *The Three Sisters*, *The Government Inspector*, *Bendigo*, *Walking Like Geoffrey*, *The Churchill Play*, *Comedians*, *Touched*, *The Cherry Orchard*, *Pygmalion*, *The Plough and the Stars*, *Bartholomew Fair*, *The Alchemist*, *Othello*, *Hobson's Choice*, *Travesties*, *A Flea in her Ear*, even *The Wizard of Oz*; many actors whose names from that vintage now resonate like the chateaux of Bordeaux – Jonathan Pryce, Tony Sher, Alison Steadman, Jimmy Jewel, Stephen Rea, Zoë Wanamaker, Celia Imrie, Roger Sloman, Tom Wilkinson, Marjorie Yates, Sue Tracey, Brian Glover, Malcolm Storry, Bridget Turner, Donal McCann, Mick Ford, Prunella Scales, Tim West, Daniel Massey, Sylveste McCoy . . . and more; designers John Gunter, Bill Dudley, and Hayden Griffin; and writers – David Hare, Trevor Griffiths, Howard Brenton, Adrian Mitchell, Ken Campbell, and Stephen Lowe.

The Playhouse board had a reputation for strong government. There had been a notorious episode which had resulted in John Neville shaking the dust of the city from his feet. The character of the board was largely (but unfairly) fashioned in the shape of its Chairman, Cyril Forsyth, who was indeed a character. He looked like a cross between Eric von Stroheim and the bald member of the Crazy Gang, and he was capricious, bullying, wilful, loyal and generous in equal measure. Even though I never got over the irritation of his pulling my hair and asking me when I was going to get it cut, I admired his passion for the theatre, and we developed an equable working relationship. He (and his board) never transgressed the line between the responsibilities of the board and those of the artistic director; the 'art' was my job, and if I messed that up, then it was all right with me if he handed me my cards. He didn't, and although we clashed on many occasions – a scene of Masonic induction in *Brassneck*, the bad language in *Comedians*, the politics of *The Churchill Play*, the nudity in *Touched* – we arrived at a point of mutual respect, and, if I'm not mistaken, a mutual affection.

It's not putting a sentimental cast on it to say that I loved being in Nottingham: I loved the work, my family, our house, the theatre, our friends, and the wild, sweet, reckless innocence of it all. When I left the theatre, I took down all the posters and photographs in my office, and I stood for minutes, alone, looking at the sunlight through the slatted blinds falling on the bare walls, and listening to the sounds in my head. Mostly I heard the sound of laughter, and even though it may have felt like the end of *The Cherry Orchard*, there was more of Anya in me, welcoming the new life, than her mother lamenting the passing of the old one.

The theatre seems small to me now, but if you're obliged to work in the prairie-like spaces of the Olivier and Lyttleton Theatres, almost any other auditorium feels small. It's in good hands, and when I return, even though it's haunted for me by benign ghosts, it still makes me feel pleased to be there. To paraphrase William Shawn when he left the *New Yorker* after years as editor: 'Whatever our roles, we built something quite wonderful together. Love was the controlling emotion; we did our work with honesty and love.'

PLAYHOUSE PRODUCTIONS 1948–1978

1948–9

Man and Superman	George Bernard Shaw
Othello	William Shakespeare
You Can't Take It with You	Moss Hart and George S. Kaufman, (premiere)
The Arabian Nights	Bridget Boland
The Torchbearers	George Kelly
Guilty	Émile Zola, adapted by Kathleen Boutall
Twelfth Night	William Shakespeare
The Long Mirror	J.B. Priestley
Frieda	Ronald Millar
The Romantic Young Lady	M. Sierra
Tobias and the Angel	James Bridie
Shadow and Substance	Paul Vincent Carroll
The Apple Cart	George Bernard Shaw
Caste	T.W. Robertson
The Winslow Boy	Terence Rattigan
The Merchant of Venice	William Shakespeare
The Light of Heart	Emlyn Williams
By Candlelight	Harry Graham

1949–50

The Importance of Being Earnest	Oscar Wilde
Dangerous Corner	J.B. Priestley
Pygmalion	George Bernard Shaw
Arms and the Man	George Bernard Shaw
Mrs Warren's Profession	George Bernard Shaw
Present Laughter	Noël Coward
The Guinea Pig	Warren Chetham Strode

A Bill of Divorcement	Clemence Dane
Treasure Island	R.L. Stevenson, adapted by
	R. Williams
The Taming of the Shrew	William Shakespeare
Playbill	Terence Rattigan
Design for Living	Noël Coward
The Petrified Forest	R.E. Sherwood
The Rivals	Richard Brinsley Sheridan
The Chiltern Hundreds	William Douglas Home
The Glass Menagerie	Tennessee Williams
The Constant Wife	W. Somerset Maugham
A Hundred Years Old	S. and J.A. Quintero
Hedda Gabler	Henrik Ibsen
Deep are the Roots	A. D'Usseau and J. Gow
The Lady's not for Burning	Christopher Fry
Doctor's Joy	Molière, adapted by Charles Drew

1950–1

The Happiest Days of Your Life	John Dighton
You Never Can Tell	George Bernard Shaw
Shooting Star	Basil Thomas
Amphitryon-38	S.N. Behrman
The Merry Wives of Windsor	William Shakespeare
Death of a Salesman	Arthur Miller
Eden End	J.B. Priestley
The Admirable Crichton	J.M. Barrie
Beauty and the Beast	adapted by Nicholas Stuart Gray
Hamlet	William Shakespeare
Hay Fever	Noël Coward
Here Choose I	Yvonne Mitchell (world premiere)
The Immortal Lady	Clifford Bax
Miranda	Peter Blackmore
An Ideal Husband	Oscar Wilde
Rope	Patrick Hamilton
Love in Albania	Eric Linklater
Candida	George Bernard Shaw
A Murder has been Arranged	Emlyn Williams
Home and Beauty	W. Somerset Maugham
Traveller's Joy	Arthur Macrae

Private Lives	Noël Coward

1951–2

The School for Scandal	Richard Brinsley Sheridan
A Midsummer Night's Dream	William Shakespeare
Captain Carvallo	Denis Cannan
Dear Brutus	J.M. Barrie
Venus Observed	Christopher Fry
The Barretts of Wimpole Street	Rudolf Besier
The Holly and the Ivy	Wynyard Brown
Aladdin	Various authors
Charley's Aunt	Brandon Thomas
Macbeth	William Shakespeare
His Excellency	Dorothy and Campbell Christie
The Circle	W. Somerset Maugham
Murder in the Cathedral	T.S. Eliot
Ring Round the Moon	Jean Anouilh, trs. George Calderon
The Cocktail Party	T.S. Eliot
She Stoops to Conquer	Oliver Goldsmith
Six Characters in Search of an Author	Luigi Pirandello
The Marquise	Noël Coward
Temple Folly	Bridget Boland (world premiere)
The Indifferent Shepherd	Peter Ustinov
Widower's Houses	George Bernard Shaw

1952–3

Lady Windermere's Fan	Oscar Wilde
Major Barbara	George Bernard Shaw
Colombe	Jean Anouilh
The Ivory Tower	William Templeton
Figure of Fun	André Roussin, adapted by Arthur Macrae
R.U.R.	Karel Čapek
The Biggest Thief in Town	Dalton Trumbo
Cinderella	Ronald Parr
The Tempest	William Shakespeare
A Doll's House	Henrik Ibsen
Lady Frederick	W. Somerset Maugham
The Boy David	J.M. Barrie

The Second Mrs Tanqueray	Arthur Wing Pinero
Point of Departure	Jean Anouilh, trs. Kitty Black
Daphne Laureola	James Bridie
Two Gentlemen of Verona	William Shakespeare
Hobson's Choice	Harold Brighouse
Getting Married	George Bernard Shaw
The Ghost Train	Arnold Ridley
The Springtime of Others	Jean Jacques Bernard
On Approval	Frederick Lonsdale

1953–4

As You Like It	William Shakespeare
The River Line	Charles Morgan
The Critic	Richard Brinsley Sheridan
The Deep Blue Sea	Terence Rattigan
The Love of Four Colonels	Peter Ustinov
Sylvie and the Ghost	Alfred Adam, trs. John Harrison (premiere)
The Breadwinner	W. Somerset Maugham
Jack and the Beanstalk	Ronald Parr
Carnival King	Henry Treece (world premiere)
The Waltz of the Toreadors	Jean Anouilh
Rookery Nook	Ben Travers
Julius Caesar	William Shakespeare
Dandy Dick	Arthur Wing Pinero
No Sign of the Dove	Peter Ustinov
The Noble Spaniard	W. Somerset Maugham
The Master Builder	Henrik Ibsen
Badger's Green	R.C. Sherriff
An Inspector Calls	J.B. Priestley
Macadam and Eve	Roger MacDougall
The Man with a Load of Mischief	Ashley Dukes
Canaries Sometimes Sing	Frederick Lonsdale

1954–5

Thieves' Carnival	Jean Anouilh, trs. Lucienne Hill
Storm in a Teacup	James Bridie
Marching Song	John Whiting
See How They Run	Philip King

Romeo and Juliet	William Shakespeare
Smith	W. Somerset Maugham
Nightmare Abbey	Thomas Love Peacock, adapted by Anthony Sharp
The Burning Glass	Charles Morgan
Toad of Toad Hall	A.A. Milne
The Cherry Orchard	Anton Chekhov, adapted by Sir John Gielgud
The Cat and the Canary	John Willard
'Tis Pity She's a Whore	John Ford
The Importance of Being Earnest	Oscar Wilde
The Confidential Clerk	T.S. Eliot
Lady Precious Stream	S.I. Hsuing
Mary Rose	J.M. Barrie
Double Bill:	
A Phoenix too Frequent	Christopher Fry
The Respectable Prostitute	Jean Paul Sartre
Footsteps in the Sea	Henry Treece (world premiere)
The Living Room	Graham Greene
Both Ends Meet	Arthur Macrae
The Man in the Raincoat	Peter Ustinov
The Voice of the Turtle	John Van Druten

1955–6

You and your Wife	Dennis Cannan
The Ermine	Jean Anouilh
Mirandolina	Carlo Goldoni, adapted by Ronald Magee
A Cuckoo in the Nest	Ben Travers
The Winter's Tale	William Shakespeare
Saint Joan	George Bernard Shaw
The Rivals	Richard Brinsley Sheridan
Blood Wedding	Federico Garcia Lorca
A Day by the Sea	N.C. Hunter
Blizzard	Pero Budak (British premiere)
A Pair of Spectacles	Sidney Grundy
Summertime	Ugo Betti
Misalliance	George Bernard Shaw
Tonight at 8.30	Noël Coward

Dial M for Murder	Frederick Knott
Castle in the Air	Alan Melville
Little Hut	André Roussin, adapted by Nancy Mitford

1956–7

The Dark is Light Enough	Christopher Fry
The Case of the Frightened Lady	Edgar Wallace
Alice in Wonderland	Lewis Carroll, adapted by John Harrison
Twelfth Night	William Shakespeare
Miss Julie	August Strindberg
The Bald Prima Donna	Eugene Ionesco
Journey's End	R.C. Sherriff
The Matchmaker	Thornton Wilder
The Servant of Two Masters	Carlo Goldini
The Queen and the Rebels	Ugo Betti
The Seven Year Itch	George Axelrod
Vice Versa	F. Anstey
The Country Wife	William Wycherley
Romanoff and Juliet	Peter Ustinov
Teahouse of the August Moon	John Patrick
South Sea Bubble	Noël Coward
A Murder Without Crime	J. Lee Thompson

1957–8

Pygmalion	George Bernard Shaw
Look Back in Anger	John Osborne
An Italian Straw Hat	Eugene Labiche and Marc Michel
Under Milk Wood	Dylan Thomas
Separate Tables	Terence Rattigan
Summer and Smoke	Tennessee Williams
Witness for the Prosecution	Agatha Christie
Red Riding Hood	David Waller, original music and lyrics by L. James
Henry V	William Shakespeare
The Perfect Woman	Wallace Geoffrey and Basil Mitchell
Three Sisters	Anton Chekhov
Our Town	Thornton Wilder

Summer of the Seventeenth Doll	Ray Lawler
She Stoops to Conquer	Oliver Goldsmith
The Moon is Blue	F. Hugh Herbert
The Rainmaker	N. Richard Nash
Doctor in the House	Ted Willis, from the novel by Richard Gordon
Lucky Day	Serge de Boissac (British premiere)
On the Spot	Edgar Wallace
The Banbury Nose	Peter Ustinov
Spider's Web	Agatha Christie

1958–9

Boys, it's All Hell!	Willis Hall (British premiere)
Fanny's First Play	George Bernard Shaw
A Memory of Two Mondays	Arthur Miller
A Resounding Tinkle	N.F. Simpson
Peer Gynt	Henrik Ibsen
French without Tears	Terence Rattigan
The Potting Shed	Graham Greene
The Solid Gold Cadillac	Howard Teichmann and George S. Kaufman
Towards Zero	Agatha Christie
The Black Arrow	R.L. Stevenson, adapted by J. Blatchley and W. Hall
Oedipus Rex	Sophocles
Cecile or the School for Fathers	Jean Anouilh (British premiere)
Mr Pickwick	Charles Dickens, adapted by S. Young
While the Sun Shines	Terence Rattigan
Hamlet	William Shakespeare
Reluctant Heroes	Colin Morris
Don Juan	Anton Chekhov, trs. Basil Ashmore
My Three Angels	Sam and Bella Spewack from the comedy by Albert Husson
The Man with the Golden Arm	Nelson Algren, adapted by Jack Kirkland (premiere)
The Fourposter	Jan de Hartog
The Diary of Anne Frank	Frances Goodrich and Albert Hackett

The Clandestine Marriage	George Colman and David Garrick
Flowering Cherry	Robert Bolt
The Rape of the Belt	Benn W. Levy
The Hollow	Agatha Christie
Blithe Spirit	Noël Coward

1959–60

Two for the See-saw	William Gibson
Take the Fool Away	J.B. Priestley (British premiere)
A Midsummer Night's Dream	William Shakespeare
Busman's Honeymoon	Dorothy L. Sayers and M. St Clare Byrne
The Beggar's Opera	John Gay
The Rose Tattoo	Tennessee Williams
A Christmas Carol	Charles Dickens, adapted by John Maxwell
Charley's Aunt	Brandon Thomas
Edward, my Son	Robert Morley
Much Ado About Nothing	William Shakespeare
Concubine Imperial	Maurice Collis (British premiere)
An Ideal Husband	Oscar Wilde
Any Other Business	George Ross and Campbell Singer
The Quare Fellow	Brendan Behan
The Entertainer	John Osborne
Strip the Willow	Beverley Cross (British premiere)
The Doctor's Dilemma	George Bernard Shaw
Present Laughter	Noël Coward
Beautiful Dreamer	Jack Pulman (British premiere)
You, Me and the Gatepost	An Intimate Revue (various authors)
Five Finger Exercise	Peter Shaffer

1960–1

Rhinoceros	Eugene Ionesco
A Cry of Players	William Gibson (premiere)
The Merchant of Venice	William Shakespeare
Roots	Arnold Wesker
The Survivors	Irwin Shaw and Peter Viertel (premiere)
One Way Pendulum	N.F. Simpson

Oliver Twist	Charles Dickens, adapted by R. Gotterough
The Happiest Days of your Life	John Dighton
The School for Scandal	Richard Brinsley Sheridan
A Passage to India	E.M. Forster, adapted by Santha Rama Rau
Celebration	Willis Hall and Keith Waterhouse (premiere)
Richard III	William Shakespeare
The Unexpected Guest	Agatha Christie
The Winslow Boy	Terence Rattigan
The Ballad of Dr Crippen	Beverley Cross (premiere)
The Tiger and the Horse	Robert Bolt
Triple Bill:	
Lunch Hour	John Mortimer
The Form	N.F. Simpson
A Slight Ache	Harold Pinter
A Taste of Honey	Shelagh Delaney
Lady Windermere's Fan	Oscar Wilde
The Aspern Papers	Henry James, adapted by Michael Redgrave
Second Post	Revue (various authors)

1961–2

Hotel Paradiso	Feydeau and Desvallières
A Streetcar Named Desire	Tennessee Williams
Macbeth	William Shakespeare
Alas, Poor Fred	James Saunders (premiere)
A Man for All Seasons	Robert Bolt
The Caretaker	Harold Pinter
Great Expectations	Charles Dickens, adapted by Gerald Frow
The Hostage	Brendan Behan
The Taming of the Shrew	William Shakespeare
The Recruiting Officer	George Farquhar
Maria Marten	George Hall
The Birthday Party	Harold Pinter
An Enemy of the People	Henrik Ibsen
The Enchanted	Jean Giraudoux

Look Back in Anger	John Osborne
Julius Caesar	William Shakespeare
The Rehearsal	Jean Anouilh
The Love of Four Colonels	Peter Ustinov
Yer What?	Various authors

1962–3

The Empty Chair	Peter Ustinov
Twelfth Night	William Shakespeare
The Three Musketeers	A. Dumas (British premiere)
Double Bill:	
A Subject of Scandal and Concern	John Osborne (stage premiere)
The Sponge Room	Keith Waterhouse and Willis Hall (premiere)

Waiting for Godot	Samuel Beckett
The Heap	G. Thomas
Macbeth	William Shakespeare
Salad Days	Julian Slade and Dorothy Reynolds
Photo Finish	Peter Ustinov
The Shoemaker's Holiday	Thomas Dekker
Epitaph for George Dillon	John Osborne and Anthony Creighton

Cymbeline	William Shakespeare and Shaw
Hay Fever	Noël Coward
The Zodiac in the Establishment	Bridget Boland (premiere)
Billy Liar	Keith Waterhouse and Willis Hall
A Month in the Country	Turgenev, adapted by Emlyn Williams

Man and Superman	George Bernard Shaw

1963–4

Coriolanus	William Shakespeare
The Importance of being Earnest	Oscar Wilde
The Life in my Hands	Peter Ustinov (world premiere)
Semi-Detached	David Turner
The Bashful Genius	Harold Cullen
The Mayor of Zalamea	Calderon, trs. David Brett
The Good Old Days	Various authors
Saturday Night and Sunday Morning	Alan Sillitoe

Arms and the Man	George Bernard Shaw
Memento Mori	Muriel Spark (world premiere)
Sir Thomas More	William Shakespeare and others

1964–5

The Merchant of Venice	William Shakespeare
Alfie	Bill Naughton
Listen to the Knocking Bird	John Wells and Claud Cockburn
The Creeper	Pauline Macaulay
The Birdwatcher	Georges Feydeau
Oedipus the King	Sophocles
That Scoundrel Scapin	Molière
Treasure Island	R.L. Stevenson
Richard II	William Shakespeare
Collapse of Stout Party	Trevor Peacock
The Cherry Orchard	Anton Chekhov
Volpone	Ben Jonson
The Elephant's Foot	William Trevor
The Cavern	Jean Anouilh, trs. Lucienne Hill
When we are Married	J.B. Priestley
Changing Gear	Various authors

1965–6

Measure for Measure	William Shakespeare
Private Lives	Noël Coward
Richard II	William Shakespeare
'Owd Yer Tight	Emrys Bryson
Schweyk in the Second World War	Bertold Brecht
A Christmas Carol	Charles Dickens
The Country Wife	William Wycherley
As You Like It	William Shakespeare
A Man for All Seasons	Robert Bolt
The Caretaker	Harold Pinter
The Astrakhan Coat	Pauline Macaulay
Saint Joan	George Bernard Shaw
Measure for Measure	William Shakespeare
Who's Afraid of Virginia Woolf?	Edward Albee
The Spies Are Singing	Giles Cooper
The Proposal	Anton Chekhov

Doctor Faustus	Christopher Marlowe
Moll Flanders	Daniel Defoe

1966–7

Julius Caesar	William Shakespeare
Hedda Gabler	Henrik Ibsen
Antony and Cleopatra	William Shakespeare
Fill the Stage with Happy Hours	Charles Wood (premiere)
She Stoops to Conquer	Oliver Goldsmith
Jack and the Beanstalk	John Moffatt
Death of a Salesman	Arthur Miller
Beware of the Dog	Gabriel Arout
Stop It, Whoever You Are	Henry Livings
The Silver Tassie	Sean O'Casey
The Miser	Molière
Bread and Butter	C.P. Taylor
A Midsummer Night's Dream	William Shakespeare

1967–8

Othello	William Shakespeare
A Long Day's Journey into Night	Eugene O'Neill
The Workhouse Donkey	John Arden
Staircase	Charles Dyer
Dandy Dick	Arthur Wing Pinero
A Midsummer Night's Dream	William Shakespeare
Tinker's Curse	William Corlett
All's Well that Ends Well	William Shakespeare
Skyvers	Barry Reckord
Boots with Strawberry Jam	John Dankworth and Benny Green
The Little Mrs Foster Show	Henry Livings
Mother Courage	Bertold Brecht
Vacant Possession	Maisie Mosco (premiere)
Candida	George Bernard Shaw
Confession at Night	Aleksei Arbuzov (premiere)

1968–9

King John	William Shakespeare
The School for Scandal	Richard Brinsley Sheridan
The Ruling Class	Peter Barnes (premiere)

The Seagull	Anton Chekhov
Whoops a Daisy	Keith Waterhouse and Willis Hall (premiere)
The Mountain King	Ferdinand Ramund
Macbeth	William Shakespeare
The Entertainer	John Osborne
The Playboy of the Western World	J.M. Synge
The Resistible Rise of Arturo Ui	Bertold Brecht
Love in a Bottle	George Farquhar
The Hostage	Brendan Behan
Widower's Houses	George Bernard Shaw
'Owd Yer Tight	Emrys Bryson

1969–70

The Hero Rises Up	John Arden and Margaret D'Arcy
The Alchemist	Ben Jonson
King Lear	William Shakespeare
The Demonstration	David Caute (premiere)
Huckleberry Finn	Mark Twain, adapted by David Teonre
The Dandy Lion	Dodi Robb and Patti Patterson
Twelfth Night	William Shakespeare
The Daughter-in-Law	D.H. Lawrence
Barefoot in the Park	Neil Simon
The Idiot	Dostoyevsky, adapted by Michael Glenny
A Yard of Sun	Christopher Fry (premiere)
Love on the Dole	Terry Hughes, Alan Flack and Robert Gray (premiere)

1970–1

The Misanthrope	Molière
Lulu	Wedekind, adapted by Peter Barnes (premiere)
Hamlet	William Shakespeare
Nicholas Nickleby	Charles Dickens, adapted by Caryl Brahms and Ned Sherrin
Waiting for Godot	Samuel Beckett
The Rivals	Richard Brinsley Sheridan

The Birthday Party	Harold Pinter
The Amazons	Michael Stewart, David Heneker and John Addison
Lillywhite Lies	Alan Richards
A Close Shave	George Feydeau
Antigone	Sophocles

1971–2

Richard III	William Shakespeare
The Magistrate	Arthur Wing Pinero
Rosencrantz and Guildernstern are Dead	Tom Stoppard
The Owl on the Battlements	Beverley Cross (premiere)
The Swallow Garden	Michael Payne (premiere)
The Life of the General	Ronald Mavor
The Tempest	William Shakespeare
The Homecoming	Harold Pinter
The Green Leaves of Nottingham	Pat McGrath (premiere)
A Doll's House	Henrik Ibsen
See How They Run	Philip King
A Collier's Friday Night	D.H. Lawrence

1972–3

Love's Labours Lost	William Shakespeare
The Deep Blue Sea	Terence Rattigan
Brand	Henrik Ibsen
What the Butler Saw	Joe Orton
The One Day Night	Michael Payne (premiere)
The Plough and the Stars	Sean O'Casey
The Three Musketeers	Alexandre Dumas
The White Raven	Maxim Gorky
The Devil is an Ass	Ben Jonson
The Malcontent	John Marston, adapted by John Wells
The Contractor	David Storey

1973–4

The Taming of the Shrew	William Shakespeare
Brassneck	Howard Brenton and David Hare (premiere)

Soft or a Girl	John McGrath
Three Sisters	Anton Chekhov
Adventures of a Bear Called Paddington	Michael Bond, adapted by Alfred Bradley (premiere)
Toad of Toad Hall	A.A. Milne
The Crucible	Arthur Miller
Loot	Joe Orton
The Caucasian Chalk Circle	Bertold Brecht
The Government Inspector	Adrian Mitchell
The Churchill Play	Howard Brenton
Bendigo	Ken Campbell, Dave Hill and Andy Andrews (premiere)

1974–5

Juno and the Paycock	Sean O'Casey
Henry IV (parts 1 and 2 condensed)	William Shakespeare
Bendigo	Ken Campbell, David Hill, Andy Andrews
Oh What a Lovely War	Theatre Workshop
The Speckled Band	Sir Arthur Conan Doyle
The Plotters of Cabbage Patch Corner	David Wood (premiere)
Canterbury Tales	Martin Starkie, P. Neville Coghill
She Stoops to Conquer	Oliver Goldsmith
Comedians	Trevor Griffiths (premiere)
Major Barbara	George Bernard Shaw
The National Health	Peter Nicholls
The White Devil	John Webster
Walking like Geoffrey	Ken Campbell, David Hill, Andy Andrews (premiere)
As You Like It	William Shakespeare

1975–6

The Widowing Of Mrs Holroyd	D.H. Lawrence
The Beggar's Opera	John Gay
Jug	Henry Livings (premiere)
A Streetcar Named Desire	Tennessee Williams
Annie Get Your Gun	Herbert and Dorothy Fields
The Pig and the Junkle	Brian Patten
Entertaining Mr Sloane	Joe Orton

Red Noses for Me	Charles Lawson
Pygmalion	George Bernard Shaw
The Servant of Two Masters	Carlo Goldini
Trumpets and Drums	Bertold Brecht
Dimetos	Athol Fugard (British premiere)
Bartholomew Fair	Ben Jonson
Private Lives	Noël Coward

1976–7

Othello	William Shakespeare
Travesties	Tom Stoppard
Hobson's Choice	Harold Brighouse
Knickers	Carl Sterheim
The Magicalympic Games	Graeme Garden (premiere)
Sleeping Beauty	Alan Brown
A Flea in her Ear	Georges Feydeau
City Sugar	Stephen Poliakoff
The Cherry Orchard	Anton Chekhov
Death of a Salesman	Arthur Miller
Twelfth Night	William Shakespeare
Touched	Stephen Lowe (premiere)
Comedians	Trevor Griffiths
White Suit Blues	Adrian Mitchell (premiere)

1977–8

The Importance of being Earnest	Oscar Wilde
Bedroom Farce	Alan Ayckbourn
Much Ado About Nothing	William Shakespeare
Charlie and the Chocolate Factory	Roald Dahl, adapted by Richard H. Williams and Sue Birtwistle
The Wizard of Oz	L. Frank Baum
The Alchemist	Ben Jonson
Shadow of a Gunman	Sean O'Casey
Deeds	Various authors – Howard Brenton and Trevor Griffiths with Ken Campbell and David Hare

BIBLIOGRAPHY

Agate, James, *Brief Chronicles* (Cape, 1943)
——, *Red Letter Nights* (Cape, 1944)
Baudelaire, C., *Art in Paris 1845/1862* (Phaidon, 1965)
Barker, Harley Granville, *Prefaces to Shakespeare* (Sidgwick & Jackson, 1945)
Brown, Ivor, *Shakespeare* (Collins, 1949)
——, *Theatre 1954/1955* (Reinhardt, 1955)
——, *Theatre 1955/1956* (Reinhardt, 1956)
Chekhov, Anton, *Letters* (Bodley Head, 1973)
Eliot, T.S., *The Sacred Wood* (Methuen, 1920)
Elsom J./Tomalin N., *The National Theatre* (Cape, 1978)
Forster, E.M., *Two Cheers for Democracy* (Edward Arnold, 1952)
Hansard, *Estimates Committee Report – Grants for the Arts Session 1967/68* (HMSO, 1968)
Hazlitt, William, *Dramatic Criticism*: *Characters of Shakespeare's Plays* (Nevil, 1948)
Herbert, A.P., *Look Back and Laugh* (Methuen, 1960)
Ibsen, Henrik, *A Critical Anthology* (Penguin, 1970)
Lawrence, D.H., *Letters* (Heinemann, 1932)
Miller, Arthur, *Collected Plays* (Methuen, 1988)
——, *Time Bends* (Methuen, 1987)
Priestley, J.B., *The Art of the Dramatist* (Heinemann, 1957)
Shakespeare in Perspective 1 & 2 (BBC, 1932/1935)
Shakespeare Criticism 1919–1935 (Oxford University Press, 1936)
Shaw G.B., *Prefaces* (Constable, 1934)
——, *Our Theatre in the Nineties* (Constable, 1932)
——, *The Quintessence of Ibsenism* (Constable, 1932)
Shaw G.B.,/Terry E., *A Correspondence* (Constable, 1931)
Stanislavsky C., *My Life in Art* (Bles, 1948)
——, *An Actor Prepares* (Bles, 1936)
——, *Othello* (Bles, 1948)
——, *The Seagull* (Dobson, 1952)
Treece, Henry, *Carnival King* (Faber, 1954)

Trevelyan, G.M., *History of England* (Longmans Green, new impression, 1948)

Tynan, K., *Tynan on Theatre* (Penguin, 1964)

——, *A View of the English Stage* (Methuen, 1975)

Van Gyseghem, André, *Theatre in Soviet Russia* (Faber, 1943)

REFERENCES and QUOTATIONS

I am very grateful to the following for permission to reproduce extracts from their publications: The BBC for an extract from a *Kaleidoscope* programme transcript in 1978; Harper Collins for an extract from *Shakespeare* by Ivor Brown, published by Collins; John Johnson (Authors' Agent) Ltd on behalf of the Estate of Henry Treece for extracts from *Carnival King* and *Footsteps in the Sea*, published by Faber & Faber; The Kenneth Tynan Estate for quotations from *Tynan on Theatre;* The Longman Group UK for an extract from G.M. Trevelyan's *History of England*; Nottingham Playhouse Reviews 1948/50, 1955, 1956, 1957/60, and Programmes 1953, 1954, 1955, 1963, 1968, 1972; Penguin Books Ltd for quotation from *Ibsen – a critical anthology*, edited by James McFarlane; The Peters, Fraser & Dunlop Group Ltd on behalf of the Ivor Brown Estate for an extract from *Theatre 1955/56* by Ivor Brown; The Phaidon Press Ltd for an extract from C. Baudelaire's *Art in Paris 1845–1862*; Random House for extracts from *Red Letter Nights* and *Brief Chronicles* by James Agate and *History of the National Theatre* by John Elsom & Nicholas Tomalin, published by Jonathan Cape; Reed Book Services Ltd for extracts from Arthur Miller's *Timebends* and Preface to *Collected Plays*, published by Methuen; The Society of Authors on behalf of the Bernard Shaw Estate for extracts from works by Bernard Shaw.

I would also like to thank the following for permission to reproduce extracts from drama reviews: *Financial Times, Guardian, New Statesman and Society, Nottingham Evening Post* and allied publications, *Observer, The Times Educational Supplement;* and the Nottinghamshire Central Library (Local Studies Department) for the loan and use of photographs for illustrations.

The author and publisher have made every endeavour to contact the copyright holders of all quoted material, but in spite of repeated efforts no response has been received in a few cases, and therefore we regret any omission of acknowledgement.

INDEX